CRIME BY CHANCE

CRIME

Elizabeth Linington

BY

CHANCE

J. B. LIPPINCOTT COMPANY
Philadelphia and New York

U.S. Library of Congress Cataloging in Publication Data

Linington, Elizabeth.
    Crime by chance.
    I. Title.
PZ4.L756Cp [PS3562.I515]   813'.5'4   72–12517
ISBN–0–397–00959–3

O Thou, Who Man of baser Earth didst make,
And who with Eden didst devise the Snake,
For all the Sin wherewith the Face of Man
Is blackened, Man's Forgiveness give—
and Take!

—*Rubaiyat of Omar Khayyam*
Ed. 1, LVII

CRIME BY CHANCE

one

Sue had forgotten to set the alarm, and they'd overslept. She was rummaging frantically after clean stockings; Maddox, shaving hurriedly, had just inflicted a savage nick on his lower left jaw. "If you'd use an electric—" said Sue to his profane comment.

"Contrary to all the TV commercials, you can't get a close shave with those things, not with a beard like mine."

Sue flew out to the kitchen to find that the electric coffeemaker had done its job: coffee was ready, too hot to drink. She poured two cups and went back to the bedroom for her dress. "Eggs?"

"No time," said Maddox, buttoning his shirt and reaching for a tie. "I'll try for an early lunch. And I still think," he added, looking at her hands as she combed her hair, "I should have traded the Maserati on something with lower payments and got you an—"

"Are you back to that again? Don't be silly," said Sue. "I don't need an engagement ring. I'm quite happy with the other one, darling." She slipped into low-heeled navy pumps and trotted out to the kitchen again. The coffee was just possible to drink.

Maddox swallowed three quarters of a cup and finished tying his tie. "My God, the time. I'm off. See you." He kissed her hastily and was gone.

Sue put the cups in the sink and went back to the bedroom to put on makeup and small gold stud earrings. Five minutes after he'd left, she followed him, working-size handbag over her arm, and locked the front door of the little house set behind the Clintons' larger house on Gregory Avenue. Maddox could leave his car in the street, but there wasn't room for Sue's Chrysler; they rented a garage from old Mrs. Patterson two doors down the street. As Sue hurried down the drive, she might have been any slim young woman in her mid-twenties, neat in a plain dress, heading for any mundane office job. Only, of course, she wasn't.

Ten minutes later she pulled the Chrysler up behind the little blue Maserati, in the bay in the street across from the Wilcox Street precinct station. César Rodriguez's old Chevy was there, and Daisy Hoffman's Buick, and Sergeant Ellis's Ford. She trotted across to the old tan brick building and lifted a hand to Sergeant Johnny O'Neill on the desk as she made for the locker room. There she changed quickly into her neat navy uniform; as she came out and started up the stairs, a couple of civilians were ahead of her, evidently just started up by O'Neill. They paused on the landing and Sue said, "Can I help you?"

"That sergeant said to come up and see Sergeant Hoffman," said the man doubtfully. "It's about our daughter. She's run away." They were ordinary-looking people in rather shabby clothes; the woman had been crying.

"Yes, sir. Right here," said Sue, steering them into the office she shared with Daisy. "Mr.—"

"Rodney. I'm John Rodney."

"Sit down, won't you?" said Daisy with a smile; brisk blond Daisy didn't look like a grandmother but was. "I'm

Sergeant Hoffman. This is Policewoman Maddox." At least after six months she didn't start to say Carstairs any more.

Sue got out her notebook, resigned to listen to the old familiar tale: daughter in with a bad crowd, rebellious, dropping out, possibly on dope.

"Your daughter—" she prompted.

"She didn't have to run away!" wailed Mrs. Rodney. "There's been arguments and all, but she didn't have to. She must've left way after midnight last night, both her suitcases gone and this note—"

"Arguments," said Daisy. "About school, or her friends?"

"Well, I guess you'd say," said Rodney. "You see, we want her to go to college and she don't want to."

Sue put down her notebook. "How old is your daughter, Mr. Rodney?"

"Ella's twenty."

Sue looked at Daisy.

■ ■ ■

When Maddox got to the detective office upstairs, Joe Feinman was typing a report and Rowan was looking at a flyer. "D'Arcy and César just went out on a new call," said Rowan. "Couple of bodies."

"Homicide, that's all we need," said Maddox. "Anything in from Sacramento yet?"

"Nope. But the photostats of those drivers' licenses ought to give us something, all right."

"No bets," said Maddox. "How much does the photo on yours look like you?" But it would be a little something, at least: somewhere else to go on this bunch of kite flyers. The first batch of forged checks had showed up a month back, and they hadn't developed a lead yet. A pattern showed, but that was nearly always the case. The checks purported to be issued by big companies anyone around here would recognize instantly: Lockheed Aircraft, The

May Company, J. W. Robinson's, The Broadway, and several chains of service stations, Shell, Gulf, Standard. They weren't even very good forgeries, or so said Questioned Documents downtown at Central Headquarters; not imitations of real checks from those companies, just neatly printed checks with those company names. They had been cashed by liquor stores, chain markets, drugstores; such places didn't like to refuse checks and took in hundreds every day as a convenience to customers. They asked for some identification, of course, and in every case the identification offered had been a driver's license and a student I.D. card from Los Angeles City College, and a lot of help that had been to the detectives.

L.A.C.C. had at present no students named Patricia Gall, Joseph Ruzicka, Eleanor Wayne, Robert Gunderson, Coralee Lambert, or Richard Goslin. The registrar had no idea where or how anyone could have obtained the I.D. cards.

"I always said it's idiotic," said Maddox now. "The first piece of I.D. anybody asks you for, when you're cashing a check, is your driver's license, and it's no I.D. at all. Anybody can walk into any D.M.V. office and get a license in any name he picks at random."

"And do you take any bets we don't get another batch passed over the weekend?" said Feinman. All the checks had been cashed on weekends. None of them had been for over fifty dollars, most for sums in the thirties and forties. And just what the photostats of the licenses would give them, if and when Sacramento got around to sending them down, was debatable. The various clerks and managers who had taken the checks gave very vague descriptions: all the passers were young, they said, and young people nowadays —well, kind of alike. The girls with the long straight hair, not much makeup, casual clothes. It did emerge that of the three males none had overlong hair, but that was about all.

12

They were waiting for a kickback from the FBI on the prints of the hit-run victim found along Hollywood Boulevard on Wednesday night. They had just wrapped up a murder-three for the D.A., and Lieutenant Eden was probably downtown with all the paper on that. The last couple of weeks had been quiet except for the check passers, but as usual in March they were having a little heat wave, which might make more business for cops.

"I hope this pair isn't heading for our beat," said Rowan, looking up from the flyer. "We got a hail from N.C.I.C. overnight on 'em, and I looked up the Feds' report. They got out of Leavenworth couple of months ago, that break when seven–eight cons got loose. N.C.I.C. thinks they're heading west. Identified as the heisters at a bank in Dubuque and a liquor store in Denver. They've been a team awhile—Roy Connors and Ralph Fielding, pedigrees from here to there."

"Nice," agreed Maddox. He was rereading the reports, interviews with the people who'd taken the checks. A handful of nothing. Now if they had a hope in hell of getting photostats of those student I.D. cards— The phone rang on his desk and he picked it up. "Something, Johnny?"

"Something," said O'Neill. "Pair on the way up. A Mr. and Mrs. Harvey Easterfield, from Cincinnati. I think you'll be talking to P.R. on this one. We can't have the tourists spreading nasty lies about the old reliable L.A.P.D."

"Oh?" said Maddox. "O.K., thanks, Johnny." He put the phone down and stood up as a couple stopped in the doorway. "Mr. and Mrs. Easterfield? I'm Sergeant Maddox. You've got some complaint on the department?"

They came over to his desk rather warily; Rowan put down the flyer to listen. The man was about fifty, big and ruddy, nearly bald, well-dressed in a conservative gray suit. The woman was younger, blond by request but also conservative in a rather dowdy black dress, a little jewelry that might be real. "I told you, Harry," she said. "They weren't. That man in uniform downstairs—it wasn't quite the same."

"Won't you sit down?" said Maddox, offering chairs. They sat down. "What's it all about, sir?"

• "Well, I was mad," said Easterfield. "Then. But the more we talked it over—well, I thought Los Angeles was supposed to have a good police force. *Dragnet*, you know. Honest, I mean."

"We like to think so."

"So the more Alice says they were fakes, the more I wondered about it. Anyway, it won't do any harm, tell you about it. See, this isn't the first time we've been in California. Our daughter and her husband live here—Santa Monica—but it's the first time we drove out. Little vacation. I've got my own hardware store back home. Well, cut a long story short, yesterday afternoon we're here in town—Hollywood, I mean—on Sunset Boulevard, we'd just had lunch at Michael's up on Los Feliz, and we were heading back for the beach, and I made a left turn onto Western. And right off there's a car come up alongside and I see there's two cops in it. In uniform. And the one on the passenger's side leans out and says for me to pull over. So I did. I didn't know what I'd done wrong, but as I say I've never driven in California before and maybe I don't know all your traffic rules. So I pulled over, first empty space along the curb, and they stopped ahead of me and got out and came back and said they'd have to give me a ticket for an illegal left turn."

"And it wasn't," said his wife. "Dick told us about the left-turn rule you got here, we don't have that in Ohio, and he didn't want—"

"Excuse me, was the car a police car?" asked Maddox.

14

Easterfield shook his head. "Just a car. A green Dodge about four years old. But you hear about unmarked police cars—"

"Did either of the men show you a badge?"

They nodded. "The first one did. It was a damn nuisance. He said it was a moving violation and I'd have to go to a court hearing and all, and we've only got three weeks. I was annoyed and said so, and it was then he said I could get out of going to court if I paid the fine right then, ten bucks, and he'd give me a receipt and that'd be that."

Maddox sat up. "So you did."

"I did. I didn't want to waste a couple of days in court. He gave me a receipt—here it is," and he took it out of his wallet and laid it on the desk.

It was just a slip taken from an ordinary receipt book that any business might use; scrawled across it was the notation "Rcvd. in payment fine traffic violation" and the nearly illegible signature "R. O. Dillon." Maddox looked at it and laid it down and fetched out his badge in its leather case from his breast pocket. "Did the badge look like this?"

They studied it, and Mrs. Easterfield shook her head. "It didn't have any tower on it like that."

"That's the City Hall," said Maddox absently.

"It said POLICE around the bottom," said Easterfield, "and it was gold like that, but I seem to recall it had a star in the middle."

"Mmh," said Maddox. "What about the uniforms? Navy blue?"

They both nodded. "But they weren't wearing guns," said Mrs. Easterfield. "And I don't think it was just the same uniform as that man downstairs had on."

Maddox said, "Mmh," again. "I'm afraid you've been conned, Mr. Easterfield. They weren't L.A.P.D. men, that's sure. But this sounds like a new racket around here, and we're glad to know about it. And what a racket, come to think about it."

"How d'you mean?" asked Easterfield.

"Well, at any time of year there are apt to be a few out-of-state cars around L.A. Wearing out-of-state plates to identify them. Yes indeedy, that's quite a bright thought this pair had. Rent a couple of police uniforms at any costumers' in the county, spot the out-of-state cars and pull 'em over. I'd bet that a hundred percent of those drivers would pay that quote-unquote fine on the spot—it's not that much money—and whether they thought it was how the rules read in California or that the cops were on the take, would any of them bother to report it to us? Why should they? But we're very glad you did. Sorry you're out the ten bucks, but we'll try to put a stop to it now we know about it."

"Well, I'll be damned," said Easterfield. "See what you mean. They could cruise around all day, stop as many cars as they spotted. Well, I'm glad we decided to come in."

Maddox thanked them again, saw them out, came back and dialed Central H.Q. and asked for Public Relations. He got a Sergeant Forster, who listened to his tale and said, "Ten minutes before you called I was talking to a patrolman from University division. Man hailed him on the street and told him much the same story, just now. Said after it happened he thought it over and decided the men were phonies. I wonder how long they've been at it. Most of the marks wouldn't report it."

"Just what I concluded," said Maddox. "Do we suppose there are more than two of them? I thought you'd like to know, anyway."

"Damn right. Building a bad image, you could say," said Forster.

D'Arcy and Rodriguez came in, D'Arcy looking morose and Rodriguez as usual faintly cynical.

"I'll pass it on to the Chief's office and get something out for the press and TV. If we spread it around that it's a racket—"

"People on vacation don't always keep up with the papers or TV."

"Well, we can but try," said Forster. "Thanks very much."

"So what's the new one look like?" asked Maddox.

D'Arcy folded his lank seventy-six inches into his desk chair and sighed. "A mystery. All we need. . . . I asked Sheila again last night and she said wait and see, maybe. Her father says she's flighty. I'd like to settle her down, but—"

"*Paciencia*," said Rodriguez. "Look at Sue's example. She finally caught up to our little Welshman."

"Or the other way round," said Maddox with a grin. They'd had all the kidding they'd expected, last September, when they'd got their vacations to coincide and slipped over to Vegas to get married. "What's the mystery?"

"The baby," said Rodriguez. "Woman walking by on the street heard the baby yelling, stopped to look and called in. Couple in a Caddy parked along Sycamore Avenue, both shot in the head, cold, and the baby still in the woman's lap, not a mark on it. Ambulance men said it was about six months old, a boy. No I.D. on either body, nothing anywhere—ordinary cosmetics in the handbag, cigarettes and matches on him, but no money, nothing but this." He laid a plastic evidence bag on the desk; there was a scrap of paper inside. "Receipt from a motel in Pasadena. I'm just going to check it."

"Could've been shot by somebody in the back seat," said D'Arcy, and yawned. "Looked like a thirty-two. I

17

suppose I'd better start the initial report." He pulled the typewriter toward him. "They'll be at the morgue by now. Would any of you feel inclined to go get their prints?"

"I'll do it," said Feinman. "Looks as if business is picking up a little."

"And we've got the damndest con game going on," said Maddox, "God knows how long they've been at it," and he told them about that. Rodriguez smoothed his neat mustache.

"You know something, Ivor? If this pair—or however many are in it—sort of subtly put over the idea that this so-called fine is an under-the-counter bribe, that'd make it all the more certain that the marks wouldn't come crying to the top brass. Corrupt cops on the street, what else at the desk? I do wonder how long they've been operating, damn it."

"What P.R. said. Hardly a good image," said Maddox dryly.

"See what the lab gives us on that Caddy," said D'Arcy. "No registration in it, by the way. We asked N.C.I.C. about the plates. Florida ones."

"And your answer is just back," said Sue briskly from the door. "Computers." Since the National Crime Information Center had been operating, it had proved a godsend to cops all over the country, with its vast files and its army of computers. Rodriguez looked at the slip she handed him.

"So now we know. The Caddy belongs to one Roderick Cameron of Sarasota. It was stolen three weeks ago from a public parking lot. That tells us a lot."

"Maybe tells you that the two corpses were on the wrong side of the fence," said Maddox.

"Which means their prints might be on file somewhere, yes." D'Arcy's typewriter started ticking rather slowly, and he yawned again and said he had spring fever.

18

It was ten o'clock, and Maddox's stomach was rumbling, but he'd have to type a report on the interview with the Easterfields. Well, there was at least the coffee machine down the hall. "Anybody want some coffee?"

D'Arcy fished out a dime and handed it over. "With cream. Maybe keep me awake."

When Maddox got to the coffee machine he found a stranger in a white jumpsuit measuring the wall beside it. "And what are you up to?" he asked.

The man turned, revealing a round good-natured face with a snub nose and freckles. "Hi, you one of the officers here? We're sure glad to get the go-ahead from your head-quarters. Fred and me, he's my partner, we been tryin' for it nearly a year. Fin'ly got the word this week. I just put one in at the Wilshire station. Get yours in tomorrow."

"What?"

"Our machine, see. Our sandwich machine. There's lotsa places where people got to do overtime, work long hours, and no place near to get a sandwich, a snack. We got some of our machines out at Lockheed, and a big laundry chain, and now we get the go-ahead to put 'em in your stations and fire stations too."

"Say, that might be handy," said Maddox, interested. He could use a sandwich right now. "How do they work?"

"Just great," said their benefactor proudly. "We picked up a whole mess of 'em at a forced sale—business went broke, see. You gotta choice of four kinds. We get 'em fresh every day, all wrapped up hygienic, you know? You put fifty cents in and pull the handle, it hands you a sand-wich. It'll just fit on this wall. We got three guys already help us keep 'em all serviced, besides Fred and me."

"Fine," said Maddox. He pushed dimes in the coffee machine and the cream lever for D'Arcy's cup. He wished the sandwich machine was already there.

"Get yours in tomorrow for sure."

"Fine," said Maddox again. He went back down the hall and told the other boys about it.

■ ■ ■

Sue and Daisy had got rid of the Rodneys with a little difficulty. "After all, your daughter's of age," Daisy had pointed out. "She's out of school, you said."

"Graduated two years ago," said Mrs. Rodney mournfully. "Went right to work, learned to be a beautician. And we had it all planned for her to go to college!"

"I got nearly four thousand saved toward it," said Rodney. "And Ellie said it was foolishness. I couldn't argue her into it no way."

"Well, after all—" said Sue.

He shook his head. "Kept sayin' she had better things to do with her time than listen to a lot of egghead professors without any common sense. I tried to tell her she'd get a better job, earn more—"

Sue turned a giggle into a cough. "Well, it's really her own choice, isn't it, Mr. Rodney? In any case, she's of age."

"People, people," said Daisy when they'd trailed out forlornly, and they both forgot the Rodneys, unaware that the Rodneys marked the beginning of a little spate of offbeat items.

They got a call from The Broadway, a pair of shoplifters, and both went out on that. The shoplifters turned out to be a mother and teen-age daughter, both of whom had been picked up before; they were equipped with the fake wrapped packages with a concealed mechanism that quietly picked up any object they were set down on. There wasn't much the L.A.P.D. could do about shoplifters, pro or amateur; with the rate of shoplifting astronomically up, it was hardly worth the time in court to prosecute them just to have a judge put them on probation. Perhaps this pair might draw more; a check with Central showed they'd been picked up four times in the last two years and always went for the real jewelry. Pros, you could say. Daisy spent a while on the phone with the D.A.'s office while Sue typed a report. They ended up sending them down to the jail, where they'd probably make bail within a few hours.

A Missing Persons report was relayed up from Central, who had it from N.C.I.C.: just another juvenile runaway, but this one a Congressman's daughter from back east. It didn't match any of the bodies L.A. currently had on hand, or anybody in jail downtown. They filed it.

"You mind if I take off for lunch?" asked Daisy. "I've got to lose ten pounds, so I skipped breakfast."

"So did I," said Sue. "I forgot the alarm."

"You newlyweds."

"Hardly, after six months. All right, you go on."

"We're going to have a sandwich machine," said Daisy. "George Ellis was telling me about it this morning. It should be very handy."

"It certainly should," said Sue, her stomach rumbling. But she finished the report on the shoplifters ten minutes later and drove up to the Grotto on Santa Monica Boulevard for lunch. Maddox and Rodriguez made room at their table. Hearing about the new bodies, she said, "What a miracle that baby wasn't hurt. Poor thing. I wonder if you'll turn up any relatives."

"Our new con game is what worries me," said Rodriguez. "We try to keep a tight force here, and these jokers are ruining our image."

So she heard about that. "For heaven's sake," she said, amused. "I must remember to warn Aunt Evelyn. She's driving over to stay with Mother awhile. What a thing. But did you hear about the sandwich machine?"

21

When she got back to the station, Johnny O'Neill was leafing through *The American Rifleman* and whistling "The Patriot Game" softly. "Oh, Johnny, have you seen your report yet?" O'Neill had been assigned temporary desk duty on account of a bullet in one ankle, the result of a shoot-out with some bank heisters last year; he was hoping to be reported fit for active duty again.

"Ought to come through Monday," he said, smiling at her. "Then wait for the powers that be to see fit to reassign me."

"It'll all come right," said Sue reassuringly. She hoped so; she liked Johnny. Johnny had been a big help in opening Ivor Maddox's eyes to the junior division.

"You'd better get back to work. Funny sort of thing just now. I sent 'em up to Aunt Daisy."

"Why funny?"

"I don't know—what I got, no handle to it."

Upstairs, Sue found a pair of young women sitting beside Daisy's desk. They looked up at her. "This is Policewoman Maddox," said Daisy. "Sue, Mrs. Teresa Fogarty and Miss Sandra Cross."

Sue nodded, sat down and got out her notebook. "Now just tell it in detail," said Daisy. "You're worried about this friend? Why? You said her name was—"

"Theodora Mayo," said Sandra Cross. "Only everybody calls her Dorrie. And she wouldn't go away like that without saying anything—telling people! Only where is she? And where's Monica?"

"Let's take it from the beginning," said Daisy patiently. "Monica? Is Dorrie married?"

"No—yes—she was," said Teresa Fogarty. She was a slim dark young woman in the mid-twenties, pretty, in a plain tan cotton dress and brown loafers. The Cross girl was a little younger, tawny blond, a little plump, neatly dressed in navy-blue crepe with fake pearls. They were both obviously distressed and upset. "Her husband, Ken—he was killed in an accident when Monica was only a month old. It was terrible, this drunk driver ran into him on the freeway—he was only twenty-seven. Dorrie's only twenty-four now."

"When was that?"

"Oh, last year. Monica's fifteen months old now. And Ken's mother wanted Dorrie to go back east and live with her. I ought to say," explained Teresa Fogarty, "we knew Dorrie and Ken because they'd just started to buy the house next to us—we live over on Roseview in the Atwater section—but of course Dorrie had to give it up. There wasn't much insurance. But she didn't want to go back east because of the winters."

"Her husband's brother and his wife live there too," said Sandra, "and they offered to take the baby; she could come and visit—but she wouldn't do that. It wasn't easy for her, you can see."

"Where back east?" asked Daisy.

"Oh, Danbury, Connecticut. That's when she got the job at Robinson's. She gave up the house and started to work for Robinson's—she's in Fine Jewelry and I'm in Cosmetics, the next department—and we made friends, we always go to lunch together, and if she was going to move or go back east or anything she'd have told me! But she didn't say a word, and she's gone."

"Just a minute," said Daisy. "Hasn't she any family of her own?"

"She was an orphan," said Teresa. "She was brought up in a home—an orphanage—in Fresno. She doesn't have a soul, except Ken's people. They've been nice to her. I know they kept in touch—his brother came out for the funeral and helped her settle about the house and everything. But she would have—you know—told everybody, all her friends, if she was going away. I guess between us we know everybody she knew, and we've asked, and she didn't say anything to anybody as far as we can find out. And that's not like Dorrie."

"But where could she be?" said Sandra. "It doesn't make any sense!"

"Where does she live?" asked Daisy.

"She's—she had an apartment on Lexington." Teresa added the address. "It doesn't make sense, all right. I mean, Dorrie's not secretive, or queer any way. She's just—well, like anybody else. If she was going to move, she'd have told her friends. Like anybody. The way it happened— well, with her working, and we've got two children, it wasn't so often we saw each other, but we'd talk on the phone a couple of times a week, and—"

"Oh, Mrs. Fogarty, it couldn't be anything to do with Brian Faulkner, could it?" said Sandra suddenly. "I don't see how, but—"

"Let's back up and get details," said Daisy. "She's moved from her apartment?"

"We don't know where she is," said Sandra tearfully. "Or Monica! You see, I thought of Mrs. Fogarty—I mean, you see, I didn't know all Dorrie's other friends, that she'd known before her husband was killed, but I thought of—"

"I g-gave a birthday party for Monica," said Teresa, suddenly looking as if she wanted to cry. "Last December. Her first birthday."

"She's such a darling," said Sandra. "A real doll, and that cute blue outfit Dorrie made for her—"

"And Dorrie asked me to invite Miss—Sandra. And so when—"

"Now, when did you see her last?" Daisy was business-like.

"L-last Saturday." This was Friday. "At work. And she

24

was just like always," said Sandra. "She never said a thing about going anywhere, or moving. And then on Monday she wasn't at work, and I wondered if she was sick, or the baby, and I phoned the apartment at noon but nobody answered. I tried to phone her that night too. And she wasn't at work on Tuesday, so I asked Mr. Simon—he's head of Fine Jewelry—and he just said she hadn't called in sick. He was mad. So on Wednesday—I haven't got a car, but I got my brother to drive me up here that night (we live in Santa Monica), to the apartment, I mean, and nobody was there. There isn't a manager. Nobody knew anything. So then I thought about Mrs. Fogarty."

"And I don't know anything," said Teresa. "Dorrie never said anything to me either. I talked on the phone with her last Sunday morning, and it was all just—just casual, you know. But I did know that apartment building's owned by a big realty company—that's who she paid rent to. So yesterday I went there and asked, and they tried to give me the runaround but I kept on asking, and finally they told me that Mrs. Mayo had informed them—that's the way they put it—that she was giving up the apartment. They were annoyed because she hadn't given them any forwarding address and they'd owe her a rebate on the rent. They asked if I knew a forwarding address."

"But what could have happened?" wailed Sandra.

"And she doesn't have a typewriter," said Teresa, "but she left a typed note on Mrs. Littleton's apartment door. Mrs. Littleton was the only tenant there she'd got friendly with, but she works too, at Sears, so if Dorrie left in the daytime she'd know she wasn't home, but—"

"We just thought about Mrs. Littleton last night," said Sandra. "Dorrie'd mentioned her once or twice."

"And I got Jim to drive me over and asked if Dorrie'd said anything to her, and she told me about this note—"

"Scotch-taped onto her door," broke in Sandra, "saying Dorrie was going back east to live with her mother-in-law. And she never said a *word*. But Mr. Simon—"

"Just a minute," said Daisy. "Who's this Brian Faulkner? She had a—Mrs. Mayo had a boy friend?"

"Not really," said Teresa. "She met him at our house, actually. I don't know him very well. He and my husband went to school together. He seems nice enough, and he fell for Dorrie, asked her to marry him, but she didn't want to. She hadn't—you know—got over losing Ken. Yet. He wouldn't have anything to do with her going away. But where could she be? And Monica?"

Daisy looked at Sandra. "Mr. Simon?"

"I asked him this morning," said Sandra, "if he'd heard anything about Dorrie. And he said she'd quit her job. The store had a letter, he said. But why should she? Without telling us? And I was so—upset—I just walked off at lunch hour and went to see Mrs. Fogarty, and she thought it was all awfully funny too." She looked at them helplessly.

Sue looked at Daisy. "Funny peculiar?" she said.

On the face of it, it wasn't anything much: the letter to her employer, a note to a casual friend. Other, older friends not told. Why?

"Where did she leave the baby all day?" Daisy asked.

"Oh, we never thought of Mrs. Moran!" gasped Sandra. "Of course she'd have said something to her! Mrs. Moran looked after Monica all day. Dorrie said she's such a nice woman, a widow—she lives on Virginia Avenue just a block over from the apartment—she loves children and she only charged Dorrie a dollar a day."

"I don't know what the *police* could do," said Teresa, "but we thought—put it all together—it's funny."

Sue put down her notebook. She felt a little tingle up her spine. "It *is* funny," she said. "An ordinary young woman, Daisy."

"She isn't ordinary!" said Sandra, and burst into tears. "It nearly killed her when Ken was killed—that way. They'd only been married two years—but she was b-brave as anything and she meant to bring up Monica right, and she worked so hard and never complained and—"

"Funny," said Daisy thoughtfully. "It's a word for it. See which of the brains is in, Sue?"

"I think so," said Sue. She went across the hall to the big detective office. Of all the brains, only her spouse was currently there; she regarded him fondly. Ivor Goronwy Maddox; quite a coincidence that her mother's little Welsh Corgi bore his middle name, signifying Fierce Protector. Thin, dark Maddox who had just got into the force at five-nine, Maddox with the mysterious attribute making him irresistible to anything female. He was leaning back in his chair, tie pulled loose to expose part of the mat of dark chest hair, studying some papers.

"We have something," said Sue, "we'd like the superior brains to look at."

"Mmh?" Maddox looked up. "Sacramento finally sent us photostats on the drivers' licenses. Worth damn little. It's a bunch of kids. We knew that. Well, early twenties maybe. What the hell are the photographs worth? The one on mine makes me look like a gangster. What?"

"Something," said Sue, "funny. Maybe. I know you can't rely on hunches, but there's a sort of feeling in my bones—it just could be a snatch, Ivor."

"Kidnaping?" He snapped to attention. "Don't tell me! Have you contacted the Feds?"

"Not that definite. It doesn't make much sense. There doesn't seem to be much money. Though of course the family back east might have some. But I've just got a feeling—"

"Lady cops," said Maddox. "Fill me in."

two

The manager of the Astro motel on the outskirts of Pasadena had given Rodriguez a little something. The Caddy with those Florida plates had driven in last Tuesday and three people had registered into a double: two men and a woman. By his vague description, Mr. and Mrs. Stanley Kelleher seemed to fit the bodies: early thirties, the man balding, the woman dark, a little too plump. "What about a baby?" asked Rodriguez.

"I didn't see a baby, but there could've been. Well, the other man, I never laid eyes on him either. This is a big place, and I think they were out, mostly. It was only a couple of days. Kelleher registered for the other guy, put down the name as Gary Rowe. And they paid up in cash yesterday and went off, and that's all I know. They done something?"

Rodriguez thought it was likely. Feinman was back by then with the corpses' prints; they dispatched them to Central and also the FBI. Joe Dabney did a lot of the printing and it was his day off, but they were all trained at that job, so Rodriguez, D'Arcy and Feinman went out to the garage where the Caddy had been towed in by now and started to dust it for latents. It was immediately obvious that nobody had been taking care about leaving latents in it; there were hundreds of them, good, bad and indifferent. They hadn't finished with the car before lunch, and afterward they took what they had up to their little lab and looked at some of the prints under magnification.

"I'm no expert," said Feinman, "but just from a look at the prints off the bodies, a lot of these are theirs. Of course they'd had the car three weeks or so, if it was them picked it up down there."

Rodriguez didn't think the Caddy was going to tell them much. Sometimes the lab was very helpful, sometimes not at all. They were still looking at the prints when the expected kickback came in from the Feds on Wednesday night's hit-run victim. They didn't have his prints, didn't know who he was. Well, he had looked like a derelict: about seventy, forty cents on him, and by the autopsy he'd been drunk.

Rodriguez left Feinman to package the lifted latents for the lab downtown, called Dr. Bergner and reminded him about the bodies. "I'll get to them," said Bergner irascibly. "Don't rush me."

"Well, if you do get the slugs out in any shape, we'd like to see them," said Rodriguez. They hadn't found any bullets or ejected cases in the car; ten to one the slugs were still in the bodies. Bergner said he knew that, for God's sake, and about then Sergeant Ellis came in looking mad and began to swear.

"I swear to God," he said, "what the holy hell are we doing here, César? Just what? Work our tails off to catch up to these bastards and killers and thieves, and the goddamn courts—"

"Who'd they let go now?" asked Rodriguez, lighting a cigarette.

"That goddamned rapist, Blye. I wasted the whole damn

morning in court waiting for the damn case to get called, and by God—by *God*—that damn fool calls himself a judge—not even a lawyer, some petty political appointee, who knows if he even graduated from high school—this damn *judge* puts him on two years' probation!" Still seething, Ellis planked his solid self down and groped for cigarettes. "That's a violent one, you know—he knocked a woman down on her own front porch, beat and raped her. She was in the hospital a week—and he doesn't spend a full day in jail! It's enough to make you—"

"Well, you took the oath of your own free will," said Rodriguez wryly. "We see all the dirt and blood, George. By the time it gets to court, it's all tied up in the three-syllable words." Ellis growled and asked if the Lieutenant was in.

"He'll go straight up in the air. These goddamned—"

About three minutes later, raised voices from Lieutenant Eden's office fulfilled this prediction. Rodriguez wandered back up the hall to see if those photostats were in yet, and as he came to the door of the detective office Sue and Maddox came out of it.

"Those photostats are in," said Maddox. "Four sets of 'em. Sue thinks she's got a mystery." He followed her toward Daisy's office. Rodriguez stood where he was for a moment; he was always slightly amused at Maddox in action. The open door revealed two anxious-looking females; within ten seconds, at Maddox's deep voice on the amenities, they began to look visibly reassured. Here was a man to take charge and solve all problems, what had been needed all along, said their expressions.

"*¡Qué interesante!*" he said to himself. "How does he do it?" In the office, he picked up the set of photostats on his desk and looked at them. Apparently D'Arcy had gone out to do some legwork on his. The photographs, even as Maddox had predicted, were not going to be much help to

30

them. Of the six young people, the oldest was twenty-one, and it was very unlikely that any of them had been involved, up to now, in anything serious enough that they'd have mug shots on file somewhere. But there was this and that about the licenses to say something. No thumbprint was asked for now. But three of these licenses had been issued at the D.M.V. office in Hollywood, on Homewood, one at the Bell office and the other two at the downtown office on South Hope. And the oldest one had been issued last November, the newest in January. That said something. Or did it?

■ ■ ■

From Sue's brief rundown on Theodora Mayo, Maddox didn't think there was much in it, but when he'd heard about the typed note and the letter to the store he rubbed his jaw and reflected.

"She doesn't type at all? Never owned a typewriter?"

Sandra and Teresa shook their heads. "She wasn't trained for office work. That's why she had to take the job at Robinson's," said Sandra. "She always says she'd hate office work, and it doesn't pay all that much more. She likes to be meeting people. She worked in a store before—I mean, before she was married."

There was something just a little funny about it, all right. "What about her in-laws back east? Is there any money there?"

They looked surprised. "Why, I don't think so," said Teresa Fogarty. "She never said—and after all they're Ken's people. If they could have afforded to help her she wouldn't have been too proud. Oh, it's a good family, an old family, but—Ken's older brother's a lawyer, I know that. And his father's dead. His mother still lives in the old house. Dorrie wrote her regularly."

"What was her husband doing before he was killed?"

"Well, he got sent out here when he was in the service, and he liked it, so he came back afterward. Ken wasn't very ambitious—I mean for a prestige job or like that. He was easygoing. He was trained as an electrician in the army; he was working at Mactolf-Doll in Glendale. Good money, but not— Why?"

"Just thinking around it," said Maddox. "It does look a little fishy, Sue."

"But what can you *do?*" asked Sandra. "There's nowhere to look."

"Well, first thing we'll do is find out if she has gone back east," said Maddox. "But I'm bound to say— Well, I'd better have a description." He got out his notebook.

"Of Dorrie? She's a little bit of a thing," said Sandra. "Five feet, about a hundred pounds. She's got a kind of olive complexion and dark brown hair—and blue eyes."

"How does she wear her hair?" asked Sue.

"Oh, kind of short. It's naturally curly, she doesn't have to fuss with it, and if she lets it grow the curl comes out. But why d'you want a des— *Do you think she's dead?*" She looked horrified.

"No, no," said Maddox. "Looking for somebody, you want to know what they look like."

"You *are* going to look?" said Teresa. "You don't think we're—imagining things, Sergeant?" She looked at him and Sue curiously.

Maddox said soberly, "No, Mrs. Fogarty, I think you had good reason to come to us. But let's hope you are imagining things."

"Because there's the baby too—Monica. Only fifteen months. Dorrie just—just going off into the blue—"

"Now, we'll be in touch, there's nothing more you can do. Leave it to us," said Maddox.

"It isn't anything much," said Daisy when the two

women had been shepherded out. "It's just—what there is, is wrong somehow."

"Find out if she's in Connecticut anyway." Maddox went down to the Communications room and sent off a teletype to the chief of police in Danbury: Was Mrs. Theodora Mayo staying with her in-laws there? He had a look at the atlas, and the population of Danbury was listed as twenty-four thousand; but it was an old atlas. Not a village, but it wasn't as if her name was Smith. He presumed any chief of police worth his salt, even in a town that size, could find the right Mayos. It was then three thirty, six thirty in Danbury. Possibly they wouldn't get an answer until tomorrow. But if somebody back there got on the ball, an answer could come through tonight. Do no harm to call in and ask around nine or so. Ken Donaldson and Dick Brougham were doing night watch.

He pulled out those photostats and frowned at them again. Damn little, he thought. Well, two birds with one stone. The Robinson's department store in Beverly Hills, where Dorrie had worked, was also one place one of the checks had been passed.

He went out and headed the Maserati toward Wilshire Boulevard. She hadn't, so said Sandra and Teresa, had a car, with the one they'd had demolished in the accident and no money for even a used one immediately. She'd been saving to buy one; the buses were inconvenient.

It was a big and beautiful store, with impressive "levels" instead of mundane floors, plush carpeting and glittering merchandise. He rode up to the restaurant, spent a while fruitlessly hunting means to rise higher to where he'd been told the business offices were, and finally found a single elevator hidden behind Lost and Found. In Personnel, he showed the badge and was admitted to see a surprised and flustered Mr. Wren.

"I'd just like to see the letter," he said. "When did you get it?"

"Very likely the inactive file—I'm afraid I wouldn't know. When this woman quit voluntarily, we might not—" He simmered down when Maddox put the badge away. "But what have the *police* got to do with this?"

"Maybe nothing. We'll see. How long had she been here? Good record?"

"Really, we have so many employees, I'm not familiar— my secretary might be able to find—" The secretary was a plain, efficient girl who just nodded at the name.

"Mr. Simon was furious," she said. "He liked her—she showed off the jewelry, he said. The clerks in jewelry wear some on duty, you know. He came up that first morning she didn't come in, asking if she'd called. Well, I guess he's temperamental or something. Of course he owns that concession—the store just lets it out."

"And he has no right to complain of the alarm system," said Wren fussily. "The most modern— But what about this Mayo woman, Betty?"

"I don't suppose the file's been transferred yet, Mr. Wren. I'll look." Five minutes later she presented Maddox with a manila folder; it contained a concise rundown on Theodora Mayo's employment record.

She'd applied for the job just thirteen months ago and been hired immediately. Her hours were nine to six, an hour off for lunch, except for two Saturdays in alternate months when she had the afternoon off and worked in the evening. She was paid $510 a month take-home. There wasn't a mark on her record, no sick leave, no complaints. One of the few papers was the application form she'd made out; he scanned it rapidly.

Neat, small writing. Under *Education* she'd marked *High school. Nearest relative*—well, that would be a help if the chief of police was dimwitted—*Mrs. Kenneth Mayo,*

Sr., 118 Holly Rd., Danbury, Conn. Marital status: widow. Age: 23. Vital statistics he'd heard from Sandra and Teresa. A little bit of a thing, he saw her, a dark little thing, so brave and hardworking after Ken was killed. . . . Previous employers. They'd said she'd worked in a store, before. Sears, Roebuck, it had been, nearly six years back, and then the hiatus of a couple of years after she was married.

He found the letter. Today was the tenth of March; the letter was dated last Monday, the sixth. It was typed on a plain sheet of typewriter-size paper—no watermark, not bond. There was no address listed at the top, and it was addressed impersonally to *Personnel Dept., J. W. Robinson*, at this store's address. The type was square pica and very clean, no ink smudges, no erasures, no chipped edges. And the signature was typed.

He looked at it thoughtfully. "Who's handled this?"

They looked surprised, confused. "Well, I opened it," said the secretary. "I don't remember if Mr. Wren actually read it, I just told him about it."

"Yes, and I was annoyed," said Wren. "It was irresponsible, just walking off like that with no warning. I don't blame Simon for being angry. Leaving us shorthanded without notice."

"But she hadn't been irresponsible up to then, had she? She had a very good work record, no sick leave."

"Well, I suppose so. I really don't keep track of every employee personally. But what the *police*—"

Maddox wished he had an evidence bag on him. Fingerprints were queer; sometimes careful lab work turned up good ones where you'd least expect to find any. He smiled at the secretary. "Do you think you could find me a new envelope?"

She thawed. "Certainly, sir."

The letter had been folded lengthwise twice, to fit a business-size envelope. He folded it back, touching it as lightly as possible, and slid it into the envelope she gave him. "I'm afraid I'll have to take this, Mr. Wren. You can probably have it back eventually if you want it."

Wren just shrugged massively. "Why the *police* are interested is beyond me."

Maddox found the elevator again and went down to the lower level and men's clothing. The middle-aged clerk he'd talked with before recognized him and came forward, to the annoyance of a bright young salesman in a snappy mod outfit who was about to buttonhole him.

"Hello, Sergeant. Don't tell me you've nabbed one?"

"Here—" said the young clerk.

"Your prices are a little too steep for me. Sorry," said Maddox. He pulled out the photostats of the licenses. "Recognize any, Mr. Ahearn?"

Ahearn pored over them. "It was this one. Richard Goslin. It's not a very clear picture, but I remember the name, of course."

"Would you have recognized the photograph if you hadn't seen the name?"

"Now, that's a question," said Ahearn. "I honestly don't know, Sergeant. You know, young people these days—the same kind of clothes, and the hair. All I was going by"— and he looked indignant—"was identification. The kind the store asks us to get. And that he had. The driver's license, the student card. It was a check from Lockheed. I told you he said he was working part time there. A lot of the students at L.A.C.C. are working their way."

"Hey, this the guy that stuck you with that check?" asked the other salesman.

Maddox looked at the photograph. It was about an inch square; the whole license three and a half by two and a half. The young man in the photograph had light hair, not overlong but straggly, straight; a thin face, the only word for it nondescript. Richard Goslin, male, white, six feet, one-eighty, blond and blue, age twenty-one. Short and sweet.

"Well, thanks anyway." The photostats would be useful after they'd caught up to the kite flyers, but not much help in locating them.

Dorrie hadn't known how to type, had never owned a typewriter. That letter was so evenly and cleanly typed. By a pro typist? Ask Questioned Documents. It really looked like it.

After they'd dusted it for any possible latents, he'd pass it on downtown. He should have asked if Dorrie had ever been printed for any reason. . . .

■ ■ ■

D'Arcy, feeling somewhat depressed, was saying, "Do you recognize her?" and thinking about Sheila Fitzpatrick. Flighty, said her father; taking pictures of society people at this night club. Earning too much money; he'd like to see her settled down. So would D'Arcy, but she kept putting him off. Maybe someday, she'd say airily, maybe someday, Drogo. And that was something else, her discovering his funny handle and actually liking it. It sounded all the funnier to him after so long; he'd kept it a secret for years and had the other boys trained never to use it. Damn that girl.

"Listen, Mr. D'Arcy," said Mr. Steiner, "does a face mean anything, it asks me to cash a check? I may be smart —if not quite as smart as I thought—but that smart I'm not, to tell by a face is there a bank account. I wasn't looking at her face, I was looking at the identification she showed me. The name, that I remember—Coralee Lambert. Such names these kids got nowadays. The driver's license is all kosher, likewise the student card. She bought some cosmetics—five dollars and eighty cents' worth. My girl Lois, usually she works the cosmetic counter, she's off on her break." Mr. Steiner was the pharmacist owner of this patently successful store on Fairfax Avenue. "So I wait on her. And she gives me this check from The Broadway. Probably a part-time job there, I think. It's for thirty-eight seventy-five."

"Yes," said D'Arcy. Mr. Steiner's pharmacy was cool with air conditioning, a welcome change from the heat outside. "But—"

"So I took the check, I put down on the back the number of the license, like you see right there. I put down the serial number on the student card, and I give her thirty-two ninety-five in cash. And the next day I bank all the checks I got, and that one bounces."

"Yes," said D'Arcy. "But did—"

"Faces!" said Mr. Steiner. He looked at the small picture on the photostated license before them: a female, all right, the license said twenty years old, with a lot of blond hair piled on top of her head. "Now I see this, maybe if she comes in again I'd recognize her."

And that was about as likely, thought D'Arcy, as it was likely that Sheila Fitzpatrick would turn into a sweet little domestic housewife overnight.

■ ■ ■

Sue had hoped to get home a little early, to start work on that special beef Stroganoff recipe; but five minutes after Maddox had gone out, Patrolman Carmichael brought in a couple of female juveniles, looking sullen. "Staging a hair-pulling contest on the corner of Hollywood and Highland," he reported. "Disturbing the peace at least. And the blond one had this on her." He laid down a little plastic bag on Daisy's desk; it was full of pills. Red devils, thought Sue sadly. How could anybody believe this generation was so smart? Killing themselves by degrees, brains first.

"All right," said Daisy. "Names?"

"We don't hafta tell you anything!" said the blond one. They looked about sixteen; they also looked dirty and unkempt, in mud-colored pants and sleeveless shirts hanging out. Inevitably they both carried fringed fake-leather shoulder bags, had long straight hair parted in the middle and uncurled, and wore thong sandals on dirty bare feet. But it makes you tired, thought Sue. Were they deliberately trying to make themselves as unattractive as possible, or didn't they really know they were?

"No names?" said Daisy. "Well, I suppose you're both carrying identification of some kind. We can go the long way around."

"The fuzz," said the dark one sullenly. "Helen Eiler. We didn't do anything."

"Where'd you get the pills?" asked Sue.

"None of anybody's business."

It wasted a lot of time, that kind of thing, and it was frustrating and also frightening. Too many kids like these, all over. Where would they end up? And when they had finally got the blonde's name—Linda Davis—and called her mother to explain that Linda would have to appear in juvenile court on the possessions count ("Yes," said Sue, "and be put on probation") they got a tirade of profane abuse, the damn fuzz just picking on kids and if they thought she was coming all the damn way down there after that damn kid now, they could think again.

They sent Linda down to Juvenile Hall, and Sue got home at a quarter past six, before Maddox. No beef Stroganoff; it took too long. She investigated the freezer and got out some breaded veal chops; they didn't have to thaw. She had the white sauce warming and was slicing baked potatoes for frying when he came in.

"Damned heat wave," he said. He kissed her first, pulled off his tie and went to build himself a mild drink with plenty of ice. He told her what had showed at Robinson's. "Funny," he said, "all right. Professionally typed letter, neat and clean."

"But what could be behind it?" asked Sue. "If she didn't type that letter, why should she just walk away like that, without telling?"

Maddox swallowed bourbon and water. "If she didn't type that letter, she didn't intend to walk away. I'd like to see that apartment—and the letter the realty company had. I want to know more about Brian Faulkner, about other people she knew. I think I'll go see this Mrs. Moran tonight."

"It's a mystery—which we don't often run into."

"May be the reason I'm intrigued," said Maddox, massaging his jaw. At this hour he needed another shave. "So we'll go to see your mother tomorrow night instead. Better yet, invite her for dinner."

"It's not my day off," said Sue. "I swear to goodness, half the reason you married me is Mother!"

"Well, twenty-five percent." Maddox grinned. "It's nice to have a family again, love."

■ ■ ■

"And I must say I was that glad to hear it," said Mrs. Moran comfortably. "Best thing for her to do, and she should've done it before. When her poor young man got killed. Best for the baby and everybody. A person needs a family around, like it says right in the Bible."

Maddox had found Mrs. Wilda Moran in the phone book; she lived on Virginia Avenue, a block from the apartment where Dorrie Mayo had lived. He had driven past that building on his way and evaluated it instantly. In some of the smaller apartment houses in central Hollywood, four to eight units, neighbors knew each other, marked comings and goings. But Dorrie's was older, an old-fashioned place of three stories and perhaps thirty apartments. Neighbors would be anonymous; nobody would take note when the Smiths were out late or the Joneses were home with flu or the Robinson hussy had a late caller. In that building, anybody might come and go without remark.

"You said Monday morning," he prompted, to get her back to the point.

"That's right. About nine o'clock, far's as I remember." Mrs. Moran was in her sixties, fat and dumpy and bright-eyed, and she rocked gently with a calico cat asleep in her lap. "I'd wondered why Mis' Mayo hadn't brought the baby—little Monica. A cute baby, cute as a bug in a rug. And a good baby. I oughta know, raised seven myself." She chuckled. "And all turned out good, too. Mike's doin' real well— But I get to rambling. What was it you asked?"

"The telephone call," said Maddox. "It wasn't Mrs. Mayo?"

"No. No, it wasn't. It was somebody said she was a friend of hers."

"A woman. You're sure?"

"Surely I'm sure. I can't make out why you're asking all this. You said *police*. Nothin's happened to Mis' Mayo or little Monica, has it?"

"Well, we're not sure. Just tell me what happened."

"I already did. This woman phoned. Said she was a friend of Mis' Mayo's and Mis' Mayo asked her to call and tell me as she was goin' back east with her husband's family. She'd decided all of a sudden. I already knew they wanted her to, her mother-in-law did—wanted see the baby grow up, and only natural. And Mis' Mayo, no flesh and blood of her own atall, it'd be a good thing for her too. So I said I was glad to hear about it."

"She didn't give you any name?"

"No, sir, she didn't. Wasn't any need, I suppose, though it'd have been polite. She just said Mis' Mayo was packing her things and asked her to call."

"You weren't surprised?" asked Maddox.

She considered, rocking. "Well, one way I was and another way I wasn't. I know once she said they were always after her to move back there, but she'd grown up in California and liked it, and there's all the snow in winter back east. But then once she said she'd never known what it was to have a family and maybe it wasn't right she should bring up little Monica all alone, when there was family back there. No, I don't know as I was surprised. I just thought, She's decided the right way."

Maddox looked at her. A nice woman, maybe not very brilliant, but nice. "What kind of voice was it on the phone, could you say?"

"I don't know," she said vaguely. "Just a voice. A woman's voice. Oh, kind of ladylike, that's all. I miss the baby, you know. I got used to having her. She's a good little thing—going to be pretty too. Like Mis' Mayo. It'd be nice, her widowed so young, if she found a good young fellow back there and got married again."

On his way home Maddox parked down the street from that apartment building and went in. He knew what it would look like inside. Ancient flowered carpet in the dim lobby, on the stairs, along the narrow halls. Dim light. Very quiet. It was an old building, shabby now but still well built. In the new, cheaply built places, sounds of neighbors came through the walls; not here. He walked down the length of the ground floor, looking at the name slots on doors. *Littleton* appeared halfway down on the left, and he pushed the bell, but it rang emptily and the door stayed shut. At the far end, on the right, the door labeled 12 bore a hand-lettered slip in the slot: *Mayo.*

He felt frustrated. As Johnny had said, there was no handle to it.

■ ■ ■

Donaldson and Brougham were sitting on night watch, talking desultorily, at a quarter to twelve, when a teletype started coming through. The sleepy Sergeant Hopewell on the desk called their attention to it, and Donaldson looked at it in some perplexity.

"It's something of Maddox's, addressed to him, but what the hell? THEODORA MAYO NOT HERE FAMILY KNOWS OF NO PLANS TO TRAVEL MUCH CONCERNED PLEASE ADVISE SOONEST LAPD INTEREST AND ALL RELEVANT FACTS IS SHE IN TROUBLE OR NEED REPLY DIRECT MRS KENNETH MAYO SR 118 HOLLY RD DANBURY CONN THOMAS F SUTTNER CHIEF OF POLICE. What the hell, Dick? We can't call Maddox at this hour."

Brougham said it could probably wait. "They wouldn't expect an answer, whatever it is, overnight. My God, it'll be three A.M. there. Of course this was probably transmitted before."

They forgot the teletype when the phone rang. "You've got an assault and robbery, it looks like," said Hopewell. "Cherokee just above Hollywood, in the parking lot. Gomez has called the ambulance."

"Business picking up," said Donaldson, getting up.

"The heat wave. Thank God it doesn't usually last long. What gets me is this new racket, the con men impersonating officers. . . . Take my car?"

Up on Cherokee, dark and silent at this hour, they found the squad car waiting, Patrolman Gomez smoking beside it. "I'd just swung around the corner when the headlights hit him," he said to the detectives. "He took quite a beating, by the look of him." The ambulance came around the corner and stopped.

Just looking at the victim, Donaldson and Brougham

would take no bets he'd make it. He was lying just inside the parking lot past the sidewalk, and the squad car's headlights lit up the scene mercilessly. He was a middle-aged man, ordinary, middle-sized, in a shabby gray suit, white shirt dirtied now from the asphalt, no tie. He lay doubled up, pockets pulled inside out, obviously assaulted for robbery; he had been beaten severely around the head and neck, probably some weapon used. They looked and found a piece of two-by-four stained at one end. Not likely the rough wood would take prints, but they'd take it in for the lab. There was a wallet on the ground beside him, empty of cash but it had some I.D. in it: Walter Ilinsky, an address on St. Francis Terrace a block and a half away.

"On his way home," said Donaldson. "Maybe he'd walked down to the boulevard for a pack of cigarettes or something. Married. It says notify the wife. Damn it, I hate these things, Dick."

"So why'd you pick the job?"

"I thought about something," said Gomez. "Just an idea." They looked at him. "This isn't a public parking lot —I mean a city lot. There's an attendant up to nine P.M. It's a free lot for all the places along this block of the boulevard. And I've been riding swing watch along here the last six months."

"So?" said Brougham.

"So," said Gomez, "even riding a black-and-white, which isn't like walking a beat, you get to know this and that. This lot's chained at nine P.M. every night and the attendant goes off duty. It's right in the middle of town but dark and quiet as hell, you can see. And I'd say"—he looked at the flaccid bloody victim as he was loaded into the ambulance—"that happened maybe a couple of hours ago. So I thought about Pops Keenan and Eddy Smith."

"And who the hell are they?"

"Well, a couple of characters," said Gomez with a grin.

"They're retired actors. When I say that I mean extras, Central Casting, hired for ten bucks a day to make up the crowds. You know. They're on pension or whatever, both old bachelors, and they live in a cheap room up on Las Palmas, a block from here."

"Have you got a point in mind?" asked Donaldson.

"Well, they're winos," said Gomez. "Harmless. They don't get falling-down drunk. They usually get home all right. But a lot of times I've found 'em right here in this lot, ten–eleven o'clock, midnight. The lot attendant's got a bench and table over at the side there. They tell me their room's awful stuffy. A warm night comes along, and this is a nice peaceful place to sit." He laughed. "It just occurred to me, it's a warm night tonight. Just maybe they were here, and just maybe they saw something."

"My God," said Donaldson disgustedly.

"I mean, that bench is against the back of the buildings along the boulevard. In shadow. Whoever pulled that"— the ambulance was just turning out to the street—"might not have noticed, if Keenan and Smith were there."

"My God, a couple of drunks as witnesses?" said Brougham.

"Characters," said Gomez. "Just harmless winos. You might see 'em and ask, just in case."

three

They found that waiting for them on Saturday morning. Brougham had left a report centered on Maddox's desk; he and Donaldson had seen Walter Ilinsky's wife. He was in critical condition at Hollywood Receiving Hospital a couple of blocks up Wilcox. Mrs. Ilinsky said he'd walked down to Ace's Bar and Grill on the boulevard, as he did a couple of times a week, for a few beers and maybe a game of checkers; he'd probably have started home by nine or a little later.

"Witnesses!" said D'Arcy, reading that over Maddox's shoulder and coming to Brougham's sardonic mention of Patrolman Gomez's little idea. "A couple of drunken bums?"

"Sometimes we take what we can get," said Rowan philosophically.

"Try the bar," said Maddox. "Somebody should remember what time he left, and maybe somebody followed him out."

"And we ought to get something from the Feds today on those bodies," said Rodriguez. "Not that I suppose either of them was much loss."

By then Maddox had discovered the teletype from Danbury, and said, "By God, so now we know there *is* something very funny about it. I do wonder—"

"About what?"

"You haven't heard about it—you'd better." He filled in the story, and Rodriguez laughed.

"*Nada absolutamente.* You've got nothing says it's funny, much less anything for us. Girl gets fed up, decides to cut all ties. Maybe she didn't like Sandra and Teresa as much as they like her. Maybe she got tired of the in-laws trying to pressure her."

"That letter," said Maddox. "That beautiful typed letter —and there was the realty company. The Fogarty girl said something—and she doesn't sound like that kind of girl, César."

"So chase her down," said Rodriguez, "and I'll bet she won't thank you. Maybe found a fairy godfather."

There wasn't anything more they could usefully do about the check passers. Maddox agreed with D'Arcy when Ellis came in asking for the latest on that. "Well, just looking at what we've got," said Ellis, "I'm bound to say it doesn't look as if they're pros. A bunch of amateurs—and ten to one most of 'em attending L.A.C.C., else why think of the student cards for I.D.?"

"I had also got that far," said Rodriguez, smoothing his mustache. "Have you any suggestion where to go from there?"

"I damn well might have. Somebody said you'd got photostats of those licenses from Sacramento. Can't do anything today, but Monday we could fan out on that campus and try to match some faces."

D'Arcy laughed. "Take a look at the photostats!"

"So pour the cold water," said Maddox. "I still think we've got something here." He folded the teletype into a pocket and started out, and Rodriguez said they had too much legitimate work for him to run off on a wild goose chase. "Geese," said Maddox absently. "There's the baby too. I'm going up to that realty company." But he went across the hall to show the teletype to Sue first. They had synchronized time better this morning and managed breakfast.

"So she's not there, wherever she is," said Sue. "And you know, Ivor, I had a second thought. If she just wanted—"

"Mmh, César got there too. But I don't think so. There's that letter. Something a little fishy about that letter, my love. Don't tell me I'm goofing off. We'll look a little further here. I want a search warrant for that apartment."

"Anything turned up on the Mayo girl?" asked Daisy, coming in as he went out. Sue had her mouth open to tell her about the teletype when the phone rang and Daisy picked it up. "Wilcox Street, Sergeant Hoffman. . . . Yes, sir. . . . I see. . . . Yes, certainly, sir, we'll be glad to help however we can. We'll expect you, then. Sergeant Manuel and Sergeant Walgren, half an hour." She put the phone down resignedly. "Central, Narco. They want us to tag along on some pickups here. What their own junior division is doing they didn't say. They've got some names— sellers and pushers—operating out of Hollywood High. We go along to hold the females' hands and soothe the mamas and papas."

"Oh, Lord," said Sue. "Well, all in the day's work."

■ ■ ■

Ace's Bar and Grill wouldn't be open until eleven o'clock. From what they'd heard about it, it sounded like a homey place where the same familiar crowd gathered most nights, and probably the owner and/or bartender could tell them about when Ilinsky had left and who'd been there at the time. It might be a waste of time even to ask. The assault on Ilinsky had been pretty crude, very possibly a spur-of-the-moment thing. The kind of thing, in fact, coming to be discouragingly common of late.

"With the judge saying, You be a good boy and don't do it again, and a year's probation," said Rodriguez as he and D'Arcy came out to the street.

D'Arcy didn't ask what he meant. "Oh, yes, the prime cause, of course. But not all of it. Just the general preaching of violence all over."

"And a general lack of empathy. Not many brothers' keepers around."

Brougham had put down the address. It was an old sprawling California bungalow at the top of Las Palmas Avenue. "Talk about wild goose chases," said D'Arcy. He let Rodriguez exercise the charm on the dumpy elderly woman who answered the door. She looked rather jolly, with bright blue eyes, and her cotton dress and apron were spankingly clean. She looked at the badge and said she was Mrs. Higginbottom. When Rodriguez asked about her roomers, she laughed.

"You want to talk to Pops and Eddy? Mister, you're early birds for them. Questions, hey? What about? Well, I'll see what I can do, get 'em up and halfway sensible. Early in the month like this they still got money to spare. Beats me what you want to talk to 'em for." She was mostly incurious.

"Do you know what time they came in last night?"

"Along about eleven thirty, bit later. Pretty usual. They were on their feet, but just about." She cocked her head at them. "You don't want to think they're—you know— dirty old bums. They're not. Nice old fellows, and it's about all the fun they get outta life any more. Live and let live, I say. They're clean, I wouldn't have 'em here if they wasn't, and they never get ugly or swear or nothing

—it just makes 'em happy. Well, I'll see what I can do, get 'em awake for you. You can set on the porch if you want." She went away smiling.

They sat on the porch, on two sagging old armchairs, and waited in the warm morning air. It was about time for the heat wave to end. D'Arcy had smoked two cigarettes and Rodriguez three before the screen door opened and their hostess ushered two old men out to them. One was short and thin, one was taller with a little round paunch; both were gray and mostly bald, with patently store teeth. They looked clean if unshaven, in shabby pants and tieless shirts.

"Mr. Smith? Mr. Keenan?" said Rodriguez.

"I'm Smith," said the smaller one. His eyes were a little bleary, and he looked alarmed. "Say, Mildred says you're police. We didn't *do* anything, did we? We never do anything, however little bit high we might—"

"Not that we know of," said Rodriguez.

They both sat down in the old porch swing and Keenan yawned, blinking his eyes.

"We understand that you sometimes hang around that parking lot between Cherokee and June. The patrolman on the beat—"

They looked at each other. "Gah," said Smith, shaking his head. "You know, we shoulda done something, Pops. We did see that, I guess. Is that what you're askin' about?"

"I don't know," said Rodriguez. "What did you see? In that parking lot?" As usual he was very neat and dapper, and possessing the coldly logical Latin mind, he looked at this happy-go-lucky pair of senior citizens rather disapprovingly.

"Neither of us was in a state to do anything, Eddy," said Keenan solemnly. "Tell the truth, we wasn't all that sure we really seen it. Your brain gets to imagining things sometimes."

50

"All right, were you there last night and what do you think you saw?"

"We was there," said Smith. "Like my wife used to say—"

"I thought you were both bachelors," said D'Arcy.

"Oh, no, that is abso-tootly incorrect," said Keenan. "We both had wives and lost 'em. I lost two and Eddy lost three. I got a married daughter in Pasadena. But we always got along fine, Eddy 'n' me, and it's handier to pool our resources as you might say. What did your wife always say, Eddy?"

"About it's not the heat so much as the humidity," said Eddy, making three tries at the word. "It was a muggy kind of evening, last night. Almost like summer. And our room here—"

"Gets stuffy," said Rodriguez. "So you were sitting in that parking lot, on that bench. How high were you?"

"Well, middling," said Keenan. "Middling, I got to say. We got some pretty good port at the market—three bottles. I guess we'd killed the second one."

"Do you have any idea what time it was, when you saw whatever you saw?"

"Now that I couldn't say," said Smith, "except that I got to agree we'd killed the second bottle."

"And what did you see?"

"A fight. Seemed like two fellas fighting another guy. On the street there. It wasn't very light—there wasn't any moon—but it was a ruckus some kind. We both heard it."

Rodriguez looked at Keenan.

"Well, a ruckus," he repeated. "That's it. Two—well, I don't know, Eddy, them two, just the best I can think back, they wasn't very big. Not as big as the fella they was hittin'. But like you say, the light—"

Rodriguez was annoyed with all this vagary. "There was a man assaulted and nearly killed there last night. Are you sure of what you just said, you saw two men attack another?"

They nodded, both still a little bleary. "It didn't go on but a minute or so, and then it was all quiet again. I figured a fight, and they run off."

"You didn't go to look, didn't see the man on the ground?"

"Mister, I guess we got to the third bottle after that," said Keenan frankly. "I wasn't quite so bad as Eddy. We got home some way, me helpin' him. I thought they'd gone off. Say, that's terrible, fella nearly gettin' killed. I sure wish we could tell you more about it."

"Well—" Rodriguez didn't know what he had to thank them for. They did agree: two muggers. Something. If Ilinsky ever woke up to confirm that, a small lead.

"Witnesses!" said D'Arcy again as they got into his old Dodge. "Damn drunks. If they hadn't been stinko they might have helped Ilinsky fight them off."

Rodriguez laughed suddenly. "They wouldn't have been there at all." He lit another cigarette. "It is always so much tidier in books." A while back Rodriguez had suddenly become a detective-fiction fan; at the moment he was still working his way through John Dickson Carr.

■ ■ ■

Today the stories Public Relations had fed the press and TV would get an airing, about the phony traffic cops, about the amateur check forgers. Nothing much to do on that but wait on opportunity and a helpful citizenry.

Maddox had the name of the realty company from Teresa Fogarty; it was far out on Santa Monica. Once there, he was frustrated for forty minutes, shuttled from one person to another, none of whom knew what he was talking about, until by chance he mentioned Mrs. Fogarty's name. A spasm of annoyance flickered across the face of the anonymous salesman he was talking to. "Oh, yes, on Thursday—a most obstinate woman. She was really rude, but I think Miss Winkelstein got rid of her finally."

"I'd like to see Miss Winkelstein," said Maddox. "I did mention that this is police business?"

"Oh, for God's sake," said the salesman. He went away and came back ten minutes later with a female in tow. "Miss Winkelstein. He says he's a cop, I don't know what about."

"Miss Winkelstein?" said Maddox.

"That's me." She looked at the badge interestedly. She was probably nearer forty than thirty, but still good-looking. Bright-eyed and bushy-tailed, thought Maddox. Black hair with a white streak, smart black-and-white dress, good figure and very good legs (not as good as Sue's). She had a narrow dark face, not pretty but handsome, and snapping dark eyes. "What's it all about? We can sit down."

There were two very modern chairs and a table with a lot of land prospectuses on it. They sat down. He offered her a cigarette and lit it for her and told her what it was about.

"Oh," she said. "I remember that Fogarty girl on Thursday. The way it happened was—funny"—and she shrugged —"but what business was it of mine? This Mayo woman wants to take off with us owing her a rebate, it's her business. That's all I know, and that's what I told the Fogarty girl. You aren't telling me it's your business?"

"Maybe. How did Mrs. Mayo—er, I think you said 'inform' you of her moving? Did you get a letter?"

She sighed impatiently. "Not exactly. It looked to me as if something'd come up in a hurry and she didn't want any red tape. Her business, as I say. Look, if I have to tell it in words of one syllable, that apartment house is one of a dozen or so old Waldemar owns—retired broker, he lives in Monterey. We handle the business for him—maintenance, rent collection and so on. The tenants pay us and we pay him. We usually ask a month's notice of moving, and of course they pay two months ahead when they move in. So. We've got a maintenance man—fancy name for janitor. He's there—that place and the rest—once a week, cuts the strip of lawn in front, puts out the trash for the refuse truck, any odd jobs. Got that? All right, let's see, it was last Tuesday morning he found the note."

"A note. Where?"

"Scotch-taped on the door of Mrs. Mayo's apartment. In an envelope. It was addressed to the manager."

"Wait a minute. You mean literally?" asked Maddox. "Quote *To the manager* unquote?"

"That's right. He didn't know what to do with it. He brought it here and happened to give it to me. And it said the Mayo woman was moving out, sorry for any inconvenience. The door key was in it."

"Do tell," said Maddox gently.

"Look, I read it, especially when this other woman came asking about her—maybe she was getting out from under something. Cut ties to a boy friend or whatever. Good luck to her. I wasn't about to—"

"You told Mrs. Fogarty there was no forwarding address. Was there?"

"No," she said. "Just what I told you."

"Well, well," said Maddox. "Wild geese indeed. If that's not fishy I've lost my sense of smell."

"What?"

He looked at her. Whatever it was about unhandsome, unremarkable Ivor Maddox that drew the females, he'd never know, but she was reacting to him. "Tell me," he said, "the tenants make their rent checks payable to this company? Was Mrs. Mayo's rent paid up?"

"Yes. I went and looked when I read the note. Her check had come in the mail on the first. Ninety bucks."

"Check payable to the company?"

"Yes." She was impatient.

"So she knew—like every tenant there—that there wasn't a manager on the premises. Can you describe the note for me? Typed or written?"

"Typed," she said automatically. "My God, I never thought—"

"I suppose it's too much to hope for that it's still around somewhere?"

"No, I threw it out. I didn't think—but I don't understand. What's it mean? Has something happened to this woman? Police coming—"

"I don't know," said Maddox, "but I really don't think she intended to—mmh—walk away." There was also Monica, fifteen months old and cute.

"We haven't arranged to clean the apartment yet."

"Don't," said Maddox. "There'll be a seal on it, and a search warrant." He'd got O'Neill to start the machinery on that before he left the office; it would be slow, on a Saturday, but it might come through by tonight; he hoped so.

And what was he going to answer to that agitated-at-one-remove teletype from Danbury, Connecticut?

■ ■ ■

He found a public phone and called Teresa Fogarty. Sooner or later they'd get the search warrant, and he'd like her to look at the apartment. "You'd be familiar with it—her furniture and so on?"

"Well, I've only been there a couple of times, but I'd know her things. They'd only started to furnish the house when Ken was killed. She didn't have much or keep much.

It's a furnished apartment. But she kept a couple of pictures and her small appliances—her mixer and a vacuum and a blender—"

"Fine. I'll let you know. What can you tell me about this Brian Faulkner?"

"Jim knows him—we don't know him well. Please, have you found out anything? About Dorrie?"

"Still looking. Is your husband there?"

He was. He sounded a little surprised at the detailed questions but answered amiably. Faulkner, he said, had been in his graduating class at Hoover High in Glendale. He hadn't run into him since, until about six months ago Faulkner had got a job in the same firm, a tax-accountant office in Hollywood, Giese and Weekes. The only time they'd had Faulkner to the house was when they gave a big back-yard party last fall and asked practically everybody they knew; he guessed that was when Faulkner had met Mrs. Mayo. He didn't even know where Faulkner was living. The office, of course, was closed today.

It was all unsatisfactory and up in the air. She must have had a bank account somewhere; couldn't get at that until Monday. Maddox called Wilcox Street and asked about the search warrant. "Well, you know Saturday," said O'Neill. "I haven't heard. Just be thankful you're out of uniform."

"Why?"

"The—er—younger generation," said O'Neill, "is staging a mammoth rally in the pure name of ecology, up in Griffith Park. There've been cars diverted up there to keep an eye on it. Traffic shift just changing, and the boys are saying this and that. Already the biggest mess up there you ever saw, litter and food thrown around and sandwich bags and cigarette butts and—"

"And, I wouldn't doubt, reefer butts," said Maddox.

"Oh, yes, and the former containers of H and acid. Ecology. I hear you're after a wild goose."

"Wild geese," said Maddox, and hung up. Dorrie Mayo was a little thing, but "brave." And adult. But he was beginning to worry about Monica.

■ ■ ■

By three thirty D'Arcy and Rodriguez had talked to the owner of Ace's Bar and Grill and to the bartender on duty last night. They had the names of seven men who were regular customers and knew Walter Ilinsky, had been there last night. It was a family place, all right, where men sat over a few beers, talked, played cards or checkers.

They had found three of the seven men to talk to. Everybody was alarmed and sorry to hear about old Walt, and nobody knew anything. Nobody had left the place just after he had; anyway, nobody there would want to hurt Walt. He'd left about nine fifteen; he'd only had about three beers and he wasn't tight, not anywhere near.

They had called the hospital and heard that Ilinsky was a little better, after surgery to repair a skull fracture. He'd probably wake up eventually, but he might never have gotten a look at whoever had jumped him.

They went back to the office then, and as they walked across toward the door a black-and-white pulled up in front and Daisy and Sue got out of it. "Thanks very much," said Daisy to the driver. They both looked tired and irritable.

"Why I ever picked this job," said Sue.

"You sound as frustrated as we are," said Rodriguez. "Where've you been?"

"Obliging Central," said Daisy crossly.

■ ■ ■

It had all been fairly exasperating. The Narco men had names, no addresses; they had pressured various school officials, who kept passing the buck, and finally an assistant vice principal or assistant counselor or whatever had turned out to open the school files for them. He was a little fat man with a beard, no inhibitions about expressing opinions, and he told them they were violently prejudiced against Youth. They lacked the Open Mind, he said, his beard waggling; they harbored Automatic Suspicion, which bordered on Paranoia. His name was Holderby.

"You Gestapo cops never make allowances," he said.

The tall dark Narco sergeant said to Sue, "Funny they never think to compare us to the KGB, isn't it?"

"But they've got open minds," said the blond Narco sergeant.

They got addresses from the files, three boys and two girls. They went looking. They did a lot of talking to the parents (four sets horrified and cooperative, one set indifferent and annoyed at the fuzz for interrupting a serious drinking party), they pried at three males and one female, definitely tied up to a selling ring of the hard stuff, who were unrepentant, wary and contemptuous, and one tearful female who hadn't known what she was getting into.

"Betty just asked me to give that package to Julie. She said it was a pair of panty hose. I didn't know—honestly I didn't—"

That one, they believed: a simpleton, merely. The rest they took down to Juvenile Hall, except for one who was turned eighteen; he got the County Jail. They had found, in various hiding places, about a pound of marijuana, an assortment of barbiturates, and ten decks of H.

"New shipment due in," said the dark Narco sergeant. "Running low. Good thing we know where the drop is and when to expect it."

They snarled at him.

Central sent Daisy and Sue back to base in a squad car, which was polite of them.

58

■ ■ ■

"And I know all about dedicated officers," said Sue as they climbed the stairs, "but I am starving. I think those Narco cops could at least have bought us lunch."

"They didn't?" said Rodriguez. "I call that ungentlemanly. The least we can do is— Well, there, we said it'd come in handy. Our new sandwich machine."

"He just put it in," said Rowan from the door of the detective office. "Why it made so much noise I don't know. It isn't fastened to the wall. Wonder if it works."

"Be my guest," said Rodriguez, fishing for change. Sue and Daisy looked at the sandwich machine. It was about five feet high and four wide; it had four vertical columns with a slot and lever for each, and, at the bottom, some two and a half feet from the floor, a long open horizontal slot. The columns were labeled *Cheese, Beef, Ham* and *Egg*. "Come on, try it. What do you want?" He handed Sue a half dollar.

Sue put it in the coin slot marked *Egg* and pulled the lever. Nothing happened. She pulled it harder and the sandwich machine began to mutter. It gave a clank and then stopped.

"Damn machines," said D'Arcy. "Half the time they don't work—"

Rodriguez took hold of the machine by both sides and gave it a hard shake. The machine clanked again and ungraciously delivered a cellophane-wrapped sandwich into the bottom slot. Sue picked it up. "It feels nice and fresh. Thank you, sir."

D'Arcy gave the machine a suspicious look and followed Rodriguez into the other office. "You've got a make in from the Feds," said Rowan.

"And about time. They've got computers too, haven't they?" Rodriguez picked it up. "*Así, así.* So now we know who the corpses were. Rex Hahn, pedigree too long to detail—armed robbery, bank heists, armed robbery—time served in the Federal pen, Leavenworth, Quentin. Originally from Fort Lauderdale, Florida. Thirty-nine, Caucasian, et cetera, but prints don't lie. The female is Edna Gifford, also quite a pedigree—prostitution, accomplice to burglary, receiving stolen goods. He was on parole from the Florida pen. She was clean, technically speaking—served two years in Illinois for the receiving charge. She's got a family in Chicago. I suppose we'd better notify them —they might want to pay for a funeral."

"Anything on the second man?"

"*Nada*. We only sent those prints from the Caddy in today. See if they make him. A little farther on anyway."

"Which is more than we are on Ilinsky," said D'Arcy.

"That could've been any lout—or pair of louts—in the county," said Rodriguez. "His wife said he wouldn't have had more than ten bucks on him." Ilinsky worked for a tree-trimming outfit. "He can offer thanks he's alive." He sounded cynical, a little sad. He wandered over to the window and looked down at Wilcox Street, a quiet orderly avenue without much traffic, a backwater in the midst of the all too often violent city.

■ ■ ■

At about the same time Patrolman Ben Loth was wondering what this odd little incident added up to. Nothing much, he guessed, but it was—funny. He'd been riding this particular beat in central Hollywood for upwards of three years, and he knew it well: he knew old Rudi Wechsler and the little mama-and-papa grocery on Fountain as an ordinary, humdrum sort of place. Not a place you looked for the wildly unexpected.

"Are you O.K.?" he asked the boy.

"Sure. I guess so." The boy was about nineteen, big,

open-faced and nice looking without being handsome. He had a close haircut and clean T shirt and jeans. He put a hand to the back of his head. "I guess," he said uncertainly, "I got sort of confused, but it sure looked like—well, gee, I'm sorry if I was wrong."

"As long as you're O.K."

"Sure," said the boy. He started up the street slowly. Loth got back into the squad car. In Hollywood they ran one-man cars; for a minute he wished he had a partner to consult about this. Put in a report or not? Old man Wechsler—it was silly.

But just being thorough and careful, maybe better make a report at the end of the tour.

■ ■ ■

Maddox came back to the office at five thirty; he'd wasted most of the day. He'd tried to get in touch with some official of Jim Fogarty's firm, to find out more about Brian Faulkner, with no luck. In Maddox's experience, when anything unusual, peculiar, or violent happened to a young woman, it was attributable, ninety percent of the time, to any current man in her orbit. As the French put it, but the other way around.

He had gone looking for other friends of Dorrie's, names supplied by Teresa, but on this warm Saturday afternoon none of them was home. Working girls, young housewives —out shopping, at the beach, on dates.

By what Teresa and Sandra said, Dorrie hadn't been interested in Faulkner; he had been in her. But did Teresa and Sandra know everything about Dorrie Mayo? Unlikely.

He veered into the office across the hall and told Sue what he'd got from Miss Winkelstein. "But," said Sue, wrinkling her nose, "it's up in the air, Ivor. She could have been—just getting away."

61

"Dragging your heels. She knew there wasn't a manager."

"That note could've been just a shortcut. The easiest thing to do," said Sue.

Rowan looked in. "You've got a telegram."

Naturally, thought Maddox. He hadn't answered Thomas F. Suttner, Chief of Police.

The telegram was from an evidently forceful character who signed himself David M. Mayo: DEMAND ANY AND ALL INFORMATION POLICE INTEREST IN THEODORA MAYO. IS SHE ALL RIGHT? FAMILY MUCH CONCERNED. LATEST LETTER TO MRS. MAYO SR. DATED MARCH 2ND RECEIVED MARCH 4TH. NO MENTION MOVE OR CHANGE ANY SORT. WHAT IS WRONG? PLEASE TRANSMIT INFO TO UNDERSIGNED OR MRS. MAYO SR. SOONEST.

Concerned, thought Maddox. They would be; by all he'd got, an ordinary nice family. Concerned. And just what the hell might he wire back to David Mayo? She's gone. We don't know where or why. With Monica, fifteen-month-old Monica.

They'd said Sue could go on working a year or so, and then they'd start a family.

Had she meant to walk away? For some reason? No, thought Maddox. The letter. The note "to the manager." No manager, which she knew.

A snatch? That was silly. No money showing. There was no handle to this thing at all, from any side.

"Damnation," he said, and jumped as the phone went off at his elbow.

"I hope you appreciate the special service, Sergeant, avick," said O'Neill. "I kept after it, from the underlings working overtime at the D.A.'s office on up. Your search warrant just came through. Fifty-six-sixteen Lexington, apartment twelve, ground floor. You can execute it any time."

"Thanks, Johnny!"

"It's after six," said Sue from the door. "Are you coming home, darling? I thought those sirloin-strip steaks in the freezer, and blue-cheese dressing—I know you don't go for the rabbit food but this heat—au gratin potatoes? I've had rather a day and I'd like a solid meal."

"Fine," said Maddox. "Yes. I'm just leaving. And we were going to see your mother. But this search warrant—"

"I'll see you at home. Fifteen minutes?"

"Fifteen minutes," said Maddox. He said it absently. He was thinking about Monica again.

four

Maddox phoned Teresa Fogarty before he left the office. When he got home, the front door of the little house behind the Clinton house was wide open behind its screen, the room air-conditioner unit in the bedroom was on and all three electric fans.

"It's the one drawback, and a sizable one," said Sue, putting down the head of lettuce to return his kiss. "With the place shut up all day, or even with the windows open, in summer it'll be—well, last October was a sample."

"We'd better start looking for a house. With air conditioning."

"At the asking prices these days? I'll settle for two more room conditioners."

"Compromise," said Maddox, getting out ice. "She'll meet us there at eight—Teresa Fogarty. Join me in a small drink?"

"You know I don't like whiskey," said Sue. "But there's one mixed gimlet left, I think." Maddox found it and poured it over ice. "Ivor." She abandoned the salad and sat down at the kitchen table, tasting the gimlet thoughtfully. "She could have just—gone. For her own reasons. Wanting to cut all ties, the way Miss Winkelstein thought."

Maddox had his tie off and his shirt unbuttoned, leaning back in the straight chair. "Why so roundabout?" he asked laconically.

"The letter quote-unquote to the manager. But—"

"If it had been easier, I'd say maybe. If it had cut any corners for her, that letter, or the one to Robinson's. The note to Mrs. Littleton—we haven't heard about that—the phone call to Mrs. Moran. But it was roundabout. She knew who she paid rent to—how much easier to write a letter to the realty company and mail it. And who did phone Mrs. Moran? I'll say this. When we hear from Questioned Documents downtown, I'd lay a small bet they'll tell us the letter to Robinson's was professionally typed. And if, damn it, we had the note the realty company got, I'd bet they'd say it was typed on the same machine."

"But why?" asked Sue blankly. "Nobody could kidnap a woman and a baby out of an apartment—and why should anybody? There's no money anywhere."

"That's the mystery, all right. But funny things happen, Sue. All the time. One of the things any cop learns by experience"—he squinted at his glass and rattled ice cubes—"is the damned reasonlessness of things. The randomness. The—mmh—essential irrationality of too much of the human race. I wouldn't have a guess here—yet—about why or how. But we'll keep on poking for something definite."

Sue finished the gimlet and got up. "I feel better. That was nice. I'd better get on with dinner, if we're going out."

"And I'll think about those conditioners. Have I got time for a shower before dinner?"

■ ■ ■

As they left the house at seven forty, Maddox stopped on the step, went back in and re-emerged with the hammer in one hand. "What on earth?" said Sue.

"I want to see if the refrigerator's been cleaned out."

"Oh," said Sue, enlightened.

It was very dark along Lexington Avenue by eight o'clock. They stood by the Maserati at the curb, and three minutes after Maddox had parked it a middle-aged Ford came nosing up behind and stopped. Teresa Fogarty got out.

"Sergeant Maddox? Jim doesn't like me to drive alone at night. But it wasn't far. Have you—have you found out anything?"

"That's what we're still doing, isn't it? I think you met my wife yesterday."

"Yes." She looked at Sue curiously in the dim light of a nearby street lamp. "It's a little funny, your both being— Well, what do you want me to do?"

"Just look. You've been in Mrs. Mayo's apartment how often?" They started up the front steps.

"Well, let's see. She moved here just over a year ago, when the house was sold and—things settled up more or less. After the accident. We'd tried to help, and I told you Ken's brother came out to help too. He was still here, and she had us all to dinner just before he went back east. It'd be a year ago last month. Then—we were both busy, you know, we didn't have much spare time, but once or twice we went shopping. I'd call for her here and go in. And last summer we had season tickets for the Bowl. We took Dorrie to several concerts—picked her up here."

"Well, you can probably tell us something," said Maddox. They were walking down the long dim hallway, and now he stopped. "I think we'll make a little detour first." He pushed the bell beside the door to his left.

After a moment it opened, and a woman looked at them. She was young and rather pretty, with light brown hair and a friendly mouth. "Yes?"

"Mrs. Littleton?" Maddox showed her the badge.

Small apprehension came into her eyes. "Police? What about?"

"Maybe you'll remember Mrs. Fogarty." He stepped aside, and she looked at the two women.

"Oh. You came asking about Dorrie."

"We don't know where she's gone—" began Teresa; Maddox flicked an eye at her and she stopped.

"That note," he said. "We heard she left a note for you."

She nodded. "You don't know wh— but that's silly. She *said* where she was going, and I was glad she'd decided, even if it was in such a hurry for some reason. When there was any family, it's best she should be with them."

"What did it say?"

"Why, just that—I told this lady, Mrs. Fogarty—that Dorrie was sorry not to say good-by, she'd decided to go back east to live with her mother-in-law, and it'd come up suddenly, was all."

"You found it when?"

"Taped to the door when I came home from work Tuesday. Is anything wrong about it? Police. Has—has something happened to Dorrie?" She looked from one to the other of them.

"You were about the only tenant here she was friendly with, I understand." Maddox was easy, amiable, his tone relaxing her.

"I guess so. Most of the others on this floor are older people. But you see, my little girl—she'd have been about Monica's age if she'd lived, so I noticed them right away when they moved in. Dorrie and I are about the same age. It's not as if we really saw much of each other, both working, but lots of Sundays she'd leave Monica with me while she ran up to the market. But—police—is something wrong?"

"Was the note typed or written?"

She said, "It was typed. I thought it was funny. I didn't

think she had a typewriter. But—no, I didn't save it. Why? I don't understand."

"When did you see her the last time, Mrs. Littleton?"

She thought. "It'd be last Sunday morning. About nine o'clock. She was going out—she had Monica in her stroller. I had the door open for air, and she just called good morning and said she was going up to the drugstore."

"I see. Thanks very much," said Maddox. He turned away down the hall, Sue and Teresa after him, and Mrs. Littleton stood in her open door watching them.

"But is anything wrong?" Her voice trailed after them.

At the door to Apartment 12, Maddox put the key in the lock, which was in the knob. "Hands off everything," he said to Teresa. "We haven't been through here looking for prints and so on. I just want you to look and tell me if you spot anything that looks odd to you." She nodded, and he turned the knob with the key and stood back to let them in.

Stale, hot air rushed out at them; this place had been shut up, in the little March heat wave, for nearly a week. It was a typical apartment for its age, call it fifty years. Living room about twelve by fourteen, kitchen with a dinette at this end to the left, door to bedroom and bath at the right. Two double-hung windows at the back of the living room, looking out to the driveway of the building. An old flowered rug not quite as big as the room, plain beige drapes, Venetian blinds. A double-hung window at the dinette end of the kitchen. The kind of furniture ever present in a furnished apartment: round-armed couch now wearing a yellow-flowered slipcover, chair to match, a rickety desk with matching straight chair, another armchair with a floor lamp beside it; old table lamp with a round green base on the small table beside the first chair.

"Why, there's Dorrie's mission," said Teresa.

"What?"

She pointed. "That's one of the pictures she kept. San Juan Capistrano mission. She liked it. She said it was restful." It was a reproduction print, nicely framed in distressed pine, hanging over the couch. "That's queer. I'm sure she'd have taken that if she—meant to move."

"Anything else? Take your time, just don't touch." He moved into the bedroom. Smaller than the living room: old walnut twin beds, white cotton chenille spreads. He lifted one; the bed was made up. Walnut chiffonier; brass pulls with rings. He got out his knife and slid the longest blade through the rings, one by one, pulled open the drawers. They were all empty.

"And that's the other one," said Teresa. He turned. She was looking a little frightened now. "That picture over the beds. It's a seascape by Robert Wood—I mean a reproduction. It's Dorrie's own. It cost quite a lot to have it framed."

Maddox looked at it. A very nice seascape; he liked Wood too. "All right, let's keep on looking." There was a walk-in closet; he slipped the knife blade into the unused lock on the door and pulled it open. No clothes on the rows of hangers on the long rod; nothing on the shelf. No shoes on the floor. No suitcases. He got down and peered under the beds: no suitcases there either.

Sue went into the bathroom. "Clean sweep, looks like." He joined her, Teresa looking in the door. He opened the medicine cabinet with the knife. It was empty. No bubble bath, dusting powder, soap, brushes visible.

"But she'd never have left her pictures—"

"Mmh." Maddox went back across the living room to the kitchen. There were dishes neatly stacked in the cupboards, pots and pans below, silver in the drawers. "They come with a furnished apartment," said Sue.

Maddox got out the hammer from his jacket pocket and used the claw end to get a good grip on the refrigerator door. It came open, and he said, "But that doesn't."

The refrigerator had not been cleaned out. There was a half-gallon carton of milk, a baby's bottle full of something, a pitcher of orange juice on the top shelf; a foil dish of cooked bacon, other dishes with leftover asparagus, peas; a lone veal chop still encased in cellophane from the market; a package of wieners, half a pound of margarine, opened bottles of dill pickles, relish, olives. He shut the door and used the claw on the door of the freezer over the refrigerator. A modest collection of frozen foods: breaded veal chops, peas, carrots, artichoke hearts, a quart of chocolate ice cream, a couple of TV dinners. He shut that.

"People do," said Sue. "I'll bet Miss Winkelstein could tell you stories, Ivor. Just walk out and leave it, too much bother to clean out."

"Dragging your heels again," he said. "What about bedding? Also come with a furnished apartment?"

"I shouldn't think so."

"No. Neither would I. And from what we've heard about Dorrie—and this place looks fairly neat—I'd say she was a tidy, clean sort of young woman. Besides, money was a little tight with her. All that"—he nodded at the refrigerator—"represents a small investment. Wherever she was going, she'd have taken it. And her sheets and blankets." Sue was silent. "No liquor around," he added, opening cupboards again to check.

"*Oh, Sergeant Maddox!*" cried Teresa in a frightened voice. They made back for the living room fast. She was standing in the door of the bedroom, and she had something clutched to her breast, and she looked suddenly terrified.

"What is it, Mrs. Fogarty?"

She held it out. "I'm sorry, you said not to touch, but when I saw it, I—it's Monica's very favorite, you see. She got it for Christmas, her grandmother sent it to her, and she—she wouldn't be parted from it for five minutes, Dorrie said. It was the first thing she wanted in the morning and after her nap. She c-called it Kee-kee. She can't say Kitty."

It was a large stuffed pink plush cat with green eyes and a white bow around its neck. It was about a foot high, very plump; it wore a little prim smile on its face between stiff white whiskers.

"Where was it?" asked Maddox. "Show me. It's all right, that wouldn't take prints." His voice was subdued.

She turned back to the bedroom. "It was right here, under the little table between the beds. When I saw it, I— All Dorrie'd said, how crazy Monica is about it. She'd never have forgotten that if—but—"

"But," said Maddox sadly. "Yes. Put it back where you found it, will you, please? We'll want pictures."

"Something's happened to both of them," said Teresa, white and shaken. "I know it now, I just feel it. But *what?*"

Maddox wasn't often at a loss for words. He was now. There was simply no idea in his head at all; this offbeat thing presented no handle to grasp.

He went back to the kitchen and opened the last door, a tall narrow closet at the end, evidently intended for brooms and mops. Teresa said behind him, "That's Dorrie's vacuum cleaner. She kept that too. You would, you know, the price they are now. It's a Royal." She looked at them. "But nobody," she said, "could—could kidnap people out of a—a public place like this."

None of them said anything for a while; then Maddox started toward the door. "So we go on looking," he said.

■ ■ ■

When Teresa had driven off rather fast, he started the Maserati and said, "We haven't seen my in-law for nearly a week. Better check up on her."

When Mrs. Carstairs opened the door of the court duplex on Janiel Terrace, Gor was barking; he stopped when he smelled who it was. "Ivor thought you needed checking up on," Sue told her mother.

Mrs. Carstairs laughed and Maddox regarded her approvingly. Sue would look a lot like her in thirty years' time, and very nice too. "More likely he hoped I'd been making a devil's food cake, with company coming. Now don't bristle, Sue—I know when you're working a full day you haven't time—and as a matter of fact I have."

"Fine," said Maddox, sitting down and patting Gor, the Fierce Protector.

"When's Aunt Evelyn coming?"

"Driving over tomorrow, but she'll stop at Blythe and get in Monday." Mrs. Carstairs bustled to bring Maddox a piece of cake.

He took an appreciative bite. "If you," he said, "had two sons, and one of them was married and living near you— we haven't heard if they have a family, have we?—well, anyway, and the other one was married and living across the country—whoa, back up, I won't say *you*, I'll just put it to you as a female—"

"So am I," said Sue.

"Don't interrupt—and the younger son's wife had just had a baby when he was killed in an accident, would you think it was—mmh—interfering or possessive or bossy to want the girl to come and live near you?"

"Certainly not," said Mrs. Carstairs. "Quite natural. She liked the girl?"

"Apparently. Would the girl think she was being—mmh —bossy or interfering?"

"It depends on the girl. But even if she didn't want to, I shouldn't think so."

"Who's dragging heels now?" asked Sue. "That refrigerator—and the cat—"

"Oh, yes," said Maddox. "That cat."

■ ■ ■

On Sunday morning, he sent Rowan, Dabney and D'Arcy to cover the place. "And D'Arcy, there's a large stuffed pink cat in the bedroom, under the table between the beds. Get some good shots of it. Also the refrigerator, open. And bring me the cat."

"A cat. This *is* an offbeat one," said D'Arcy. He hoisted the Speed Graphic and its accessory case; Rowan and Dabney were laden down with all the printing paraphernalia. "I suppose, playing the great detective, you're going to sit and think about it."

"There is," said Maddox, "legwork and legwork—not all the same kind." But he was still at his desk when they left, smoking with his eyes shut.

Downstairs, Johnny O'Neill was listening to a dumpy middle-aged woman who was incoherent on explanation. "If Ricky's father was still alive, tell me what to do, but Ricky's my youngest, youngest of eight and all good children, but Sam's gone this nine years and I just didn't know what to do."

The detectives went out. O'Neill said, "Yes, ma'am. If you'd tell me exactly what the trouble is."

"I was awake all night worrying, something awful! It's not like Ricky. He's never a boy to do anything like that— never coming home at all, or calling or anything. I called everybody he knows, and they didn't know anything. I didn't like to worry my own family. They've got enough troubles, what with—"

"Yes, ma'am. This is your son—he didn't come home? You expected him?"

"Oh, yes! Six o'clock for dinner like always. Since he's been back from the Army. He just did his service, he got out last month, and he went out looking for a job—an ad in the paper."

"All right, give me his description and we'll start looking." If he wanted a night on the town, O'Neill reflected, he'd probably have given her a good excuse. "What's his name?"

"And then I did call Henry, that's my oldest boy, this morning, and he said, Mama, you go straight to the police. Maybe he's been in an accident, he said. So I came straight here. Well, his name's Ricky Caprio—he's twenty. Oh, he's a big boy—six feet—well, I don't know what he weighs. He's not fat or thin either." O'Neill put down *170 lbs.* "Blue eyes he's got, and dark hair, still kind of short—oh, he had on jeans and a white T shirt. I don't know how much money he had, not very much."

O'Neill reassured her, got her address, and said they'd get right on it. He started calling hospitals, starting with Hollywood Receiving up the street.

■ ■ ■

The three men didn't talk much as they moved about the drab apartment. D'Arcy, setting and resetting lens openings and speeds, reflected sardonically that he and Sheila had that much in common, the photography: if the damned girl wasn't so—flittery, he coined a word for it. She needed to grow up a little, he supposed.

He got three good clear (he hoped) shots of the stuffed pink cat. It was a funny-looking cat, he thought, picking it up afterward, and why the hell Ivor wanted it—

Rowan and Dabney squatted, stooped, bent and lay prone and otherwise, dusting every possible surface, changing powders according to the type of surfaces. Sometimes prints turned up in very unexpected places.

"I had a thought the other day about this," said Dabney, as he lay on his back with his head inside the cupboard under the sink, dusting the folding doors. "My wife's on a diet."

"What's that got to do with anything?"

"Well, I just thought, all the exercise we got on a job like this, the positions we have to get into, must be as good as jogging a couple of miles a day."

Rowan laughed. "You may have something there, boy."

But if none of them discussed it, on this technical part of the job, they were a bit more interested in Maddox's wild geese now some further evidence had shown. It certainly began to look as if the wild geese hadn't flown away voluntarily.

But the abduction bit—that idea D'Arcy still found wild; it was just too far out. He wondered, focusing on the Wood seascape, if something had spooked her. Dorrie Mayo. She wasn't very old, but anybody twenty-four might still have something in her past she wasn't proud of, something even sinister or criminal. Something she was afraid of the in-laws finding out? It was just an idea; he'd pass it on to Maddox.

■ ■ ■

The ecology rally had swelled yesterday and overnight, and inevitably the rock groups were part of it; it was very noisy in that section of Griffith Park. They'd been sending two-man cars to cruise around up there at no set intervals and had fetched in forty or fifty participants already, mostly on possession charges. It was a real mess today, reported the latest uniformed men, bringing in another bunch late that morning. The underground presses advertised these gatherings, and the kids appeared from seven counties away, some from out of state.

"Mess!" said Patrolman Carmichael disgustedly, shepherding a couple of females in to Sue and Daisy's office. "It'll take all the P. and R. men in the county to clean it up—health hazard, if you ask me. And the damn crazy thing about it is, they don't seem to have any comprehension what a laugh it is, you want to put it that way."

"Contradiction in terms," said Daisy dryly. "Ecology."

"God, yes." One of the females started to cry. "You'd better search these two. The boys they were with had a couple of decks of H on them."

They searched the two girls. They were monotonously typical: the long straight hair, jeans, sleeveless knit shirts, fake-leather fringed purses, thong sandals, no makeup, granny glasses on one. The nonconformists, thought Sue. Neither of them was carrying any drugs.

"I want to go home!" sobbed the little blonde. "I didn't know it'd be like *this*—sleeping on the ground and no bathrooms or anything! Everybody s-says ecology's so important but I didn't know it'd be like *this*. I want to go home!"

They calmed her down and asked where she lived. "T-T-Tucson." She hiccuped. "My mother didn't want me to come, she made me promise to stay right with Barbie, but Barbie went off with some fellow she met." She denied ever having used any dope, and she looked clean, in the technical sense. They sent her down to Juvenile Hall; she could phone her mother from there.

The other one was something else. She claimed to be eighteen, and had a driver's license to prove it, but looked older. She was a local product, and she'd been through this bit before; she knew they couldn't hold her. She said indifferently she hadn't known those fellows were holding any H; she hadn't seen any. No, of course she'd never used any herself.

"What about marijuana?" asked Daisy.

"Oh, pot—that's different. Everybody drags pot sometimes."

They looked at each other a little wearily when she slouched out. "Well, right now I'm hungry," said Daisy.

"And our new machine very handy." They went down the hall to it. Sue pushed two quarters in the slot and pulled the lever marked *Cheese*. The sandwich machine muttered and rumbled and presently a hygienically wrapped sandwich slithered neatly into the long tube at the bottom. "Very nice," said Sue. Daisy put a half dollar in the slot and pulled the lever marked *Ham*. The machine muttered, clanked and stopped. "It did that yesterday," said Sue. "César shook it." She tried shaking it, but nothing happened.

"Damn," said Daisy, annoyed.

Sue trotted down to the detective office. Rodriguez was sitting at his desk poring over the County Guide. "Would you please come and shake the machine again?" asked Sue. "It won't give Daisy her sandwich."

Rodriguez laughed. "I think that thing's a snare and delusion." But he came and shook it hard. The machine clanked and after a moment delivered the sandwich grudgingly.

■ ■ ■

Maddox came in at two thirty and sat down at his desk, looking abstracted. "You've got telegrams," said Rodriguez.

"I noticed them" said Maddox.

"And where've you been all day?"

"Out and about. Hearing this and that interesting."

He had had eventually to answer David Mayo's wires. He had done so via Chief Thomas Suttner in Danbury, yesterday afternoon. He had made it short and sweet: THEODORA MAYO APPARENTLY MOVED LEAVING NO ADDRESS. SOME REASON BELIEVE NOT VOLUNTARY, CHILD ALSO MISSING. FURTHER DETAILS AS KNOWN. QUERY FAMILY ANY RECENT EMOTIONAL UPSET OR OTHER TROUBLE.

Now he had telegrams, all from David Mayo. Calculating the time difference he figured that Mayo must have started wiring about ten last night and again at eight this morning. All the wires said the same thing: NOTHING KNOWN ANY RECENT TROUBLE. LETTERS JUST AS USUAL. WHAT IS GOING ON OUT THERE? FOR GOD'S SAKE SEND INFORMATION. FAMILY VERY WORRIED. PLEASE REPLY AT ONCE.

Maddox hadn't anything to reply at once. He said, "What?"

"I said," said Rodriguez, "that they've been very cute. These check passers. Once in a while we superior brains slip up a little, you know, and something just occurred to me last night. The addresses on those drivers' licenses. Could there be any lead there? Being fairly smart as a rule, instead of driving all over I've been looking at the County Guide, and they were very canny indeed. For instance, you take this one for Patricia Gall—seventeen fifty-six Harper Avenue in West Hollywood. There is no such number. Harper stops in the fourteen hundred block. Likewise the Gunderson one—ninety-nine oh one Dunsmuir. Same difference. Dunsmuir stops at San Vicente, about the thirty-five hundred block. In fact, every single one of them is like that. A known street name but an impossible address."

"Yes, I see. Very cute," said Maddox. "Obviously, as we said, they acquired the licenses as phony I.D. It also occurs to me, while we're on the subject, that there's this craze for wigs these days. Even men wearing the damn things, if not as much as women. I'd lay a small bet that going by their right names these six cute jokers don't look much like those photographs, bad as they are. The girls at least could have been wearing wigs. Of a different color than their own hair."

Rodriguez assented, and Rowan came in with a yellow sheet in one hand and the stuffed pink cat in the other. "Picked up quite a few middling good latents at that apartment. D'Arcy said you wanted this. And we've got the kickback from the Feds on the rest of those prints from the Caddy." He handed it over.

"Very expectable," said Maddox. "Birds of a feather. Only his prints known of the batch we sent. Antonio DeLucci, pedigree much the same as Hahn's, armed robbery, assault, violent in drink. And so on." He looked at the stuffed pink cat, smirking at him there on his desk. He wasn't really much concerned about the corpses in the Caddy.

■ ■ ■

Sue and Daisy had just turned another couple of females culled from the ecology rally over to Carmichael for delivering downtown when the phone rang on Daisy's desk. This was the fifth day of the heat wave; it shouldn't last much longer, but it was, right now, very hot and breathless on the second floor of the old precinct building; they had both taken off their jackets.

"I've got a citizen concerned about some kids," said O'Neill, "so I thought I'd pass it to you. Here he is."

"Sergeant Hoffman," said Daisy. "Can I help you?"

The male voice on the line sounded relieved. "You're a policewoman? Well, that's good—I mean, maybe you'd understand better. I don't like to interfere in people's own business, but when there's kids involved—well, I just don't like it, and I'm not about to sit on my hands and do nothing because I'm scared to get mixed in."

"Well, what's it about, Mr.—"

"Hernandez, Vince Hernandez, Sergeant. I manage the Green Star Motel. It's on Sunset out past Fairfax. I'm not telling you it's like a Holiday Inn, but we generally get a good type of clients—well, in my experience, thank God, most people are pretty good people, more that kind than the bastards, excuse me. But I got a setup here right now

79

I don't like the look of. Not nohow. The last couple hours, I been getting more and more worried, and so I call you, see what you think about it."

"What's the problem?"

"Well, I tell you, Sergeant. I had three people pull out this morning, so I put out the vacancy sign. And about eight thirty this old Pontiac drives in and the man takes Number Eight. It's a double, double bed and a twin and a cot. Ten bucks. I went out to check the plate, and there's him—he's about thirty, a big beefy guy. He registered as Paul Ferguson—and his wife, I suppose, kind of a fat blonde, and three little kids. That is, a baby and two kids maybe about two and four. Well, they got into Number Eight and I didn't think any more about it till I see them drive out again about ten o'clock. Ten this morning. I was outside the office watering the planting at the front and I saw them plain—the old Pontiac and this Ferguson and the fat blonde in it, in the front seat. The kids weren't in the car, see. I know that for a fact."

"Yes?" said Daisy.

"Well, Sergeant—what I mean to say is, it's now nearly four o'clock. And since those people drove out of here this morning—and the way he nearly hit the wall then, gunning her like crazy, he could've been a little high—I haven't heard a peep out of Number Eight. Those kids. The kids weren't in the car. And one was just a baby, this blonde carrying it. And I make it that's six hours, nearly, and if the kids *are* in Number Eight—left there, I mean— it's not natural, or right either. They'd likely be hungry, and I've been feeling awful uneasy about it, Sergeant, and —what do you think?"

"I think," said Daisy forcefully, "we look and see. What's the address? We'll be there, Mr. Hernandez. . . . Johnny, chase a black-and-white out there *pronto!*" She got up. "Come on, let's see what we've got here."

The black-and-white pulled into the Green Star Motel as they emerged from Sue's Chrysler. Hernandez, a rather handsome middle-aged man looking anxious, was waiting with a key. They unlocked Number Eight and without much trouble found the kids locked in the miniature linen closet between the bedroom and bath. It was about a foot and a half deep, three feet long. The biggest kid, a boy about three, was gagged with a diaper. They were all unconscious; at a guess, the temperature in there was around a hundred degrees.

"*¡Santa María!*" said Hernandez. "*¡Qué atrocidad!*" He crossed himself numbly before he bent to help the uniformed man.

They called an ambulance. Before it came, the oldest boy came to. His eyes opened slowly and he said drowsily, "Daddy was—*too* cross."

There was an empty pint bottle which had held bourbon sitting on the silent television set.

"My God," said one of the ambulance attendants, "what happened?" They got oxygen going on the other two.

"Mama was cross too. An'—she never—gave us any samwiches 'ke she—" They got oxygen on him.

Unaccountably, what Sue was seeing was a smiling big pink stuffed cat. The kids, she thought. The kids were what got you. Where—right this minute—was fifteen-month-old Monica Mayo? Where?

five

Maddox had wanted to talk to Brian Faulkner nearly since he'd heard the name. The rule was there: *cherchez l'homme*, or was that what he meant? After D'Arcy, Rowan and Dabney had gone out with the lab equipment, he called the Fogarty house.

"What did she say about him?" echoed Teresa. "I don't—"

"Girl talk?"

"Oh. Well, she didn't much. Dorrie's reserved. She doesn't talk about herself much. Actually I think she was sorry—well, embarrassed, that she'd told me he wanted to marry her. She wasn't, you know, preening herself on it, but maybe she thought it sounded that way. No, that I can tell you, she hadn't gone out with any other men, and I doubt very much that she dated Faulkner."

Maddox asked if her husband was there. Fogarty sounded, now, a little sharp; he didn't like his wife mixed into what was definitely police business. (Definitely?) "What the hell now? Look, this thing—I'm not going to have—"

"Who in your firm should I call to get Faulkner's address?" He wasn't in the phone book.

Fogarty was silent and then said in a different tone, "What the hell. I suppose Mr. Giese—he does the hiring. Is that all? Winslow Giese. I suppose he's in the book." The phone was put down emphatically.

Giese was in the phone book, an address in West L.A. Maddox played up official business, and Giese, whatever else, was a good citizen. "I don't suppose you'd know the address without consulting your files. I'm sorry to ask you, sir, but I really would appreciate—"

"Faulkner," said Giese, and was silent, and then said, "That's quite all right, Sergeant, I hadn't any plans. Suppose I meet you at our office—you know the address?—in thirty minutes." He sounded incisive and decided, which Maddox supposed a C.P.A. should be.

Maddox was waiting for him when he drove up in a middle-aged Continental. On Sunday, plenty of parking left on the street. Giese was about fifty, tall and thin and bald, in tailored sports clothes. He looked at the Maserati doubtfully as Maddox got out of it. "Sergeant Maddox?" He had a firm handshake. "If you'll come in—"

It was a fairly new block of offices, bastard Spanish with tile roof and Moorish-design vinyl flooring in its little lobby. Giese and Weekes occupied ground-floor offices to the left of the front door, a spacious big central office with a row of private ones at the back. There were rows of file cases here and there, very orderly.

"Our personnel records are back here," said Giese, leading him up the office to a large filing case against the rear wall; it stood next to the solid slab door labeled laconically in gold *Mr. W. G. Giese Director*. "Brian Faulkner." Rather fussily he produced keys, unlocked the case. "Er— excuse me, Sergeant, might I know why you—um—want to talk to Mr. Faulkner?"

"I don't know why not," said Maddox casually. "A young woman he was acquainted with seems to have temporarily disappeared, probably just some misunderstanding, and we'd like to know if he's seen her recently." If Faulkner was in the clear here, no need to alarm his employer.

"Oh," said Giese. He sounded relieved. "I see. There's no question of Mr. Faulkner being—culpable in any way?"

"Not so far as we know, sir. I'd just like his address."

"Yes," said Giese. "Yes." He looked at Maddox appraisingly. He said, "Dear me, it's sometimes difficult to know what is the right thing to do. But you *are* police, after all, and though it's nothing to do with Faulkner, so you say, I wonder if I shouldn't tell you."

"Tell me what?"

"Possibly I should," said Giese. "I'm sure you know how to be discreet, and you'd realize the—the necessity for— Yes. Or did you know that he's on parole?"

Maddox said softly, "Do tell."

"I'm interested in these rehabilitation projects. I've worked with several parole officers over some years, but it was the first time it had happened that a parolee was trained for my particular job, you see. I had an opening at the office, which Mr. Canotti knew. He asked if I'd take him on, and I did. He's been an excellent employee, very satisfactory, good at his job and gets on well with the rest of the staff. I'd be very sorry to hear that he's—been getting into any trouble."

"I see," said Maddox. Giese had come out with that stiffly and reluctantly, a man doing his duty. "Canotti his parole officer?" Giese nodded. "Well, so far as we know Faulkner's perfectly clean, but thanks for telling me. I just want to talk to him. If I could have that address?" He needn't try to pry any more out of Giese.

It was an address on Poinsettia. Maddox copied it down, thanked Giese again and went out to the Maserati. Giese hadn't come out when he started the engine. Sometimes these civilians on the rehabilitation kick, always well-meaning, couldn't stay unbiased. He wondered whether Giese was phoning Faulkner to warn him there was a cop coming to call.

He couldn't have a look at Dorrie's bank account until tomorrow, first having a hunt for which bank; weekends often frustrate detectives. But on this particular hunt he wouldn't be hampered. Very few police departments know the meaning of a forty-hour week, and the L.A.P.D. is not one of them. Twenty-four hours a day, seven days a week, are the hours kept by the L.A.P.D. Maddox went back to the office and asked O'Neill to connect him to the Bureau of Corrections downtown; when a male voice answered, he asked for the Welfare and Rehabilitation office.

A bass voice said curtly, "Welfare and Rehab, O'Donnell speaking."

"Sergeant Maddox, Wilcox Street. I'd like to get in touch with one of your P.A. men, his name's Canotti."

The bass voice changed subtly in tone, for talking to a fellow cop. "Sure. Tony Canotti? You can try to get him at home—just a minute, I'll get you the number."

By the exchange, Canotti lived in Monterey Park. A woman answered, sounding impatient; there were children's voices in the background. She apologized when he said his name, asked him to wait.

"Not even one peaceful Sunday at home," said a hearty baritone in his ear. "Did I get it right, you're Wilcox Street? Don't tell me one of my black sheep has violated P.A. on your beat?"

"I hope not," said Maddox. "Nothing says so. But one Brian Faulkner turned up on the edge of something that might be a case. His employer, after some soul-searching, righteously revealed his status, and I just felt I'd like to know a little about him before I talk to him."

"Faulkner. He's been doing fine, and of course he's not

the usual case, never a pro of any kind. I wouldn't like to see him backslide. A nice fellow. What do you want to know?"

"What was he in for?"

"Murder-two. He got seven-to-fifteen and served four years and a bit. Got out about eight months ago, and seeing he's a graduate C.P.A. I thought about old Giese and touched him for a job there. Faulkner's been doing just fine."

"Murder-two." Maddox got out a new cigarette and groped for his lighter. "Can you be a little more specific?"

Canotti said, "Well, it was a rough one, but obviously not premeditated, which made it two. He and another fellow were after the same girl—they all worked for the same company, a big accountancy in Santa Monica. The girl picked the other man. They were engaged. Faulkner admitted to me—and the judge at the trial—that he's got a temper goes off like a rocket. The staff was just leaving work one afternoon, quite a few people in the parking lot in back, when the other guy came along with the girl and said something to Faulkner, jeering at him—second-best man, something like that. Faulkner'd just got into his car, and he ran them both down. The temper going off."

"The temper going off," said Maddox. "Indeed."

"He admitted it. The man was killed, the girl critically injured, but she recovered. You can see, a one-time deal. Nothing on him before."

"If he has learned meanwhile to control the temper. That's very interesting, thanks."

"You don't think he's—mixed into anything?"

"I don't know. I don't even know for certain," said Maddox, "that it is a case—or might be one—or what kind. If it is, and if he is, I'll let you know. Meanwhile, thanks." He put the phone down.

The whole thing was fifty-fifty, he decided. He didn't

like the typed letter, the note to the manager, the refrigerator, the pink cat. That all said that Dorrie Mayo hadn't voluntarily gone away from that place. But it wasn't definite; conceivably, for some reason, she had taken off in a hurry, and somebody else had helped her cover her tracks. It *could* be.

Faulkner. So he had killed. Absolutely nothing said that Dorrie and Monica Mayo were anything but very much alive. If—which was the first thing that had jumped into his mind—Faulkner, in love with her, had lost his temper when she turned him down and strangled her or biffed her or something—well, Faulkner's kind went berserk for an instant and then either just stood still or ran. They didn't often have the impulse to cover up. And Faulkner would have had no remote reason to harm the child.

But it was, of course, interesting to know about Faulkner.

■ ■ ■

"Disappeared!" said Brian Faulkner. "Dorrie? What do you mean, disappeared?"

Maddox watched him interestedly. He'd found Faulkner at home, which was a small single apartment in a modest residential area, west in Hollywood. The apartment was impersonal, a place a man ate and slept. No decorative touches. Faulkner was a good-looking man, six feet, well built, a crest of wavy chestnut hair, a straight profile. To his credit, he didn't seem aware of it. He was in shorts and a T shirt, this hot Sunday, and he'd been watching TV. His eyes had flickered once on the badge and then stayed steady.

Maddox said comfortably, "Nobody seems to know where she's moved, that's all. Did she say anything to you?"

"No, but I haven't seen her—lately. Somebody must know."

"Just a mix-up probably, but some of her friends got anxious and came running to us."

"Well, I don't know. You—aren't thinking anything's happened to her? She's all right?"

"I don't know," said Maddox. "We hope so."

"She must have told the family. You ask them. Back east somewhere. Her husband's family. She writes to her mother-in-law all the time. They'll know."

"We heard you were interested in her. Wanted her to marry you."

"Oh, you did!" Faulkner had not sat down or invited Maddox to; he turned quickly now and anger sparked in his eyes. "So right away you looked, and found me in your files, and saw I was on P.A., so—" Abruptly he stopped and put a hand to his head. "All right, forget that. I'm sorry. I didn't mean to sound off."

"Your temper got you in trouble before."

"So it did. I've tried to learn a little sense," said Faulkner. "You don't think anything's happened to Dorrie? Oh, my God, she's had so much bad luck—no family of her own, her husband getting killed—it's got to be just some mix-up."

"When did you see her last?" Maddox leaned on the doorpost.

"I'll tell you all about it," said Faulkner dully. "If that's what you want to know. There's not much to tell. I met her last September at a party—"

"I know about that. At the Fogartys'."

"Well"—Faulkner shrugged—"I'd been leery of mixing with people I knew before, people who knew I'd been— I don't know many people, go out much, now. And I fell for her, all right. She's a beautiful girl, you know. And— and a nice girl." It occurred to Maddox that they didn't know; they hadn't seen any photographs of her at all. "I asked her for a date. She went out with me once—that was about a week later. But she said then she didn't want to date—me or anybody. She was busy with her job, with the baby, and it was too soon after she'd lost her husband. I told her I wanted her to marry me, I'd be willing to wait—until she'd got over it more. But she said no, that wasn't fair to me, maybe she wouldn't ever want to marry anyone again. I called her, I tried to be friendly, show her—but she asked me not to. I—the last time I saw her was in January. I stopped by the apartment but she wouldn't even let me in. And that's all."

"Thanks very much." Maddox looked at him another moment and went out. That sounded genuine. Very open and natural.

Damn it, he thought, if there was just one thing definite to make it sure one way or the other. . . .

■ ■ ■

So when D'Arcy, Rowan and Dabney came in as Rodriguez was maundering about those addresses, he was ready to kick it around. He looked at the stuffed pink cat sitting on his desk and brought them up to date on Faulkner. "He sounded open as all hell."

"And he could be," said D'Arcy. "I had a small notion. Could something have spooked her? So she cut and ran to—get out from under something? What I'm thinking of is something, maybe, that happened before she was married, almost anything, say she'd had a boy friend with a pedigree, or was involved in a hit-run, or knew something about some pros—and all of a sudden it cropped up again, and she didn't want to be connected, so she cut out. Probably thinking when it blows over she can get in touch with her friends again, the in-laws."

"One way I like that just a little," said Maddox. "A vaguely similar idea struck me, that she had some reason, and somebody she knew—she knew more people than

Sandra Cross and Teresa Fogarty, after all—said, I'll take care of the details. And proceeded to write the note to the manager, the letter to Robinson's, and make the phone call to Mrs. Moran."

"It could be," said Rowan a little doubtfully. He'd just scraped in at five-nine too; he tilted his head to look up at D'Arcy. "A hunch?"

"Not exactly."

Rodriguez said sardonically, "*¡Qué va!* You aren't thinking simple enough—or enough like a female."

"So, what really happened? Silence for the expert," said Dabney.

"*¡Tontería!* I never have thought this was a case for us at all, and I don't think so now. Just as Faulkner said to you, Ivor, she'd never had much luck. Or money. Here she is, poor lone young widow, working a daily grind for just about enough to get along, baby to take care of, that dreary apartment to come home to. I can just see Dorrie making up her mind that, by God, she was going to have something better out of life and seizing any chance that showed."

"Such as?"

"Possibilities," said Rodriguez. "There she is at the real jewelry counter in Beverly Hills. Every chance the jaded millionaire dropped by to pick up a bauble for his fat wife and noticed her. Faulkner tells us she's a good looker. So, how about a little vacation in Acapulco, my dear, or maybe just the discreet apartment? You don't like that? All right, how about Simon?"

"What about him?"

"He seems to have been a little upset when she didn't turn up last Monday. First time. He was upset too soon, wasn't he? For an ordinary clerk not to come in on time? There can't be all that much press of business at the real jewelry counter. Suppose he was covering up?"

"For what, for God's sake?" asked D'Arcy blankly.

"*Santa María*, you're grown up. There they were at the same counter together all day. Maybe Simon had an eye for her. Propositioned her. And the owner of that concession wouldn't exactly be a wage slave. Maybe he's paying rent on the discreet apartment."

"Then why all the mystery? Why didn't she make an excuse to people she knew—I'm moving away to a better job, or something?"

"No mystery intended, maybe," said Rodriguez. "So, enter the jaded millionaire, and she decides to have some fun out of life, and he says magnanimously, Leave the mundane affairs to my secretary."

"Look, if you're practicing to write the blood-and-thunder mysteries, do it somewhere else," said Maddox, and the phone rang on his desk. "Yes, Johnny?"

"Walter Ilinsky is conscious," said O'Neill. "You can talk to him."

"I don't especially want to," said Maddox, "but thanks. You can go talk to Ilinsky, D'Arcy. I think César is running a little fever. He'd better stay quiet here."

■ ■ ■

Walter Ilinsky, looking pale and still weak, head bandaged fearsomely, confirmed that two men had jumped him from behind. "But maybe I shouldn't say men. They weren't very big anyway. It was dark but I got the impression—maybe teen-agers. I knocked one down but the other one come at me with a club."

His wife said he shouldn't talk much. Well, that was about all he could give them anyway. Write another report on it, and of course there was nowhere to go looking for the teen-agers or whoever. They'd only got about six dollars.

But he didn't get to the report at once. As he came back

past O'Neill's desk in the lobby, O'Neill lifted a hand at him. D'Arcy plodded over. The traffic shift was just changing: the men on swing watch coming in, making for the locker rooms to change into uniform, the men from day watch coming off. A little crowd milled around in the lobby.

"Something new, Johnny?"

"A funny little thing," said O'Neill. "I took a missing report this morning, a Ricky Caprio, and he showed up a couple of hours ago at the Beverly Lake Hospital out on Fairfax. I can't raise his mother at the address she gave me, and the family ought to be notified."

"You want me to go through the phone book and call everybody named Caprio? What's the matter with him?"

A patrolman in uniform halted stride and stood there listening. "The idea is," said O'Neill, "he could tell you where else to try. The nurse sounded very snooty—that's a prestige hospital. They probably haven't much time to waste on unarranged-for patients. He's conscious now. I did get that. He walked into the hospital lobby about six last night and collapsed. He's got concussion."

"Well, I'll be damned!" blurted the uniformed man. "Excuse me, sir, I'm Ben Loth. I saw that kid yesterday— the Caprio kid. He had a wild tale, and I checked it out, but it's crazy. Just crazy. He was really hurt, hah? Then old man Wechsler must have been right."

"What happened?" asked D'Arcy.

"I was cruising along Fountain, about the end of the tour, and I saw him staggering along and stopped in case it was a D. and D. But he told me this tale. Said he'd gone to old man Wechsler's store to apply for a job and got hired. The Wechslers've had that little mama-and-papa market there for twenty years, ordinary decent people. They live in the house in the back. And this Caprio, he said after they'd hired him they invited him to have a cup of coffee, so he went back to the house with them and sat at the kitchen table, and next thing he knew Wechsler came up behind and hit him on the head. Crazy."

D'Arcy asked disbelievingly, "Why?"

"No reason. He didn't know. He got up and ran out. He was about a block away when I spotted him, so I put him in the car and went back to hear what Wechsler said. Well, I mean, sir—old man Wechsler! It was wild."

"And what did he say?" asked O'Neill curiously.

"What probably really happened. If the kid had a concussion—well, it does funny things to your memory. Wechsler said Caprio had coffee with them, said he'd be in to work on Monday and took off, only they saw him trip and take a hell of a toss on the way past the store to the street. That's probably when he did the damage. He said he was all right, but maybe I should've brought him in." Loth looked worried.

"Well, no harm done in the long run," said D'Arcy philosophically. "That's a funny one. Wonder where he got the idea the old man hit him?"

"Concussion does funny things," said Loth.

"I'll go and see him," said D'Arcy. "Clean that up anyway."

■ ■ ■

Maddox was still thinking about Dorrie, or trying to. If Rodriguez's fanciful logic was a little forced, there was an element of human nature in it: with the run of bad luck Dorrie had had, if the jaded millionaire had come along she might have been tempted. Or would she?

Teresa had supplied him with the names of other people she knew. Not many; there wouldn't be many. A young couple, occupied with each other, the new house; then her days filled with the job, the baby. The quiet humdrum life; she wouldn't have socialized much. Brought up in an orphanage. Which? Did it matter? He looked through his notes; he had asked Teresa and Sandra, and neither knew or remembered if she'd ever mentioned the name.

D'Arcy's idea; there just could be something there. Try to trace her back?

Making a Federal case of it, he thought impatiently.

Rodriguez came back with coffee and handed him a manila envelope. The autopsy reports on Edna Gifford and Rex Hahn. Not much in them. Both shot twice in the back and side of the head. Slugs looked like .32s—sent to Ballistics. Sometime they'd get a report. It was probably DeLucci who had shot them, thieves falling out.

"Have you got spring fever too?" asked Rodriguez.

"Damn it, I don't see anywhere to go," said Maddox. "On anything. You know we're stymied on these cute check passers. Until there's enough publicity on it, the type of I.D. they're using, that some clerk spots one—"

"And nabs him for us? *Nada posible.* The citizens never want to get involved, *chico.* Any righteous merchant who spots a phony, he'd just hand back the check and say, Not today."

"You've got no faith in human nature," said Maddox. "Righteous merchants sometimes have fellow feelings."

"I'll believe it when I see it."

"And what you won't believe," said Sue from the door, "is what Daisy and I just saw. This motel manager called—" They listened to that little horror story and both said, "My God."

"The kids?" asked Maddox.

"Mercifully the closet was vented through the ceiling. Otherwise they'd have suffocated. They'll be O.K., but the intern said—we went along to the hospital—they hadn't been fed much lately. Malnutrition. There's a stake-out on the motel. We came straight back and saw Captain

O'Hagan, and we'll pick up the parents sometime. Parents!"

"Like other people, they come all sorts," said Maddox, and got up suddenly, full of purpose. "I'm off. . . . I'll see you at home, I suppose," he added vaguely, and hurried out.

"What husbandly fervor," said Rodriguez.

Sue cocked her head at him. "When he sounds that vague, he's usually plotting something."

■ ■ ■

Maddox's plotting had to do with the stale, muggy heat in the old precinct building. Well, it was only March and this heat wave would go away soon; but in this climate, you could get the little heat wave any time, and before they knew it the real summer would arrive—July on. And it was bad enough to have to spend most of the day in this old building minus air conditioning, or on the street.

He had noticed an ad in the *Herald* last night, a discount house out on Western. He drove down there, narrowly avoiding several accidents as he tried to figure the square footage of the little house in his head; Maddox was not a mathematical brain. Let the salesman do it. Eventually, when they started the family, they'd get another house; the room units were portable. It wasn't fair to Sue. . . .

At the discount house, he told the salesman the size of the rooms. "Well, if you really want to do a good job, this more powerful unit will give you much better service, sir. Two should do it, with the one you have. I'd advise, for maximum utility"—he looked at the rough sketch of the floor plan Maddox had made—"one in the kitchen and one in the living room. That should give you ample coverage. . . . What? Well, of course the bigger unit isn't on sale at the moment—"

95

Recklessly Maddox gave him a check. City employees were good credit risks, supposedly, but interest did mount up. They just managed to get the two big cartons squeezed into the Maserati.

Maddox was not much of a home mechanic either. The directions claimed that installation was simple, but by the time he had the first one fitted into the kitchen window he had barked knuckles, a bruised thumb, and had run out of cuss words. The simple directions had been confusing in parts, but at least he had got the damned thing in, and when he turned it on it actually started to work.

The second one was easier; he had a better idea what he was doing now. He turned it on five minutes before Sue came up the drive. Of course she spotted the unfamiliar gray rectangle protruding from the front window and precipitated herself into the living room excitedly.

"Ivor, you *angel!* You got one! Oh, heavenly! But—"

"I got two. The man said that should cool it all. Refrigerated cool. Just like," said Maddox, "those glamour boys down at Central H.Q. have. You'll feel it more in a minute. I just turned this one on."

"Two! But can we afford it? Another payment—"

"Damn the money. Comfort is the important thing. And I gave them a check. We can afford it. The other one's in the kitchen." He kissed her again soundly.

When he let her go she looked up at him apprehensively, her dark blue eyes doubtful. "All right, break the bad news. How much?"

He told her, and she gave a small shriek. "Ivor! With the rent, and the car payments, and inflation—"

"Now simmer down, love. The comfort is worth it," he said firmly. It was beginning to be quite cool in the little house, all three units going full blast. "Stop being so mercenary."

Sue laughed, capitulating. "Yes, darling. And it *is* heavenly. After the day we had. Heavenly beautiful wonderful, to be *cool*. I told César you were plotting something."

"I think I deserve a drink," said Maddox. And a moment later, "Damn it," he said to the tray of ice cubes, "do I call every orphanage in Fresno? Why? If there was some handle to tell us even what kind of case it is—"

"What?" said Sue from the bedroom.

"Nothing," said Maddox. It was now quite frigidly cool in the house, and he carried his drink to a comfortable chair in the living room.

"Ivor!" she said, suddenly emerging from the bedroom zipping up a short robe. "But what's it going to cost to *run* them? The electric bill!"

■ ■ ■

"Now what the hell," said Ken Donaldson, "is that? And why?" They looked at the stuffed pink cat on Maddox's desk. It smirked happily back at them.

"Evidence," suggested Brougham doubtfully. "God, I hope this heat wave goes away tomorrow."

"Bound to sometime, only March."

Sunday night, they might expect a few D. and D.s, a few accidents; nothing much for them. But rather early, at nine fifteen, a couple of uniformed men came in with a sullen couple: a big beefy man, slightly drunk, and a fat blonde all the way drunk, loud on obscenities.

"Why the hell are you cluttering up our nice clean office with common drunks?" demanded Brougham.

The younger patrolman grinned mirthlessly. "A little more. They're to be booked on a charge of gross child neglect and maybe also attempted homicide by negligence. We've been on stake-out for 'em. They just showed up."

Brougham and Donaldson eyed the pair resignedly and started the paperwork on it. They got rid of them, headed for the County jail downtown, by nine forty.

■ ■ ■

Patrolman Gomez, riding a black-and-white alone on tour through central Hollywood, was having a quiet night. By ten o'clock he'd written up three traffic tickets; he had a prowler call, nothing coming of it, and then a fight at a bar on Vine. It was just a brawl, nothing serious; he was back to cruising in fifteen minutes.

There wasn't much traffic at this hour, most restaurants closed except the night clubs. He was slowing up for a stationary stop sign, on Sunset at the intersection of Morningside, when a car in the left lane swooped past him and ran the sign without braking.

Gomez touched the siren and got behind the car; his headlights showed a New York plate. Reluctantly the car, a new Chevrolet, slowed and pulled over to the curb. Gomez braked the squad car and got out.

"May I see your license, sir? You know, you ran that stationary stop back there."

"You goddamn *cops!*" said the driver, more exasperated than anything else. "Lay in wait for out-of-state cars, I swear. Make up your own weird traffic rules! Not half an hour ago I get a ticket—sneaky damn cops in an unmarked car—and get nicked a sawbuck, else I got to go to court and waste time."

Oh, oh, thought Gomez, those phony cops again. A memo had been circulated to traffic detail on that.

"Well, we'll let it pass this time," he said. "But please watch it, sir."

■ ■ ■

At eleven ten, Sergeant Hopewell flashed the detective office. "Attempted heist. Liquor store on Santa Monica. The black-and-white's there."

They went out on that. It was a fancy big store, the

gourmet foreign foods as well as the liquor. Probably a very nice profit tucked away in the till, on a weekend. The owner was there; he always closed up himself, he said. Had just come in at ten forty-five, let the night clerk go, and was about to close up. He was a thin middle-aged man with rimless glasses and a soft New England accent, Carl Filer. The would-be bandit was also there, sprawled out on the floor.

Filer said soberly, "A stitch in time. Not that I'm proud of doing it, gentlemen. No. But too much of this sort of thing. And the courts—for whatever reason—so permissive, letting the hard-core criminals loose."

"Oh, yes," said Brougham.

There was a sign tacked onto the counter by the cash register: *When guns are outlawed, only outlaws will have guns.*

"You have to protect your own property," said Filer. "I know you people do your best, but you can't be every-where, and with the courts letting all these thugs loose—I went and took that course the National Rifle Association gives, in self-protection, and got a gun."

"Very sensible," said Donaldson, looking at the body of the heist man.

"I didn't want to kill anyone, even hurt anyone. I was just protecting my own property. He came in just as I was closing out the register and showed the gun. I let him think I'd cooperate, but I keep my gun right under the counter—he didn't know I'm left-handed, of course. He fired, but the slug hit that bottle of vermouth. I never meant to kill him."

"Yes," said Brougham. "You're very lucky, Mr. Filer, that you live in California. A few other states, you could get prosecuted for manslaughter."

There'd be some paperwork on this. Probably they'd

identify the dead man by his prints; the odds were he had a pedigree.

When they got back to the office, Donaldson said, "That bugs me. It's the silliest-looking damned thing!" The fat pink cat smiled at them from Maddox's desk.

six

When the sun came up on Monday morning, hesitant and dim, the heat wave had gone away. It was overcast, slightly chilly, and the sky was darker toward the hills to the north, where rain usually came from. "You can't win," said Sue, looking at the new air conditioners, "but we'll bless them again three months from now."

It was D'Arcy's day off; he was probably out with his photographic lady taking pictures of trees or something.

Maddox came into the office along with Feinman, Rowan and Rodriguez; Dabney was late. The stuffed pink cat was sitting on Maddox's desk, and on the blotter was another telegram; he sighed at it.

"About one o'clock this afternoon," said Rodriguez, "we're going to start to hear about the latest batch of bouncy checks."

"Probably," agreed Maddox, and picked up the report signed by Brougham. "Well, well, another armed citizen foiling the pro." He told them about Mr. Filer. "Dick was obliging enough to get the corpse's prints, all nice and neat, before they shipped him off to the morgue. Now we send 'em downtown and find out who he was. Anybody want to bet he has a pedigree?" Nobody wanted to bet.

"I see Dorrie's in-laws are still concerned," said Rowan. "What do we tell them?"

"I'm damned if I know. Did anybody remember, by the way, to put out the A.P.B. on Antonio DeLucci? He's probably the X on Gifford and Hahn."

"I did," said Rodriguez. "So what about Dorrie?"

"I think I'd like to talk to that Simon," said Maddox abstractedly. "Depending what kind he is, she might have talked some to him. They were right together most of the day. I don't know." Maddox looked at the telegram without opening it and lit a cigarette. He had just squashed the stub of it out when the phone went off. "Something, Johnny?"

"I don't know what. He's asking for a ranking officer. He looks serious."

"Send him up," said Maddox. Rodriguez had taken the heist man's prints, the set of little cards, out to transmit to S.I.D. downtown; Rowan had wandered off somewhere. Maddox and Feinman were alone in the office when the citizen came in.

He was a tall thin man in the forties, clean-shaven, with a long dark face and dark eyes under a cap of black hair. He was well dressed if not sharp, a gray suit and white shirt with a blue bow tie. "What can we do for you, sir? I'm Sergeant Maddox."

The man came forward. "A sergeant," he said. "That is good." His English was strongly flavored with some East European tongue. He sat down in the chair beside Maddox's desk and looked at him searchingly. "The rest did not want me to come. Very much they did not want it. But I am here."

"Yes, sir. If you'd tell us what it's about?" The man looked at Feinman. "Oh, this is Detective Feinman."

"I am Jan Janowsky. Feinman," he said. "A Jew. Then you will understand what I am talking about." Feinman ambled up amiably.

"Yes, Mr. Janowsky?" Maddox prompted as he was silent.

"Because—" said Janowsky painfully, and suddenly a torrent of speech came out of him, "because—it was twenty-five days we were in that old fishing boat, seven of us, and afraid all the time. Afraid of the sea, the wind, the planes, the helicopters, but most afraid we would not do it, we would not get away! When there was no more water, we waited to drink until it rained, and when there was no more food we went hungry. We stole the boat up at the west point of the Danzig Gulf, and twenty-five days—we did not know where we were, we had a compass but we were not sure—we meant to make up the Kadet Channel, but we were not seamen. City men, four of us from Warsaw.

"We thought it was the Danish islands we saw, but—we were not sure. And it was an old boat. It leaked. Twenty-five days, and we had been without food for eight when we saw land ahead, and the boat was driven in the surf and all broke up around us, and we did not know, we thought it was Germany, but we could not be sure. Maybe we had been going about in circles, and were back—there.

"Some men came down the beach. They were speaking German. We had only a few words of German. But I said to them—the words I knew—'Osten oder Westen?' and they smiled and said together, 'Westen, Westen!' And so we knelt down and gave thanks to God."

He stopped. "Excuse me. I did not mean to say all this. But you understand, it is the reason I am here. That was seventeen years ago, and I am now an American citizen. I have done well here. I have my own business, a hardware store. I have a wife and two children." Suddenly he noticed the fat pink cat; he smiled and reached to touch it. "My little daughter would like this. . . . But how can I explain it to you? Was I in a slave-labor camp? No. Was I beaten, tortured? No. But always was the fear, the being afraid. So many were, for any reason, no reason. Everybody afraid. In English you—we have the saying, 'Every fish has the bigger fish to bite him.' Like that. It is fear and blackmail hand in hand, from top to bottom. The big fish says, 'Part of your wage in my hand, I don't tell the bigger fish you say wrong things so they fire you from your job and maybe put you in jail. So that little fish, he says to the smaller one below him, 'Your money and I don't put you in trouble with the boss.' And he says it to the next. *There*, you can do nothing about this. This fear and stealing. You keep quiet and pay, so you keep a job for just enough money you don't quite starve." He breathed heavily for a moment. "No, I was not ever beaten, in jail. I was a clerk in a—what we would say, store. The people's cooperative, where there is nothing ever much to sell, and what is, shoddy and poor. You see, gentlemen, I was lucky." Janowsky's mouth was straight on irony. "I had nobody. No family. They are all killed, first by Germans, then Russians. So I was able to take the chance to escape. Most aren't so lucky. They have people—mothers, fathers, aunts, uncles, grandmas. You don't take the big chance to risk your life when you know people like this will be punished for you. Excuse me, I don't mean to take all this time. But—"

"That's all right, Mr. Janowsky. Go on."

"But in America, there is not supposed to be the being afraid. That is what I said to them, the rest of them—Mr. Green at the drugstore, Mrs. Loring at the dress shop, Mr. Hanson at the bakery, Mr. Bremmer at his watch-repair shop, Mr. Gorman. I say, it is not to be afraid! Here, the law is for justice for every man. They should not pay money to these thieves, these threateners! Go to the police. But they are afraid. They tell me to pay also. They have been paying; these thieves come first to one, then another, these two–three months. They say this gang, many like them, move into a block, threaten, come and smash windows, damage, and every week they force another store to pay too. Who knows how many merchants are paying? I tell them they are fools."

"The protection racket," said Maddox sadly. "These young street bums think it's their own invention. Where, Mr. Janowsky?"

"All of us, our stores are on Melrose Avenue." He added the block number. "I don't know how many others this gang is making to pay. I only know, Mr. Bremmer pays them twenty-five dollars a week, so they don't come and make damage in his shop, smash everything. I don't know how much the others pay. From me now, they demand also twenty-five dollars a week."

"Do you know who they are? Any names? The gang have a name?"

"I don't know. Some are white and some black. The two who come to see me on Saturday, they call each other Joe and Buck. They're maybe eighteen–nineteen years, both white. Big boys. I told the other merchants, You are fools, and they say I am the fool. Sure, they say, go to the police. They arrest them, and what happens? The judges, the courts, are very easy with criminals now. In a few days they are back on the street and you get your windows smashed just the same because you made trouble for them."

Feinman said something under his breath.

"But I did not spend twenty-five days in that old boat, starving, to come to a place where it is fear and blackmail all over again. I said to them, That is not what America is supposed to be. They say to me, Please, Janowsky, don't go to the police or we are all hurt worse in the end. I think they have forgotten what America is supposed to be!"

"Let's say," said Maddox, "they haven't—mmh—quite had the last straw laid on their backs, Mr. Janowsky." He made a fist and looked at it lovingly. "But you do have a problem. Hasn't he, Joe?"

Feinman growled. "These punks," he said. "Too lazy to do an honest job—half of 'em couldn't do any kind of job. But God knows the rest of your neighbors are right, sir. We drop on 'em, and forty-eight hours later they're out on bail and mad." He swore. Janowsky was watching them anxiously. "Do you know where and when the payoff is?"

"Pardon?"

"When they come to get the protection money, do they pick it up right at the stores?"

"I think so. Mr. Bremmer is the only one tells me much. He says so. The two who come to see me, they told me I must have the money in cash ready to give them at noon tomorrow. I think they go to the others then too."

"Goddamn," said Feinman. "What they need is a good hiding. With the promise of more if they ever try it again. All that kind understand is force. Scare 'em enough, they'll turn meek as kittens."

"Mmh, yes," said Maddox. "Yes. We are—especially the L.A.P.D.—such nice gentlemanly fellows these days, respecting everybody's rights but more especially the rights of the thugs and heist men and rapists and—louts. It is a little problem, Joe. There is nothing I would more dearly love to do than tangle with a couple of those louts; none of them has any science, you know, just brute strength."

"And having seen you in action once or twice, I'd like to be there to join in," said Feinman. "But I've got a wife and family. I've been on this force for seventeen years and not a mark on my record. I wouldn't like to get fired for police brutality."

"No. Neither would I," said Maddox regretfully.

"Though I sometimes wonder," said Feinman, "why any man wants to be a cop. It isn't as if we get rich at it. Even if this force pays higher than most. My next-door neighbor, one of 'em, is a plumber, which isn't exactly a prestige job, and he's just bought a new color TV and hires a gardener to keep up his yard. Me, not even a power mower have I got."

Janowsky listened, puzzled. "You are saying what the rest of them said, it is no good? You can't help me?"

"Damn it," said Feinman, scowling. "Damn it, if there was anything—"

Suddenly Maddox began to laugh. He leaned back and howled. The other two stared at him. "Oh, my," said Maddox, sitting up and wiping his eyes. "Oh, dear, that's the brightest idea I've had all year. It really is. Mr. Janowsky"—and he pulled himself together and stood up—"don't worry. Everything'll be all right."

"But when I refused them, said I would not pay, they said they would all come, all this gang, and if I did not give them money they would hurt me and smash all my merchandise."

"Fine," said Maddox. "The more the merrier."

"Please?"

"Just don't worry," said Maddox. "And don't lose faith in Americans, Mr. Janowsky, the ones who didn't have to fight to turn into Americans. In the end, you know, they've always got one great factor going for them—that old American ingenuity and know-how. If one thing won't work, another usually will."

Janowsky gave him a little smile. "You have thought of a plan."

"I have thought of the hell of a plan," Maddox agreed.

"Then I leave it in your hands. Thank you, sir." Janowsky went out with shoulders well back.

"And just what the hell have you thought of?" asked Feinman.

"It was you made me think of it. I got talking to the Clintons' regular gardener a couple of weeks ago." Maddox explained, and Feinman was still laughing when Rodriguez and Rowan came back.

■ ■ ■

Sue was alone in the office at a few minutes past eleven; Daisy was ferrying a couple of forlorn teen-agers down to Juvenile Hall. They had stopped a car on the street and announced that they wanted to go home; they were runaways from Idaho and they'd run out of money and couldn't get jobs. Maybe they'd go home with a few changed ideas about the glamour of the big city.

"Oh, please, is this where we're supposed to—the man downstairs said—" The voice was soft and breathless. Sue looked up to find a couple in the doorway. "Rural" occurred to her instantly; the man, big and burly, wore a suit and a white shirt, but he looked uncomfortable and the clothes too tight; you could nearly see overalls superimposed. The girl was slim, rather pretty, but her blue cotton dress was a little dowdy, a little too long, and her dark hair was arranged in a ten-year-old style. They looked about thirty, both of them.

"Can I help you?" asked Sue.

"It's about the baby, Edna's baby. I'm May Weaver and this is my husband Bob. Edna Gifford. The police came and told Mother and Dad. It was awful! She was my sister. And nobody knew—nobody ever knew—why she went bad the way she did. Like that. Running around and getting arrested and doing such terrible things."

"Now, honey, don't get upset," he said.

"Why, we've never had anybody but good people in our family, decent honest people. We all felt just terrible about Edna. And when she had the baby—"

"Now, honey."

"Oh, dear, do you know—I suppose you're a police-woman so it's all right to say it to you—she didn't even know who—who— But my goodness, a baby's a baby, and it needs looking after, and I can't have any, and we just begged her—Mother did too—to let me take him. She—she came back to Mother's to have the baby, you see, and as we all said, what *kind* of raising would the poor mite have, if she—racketing around all over— Bob and I wanted him the worst way."

"Oh, I see," said Sue. Well, one happy ending at least.

"And to *think* of Edna getting killed like that! We could hardly believe it. But the police did say, I guess your police sent a wire or something when it happened, they did say about there being the baby, and Mother and Dad said, You and Bob just *go*. Because whoever, the baby was Edna's and must be some good blood. . . . We scraped together everything we had. Neither of us'd ever been in an airplane before. And oh, please, do you think we can *have* the baby?"

Sue smiled at her. "There'll be a little red tape, but when you can prove that you're a blood relative and that it is your sister's baby—"

"Oh, I can! He was just perfect except for a little red birthmark on one leg, nothing to matter—"

"Well, then, I'd better take you two down to Juvenile Hall and get the red tape started," said Sue.

"Oh, thank you! Oh, Mother and Dad'll be so glad!"

The husband patted her arm. "See he gets a good raising anyway."

∎ ∎ ∎

The identification on the heist man came in from S.I.D. downtown about noon. He was one Peter Andrew Thatcher, thirty-nine, and he had a record back to age thirteen. He'd spent a total of four years and eight months in prison, which was about par for the course now—nineteen arrests and ten charges since he turned adult.

Maddox was reading that and Feinman was arguing with O'Neill on the phone when a man marched into the office and said loudly, "Which one of you is Maddox?" Maddox stood up. "Why the hell haven't we heard from you? My mother's wild. So's my wife. Just what's going on here, and what's all this damned nonsense about Dorrie vanishing? Where's Monica? What are you *doing* about it?"

"Mr. Mayo," said Maddox. "Sit down."

"I've *been* sitting down. On airplanes. When we didn't hear any more—"

"There isn't much to tell you."

"—I thought I'd better come, see for myself just what the hell this is all about! What *is* it all about?" Mayo was about thirty, tall, craggy-faced, wide-shouldered, with rumpled dark hair and cold gray eyes.

Maddox sighed and began to tell him. Mayo kept interjecting remarks into the narrative—"That's senseless!"— "But Dorrie wouldn't"— And then quite suddenly he noticed the pink cat, and he said, "That's Monica's! Mother sent it to her for Christmas and Dorrie said she loved it, hardly let it out of her sight. Wherever Dorrie took Monica, she'd take this. Monica'd raise a fuss."

"It was in the apartment," said Maddox. "Left behind. Mr. Mayo, had your sister-in-law ever been fingerprinted?"

"Well, my God, of course not!"

"Quite a lot of people besides criminals do get printed. It'd be a help if we had her prints, that's all, could identify

110

them from others. I gather there's been steady correspondence between—"

"Well, of course. We came out for the wedding. Mother loved Dorrie on sight. We all—and she'd never had a family, You see, her own parents were killed in a plane crash when she was about two, there weren't any relatives, and she was brought up—"

"Do you know the name of the orphanage?"

"The St. Francis Episcopal Home in Fresno. We all took to her. Dorrie's a dear girl. And then when Ken was killed—my wife and I haven't any children— But for God's sake, all this isn't *doing* anything! What are you doing to find her? Where could she have gone?"

Maddox reflected sadly that it was impossible to explain some of the realities of police work even to the law-abiding citizen. He said, "Mr. Mayo, this is a big metropolis. It's not easy to look for anybody in a place like this. The latest record we have of Mrs. Mayo's being seen by anyone who knew her was a week ago yesterday morning, when another tenant there, Mrs. Littleton, saw her start out with the baby in a stroller. That same morning, Mrs. Fogarty spoke to her on the phone. Then—nothing. The notes saying she was moving—taped on her door and Mrs. Littleton's—were found on Tuesday. The letter to Robinson's was received on Wednesday. We've had a lab examination of the apartment, but when we don't have her prints we can't isolate them from any others. We haven't had a photograph—"

"Well, you have now," said Mayo, calming down a little. He brought out a manila envelope from his breast pocket. "Mother thought about that. Here's every picture we've got of her—I'll want them back—and a batch of her most recent letters."

"That'll be a big help. Thanks very much," said Maddox. He picked up the first photograph on top of the little pile. No, they hadn't seen a picture of Dorrie before; looking at it, he could understand Faulkner's persistence. She was a beauty, in a quiet, ladylike way. A kitten face, triangular, with a generous smiling mouth and wide-set big eyes. Short, crisply curling dark hair. An intelligent face too, he thought. Rodriguez and Rowan had come over to sit in, and he introduced them absently. They looked at the photograph with interest.

"I see Faulkner's point," said Rodriguez.

"Faulkner?" asked Mayo.

"Hadn't she mentioned him?" He shook his head. "Well, there you are," said Maddox. "He wasn't even that important to her. Or maybe she didn't want you people to know she was dating anybody."

"She *was*?"

"No, not really. She'd told him she wasn't interested."

"And he sounded on the level," said Rodriguez, "but was he? Did he keep after her, and—"

Maddox lit a cigarette. "That's the wrong shape, César. I don't think so."

"Look, what are you *talking* about?" demanded Mayo. "Aren't you doing anything to find her? Why should she go off like this? Isn't there something—?"

"We'll get the press to run her picture now," said Maddox. "You'd better formally report her missing. It'll carry more weight coming from a relative. We've just had these two friends of hers. If you like we can put out an A.P.B. on her."

"What's that?"

"An all points bulletin. That goes to all the police forces all around here, and they'll be automatically watching for her. Have you got a picture of the little girl?" Fifteen months, he thought, wasn't quite a baby; a face might have some individuality by that age.

112

Mayo rummaged through the pile. "That's their wedding picture." Maddox looked at it. Ken Mayo had looked like his brother, not exactly handsome but a good reliable face, the same craggy profile. "Here—" It was an enlarged snapshot of a baby sitting on grass somewhere, trees in the background. Just a baby, he thought; a pretty one, maybe, with a good deal of dark hair, a button nose, a laughing mouth. It was a color snapshot; the baby had on a blue-checked dress with white trim. Recognizable as the child seen at the supermarket, the playground? Probably not. Idly he turned the enlargement over. The same neat small writing he remembered from the application form ran across it: *Mrs. Barnes took this in the park, let me have negative—first time she had on the dress you sent!*

"But why?" said Mayo. "We wanted her to come back, be near us, and the last couple of letters Mother had, Dorrie was beginning to think about it. It wasn't exactly easy for her here. But why would she—?"

"Just maybe she didn't," said Maddox. As he explained about the typed notes and letter, the phone call to Mrs. Moran, under the smirk of the pink cat, Mayo lost some color. When he got out a cigarette his hand was shaking.

"Oh, no," he said. "No—*you don't mean kidn*— A week, *over* a week ago, and you haven't got the FBI, the—"

"Now take it easy," said Maddox. "There isn't any big money around, we gather, for any kind of ransom. We don't think it's that. But it is a possibility that she went involuntarily, shall we say. Or halfway."

"What the hell do you mean by that?"

"Now look, Mr. Mayo," said Maddox, feeling tired. "It isn't going to help if you jump down our throats at every question. We're professional police. There are questions we have to ask. Out of experience we know these questions sometimes turn up leads. We don't know your sister-in-law personally. So please don't think we're trying to insult her

113

or— Well. Now, do you know if she went around with any other men before she married your brother?"

Mayo's voice was dull now. "I'm sorry," he said. "I realize that. I'm a lawyer, naturally I've—worked with police a little. I don't know, but I suppose she had—she was twenty-one when they were married. It would be natural she would have."

"All right. Where was she living between the time she left the orphanage and when she met your brother, do you know?"

"Ancient history," muttered Mayo.

"Not so ancient. Six—seven years ago?"

"Yes. She left the orphanage when she was eighteen. She went to Los Angeles because she thought salaries would be better than in a smaller town. She didn't want office work, didn't try for that kind of training. She worked for Sears, I think—clerking, you know. Oh—she and another girl from the orphanage went together. Wait a minute, I'll get the name. Damn it, I remember her talking about—it was the same as some old movie star's name—Talmadge! Only it was Betty, not Norma. They shared an apartment awhile. Then the other girl, this Betty, got married. No, I don't know her married name."

Maddox suppressed a hasty word. There hadn't been an address book in the apartment; if she had one, it was probably in her handbag, and where that might be— Beside the phone there'd been an index with numbers scribbled, but none of any help to them: the baby's doctor, names of friends they'd already had, Mrs. Moran.

"Did she ever write anything in her letters about Mr. Simon?" he asked suddenly. "Technically her employer."

Mayo said, after a moment, "Why, yes, I think so. Just lately—in a letter to Helen. My wife. She said—Dorrie, I mean—that she was sorry for him. She liked him very much, I know."

114

Maddox looked at him, surprised for no good reason.

■ ■ ■

Mayo went off to his hotel at ten minutes to two, and Maddox realized suddenly that he was starving. He went out to the hall and found the snub-nosed freckle-faced fellow just professionally closing and positioning the sandwich machine. "Hi," he said. "See, fresh service every day. Well, except Sundays. But all wrapped like they are— How do you like it?"

"Fine," said Maddox. "Just fine." He shoved two quarters in and pulled the lever labeled *Beef*. The machine rumbled and a neatly wrapped sandwich slithered into the long tube.

"See? Must be handy for you guys. Oh, my name's Flanagan, by the way. They're good, aren't they? We buy wholesale from a place does thousands a day, for quick-lunch counters and like that. It's O.K.?"

"Fine," said Maddox.

"Well, that's O.K. then." Flanagan went off whistling.

Maddox finished the sandwich and started calling the press. Too late to get a picture in the *Herald*, but with luck get it in the *Times* and *Citizen* tomorrow. For a start.

■ ■ ■

Feinman had argued a bit with O'Neill, because it didn't sound like a job for a plainclothesman, but O'Neill said the citizen was being stubborn, and in the end he went. He didn't really mind. He was still feeling tickled at Maddox's ingenious solution of Mr. Janowsky's problem; he thought fondly of Mr. Janowsky, American citizen.

It was a big old house up in the hills, on Maravilla Drive, and the squad car was still there, with Patrolman Ben Loth in it. He said, annoyed, "Look, I know it's nothing for you. She's pretty sure a salesman took it—she's had a couple in the house today—so what she should do is contact the companies. Well, technically a burglary. I put in a report, but not as if you could find out anything with dusting for prints and so on."

A woman came bustling down the front walk to them; there was only a narrow strip of lawn between house and street. "Are you the detective?" she asked.

"Yes, ma'am," said Feinman.

"Well, good." She was a plump, pretty little woman in the fifties, with frosted blond curls and a friendly smile. "I'm sorry if I made you mad," she said to Loth, "but I know how it's supposed to go—I watch *Adam-12* all the time. And the men riding in the black-and-white never investigate burglaries. They call the detectives." Feinman and Loth looked at each other. "You come in and I'll show you just where it was."

Feinman waved a dismissing hand at Loth and followed her back to the house. The big living room was in some disorder but homily so: old, comfortable furniture, a lot of cut flowers around. "Now!" she said brightly to Feinman. "You look a bit like that nice sergeant on *Adam-12*, the one named Mac. You see, what happened is, I have rather sensitive skin—it's dry. It gets itchy and peels off, especially in hot weather. So I often take my rings off if they're bothering me, and that's what I did yesterday afternoon when it was so hot. My, I'm glad it's turned cooler, aren't you?"

"Yes, ma'am," said Feinman, "but—"

"Oh, I'm so sorry, my name's Brightman. Mrs. Alice Brightman. Mrs. Samuel really. My husband's a stockbroker with Gibson and Conway. Of course the children are both married and away from home. Are you married?"

"Yes, we've got two," said Feinman, slightly confused. "If you'd—"

"And I put them right down on the coffee table there. Won't you sit down, by the way, Mr.—?"

"Feinman."

"Mr. Feinman, and what a very nice name for a police officer, a fine man, and I'm sure you all are. I put them right down here, my wedding ring and my engagement ring, all together they're just over three carats, and I never thought about them again until I was getting ready to go out half an hour ago. And the engagement ring was *gone*. Here's my wedding ring right here—you can see for yourself." It was a platinum band set with a double row of diamonds. "I hunted all around the floor to be *sure*. And then I thought, the vacuum man! I wouldn't like to think it of the Avon lady, a very nice woman and of course I love their things, but she had been here too. This morning. Both of them sat on the couch here and could easily have—"

"What vacuum firm was it?" asked Feinman.

"Oh, he had several brands. Names like cards," she said vaguely. "Ace, and King—no, Royal—only I don't like the ones with tanks, so complicated."

"Did he leave a card?" asked Feinman manfully. They usually did.

"Why, I believe he did. If I can think where I put it—"

A harshly conversational voice inquired, "Whaddaya think o' that, kiddo?" and a swooping black something whooshed down to the coffee table. Feinman jumped, and Mrs. Brightman laughed.

"Oh, he's got loose again! Isn't he marvelous? I adore animals—the darling kitties and the dogs are out in the yard or I'd introduce you, Mr. Feinman—Sam got me my adorable Billy for my birthday last week. He's a mynah and really *so* clever. Talk to mama, Billy!"

"You can go to hell!" said the mynah bird insolently,

and dipped his beak like lightning, snapped up the diamond band and departed with a flash of wings.

"My goodness, isn't he terrible!" said Mrs. Brightman delightedly.

Feinman got up. "Er—does he have any special place he hides things? He does seem to pick up things, doesn't he?"

"*Oh, my goodness alive!*" said Mrs. Brightman. "Do you think *Billy* could have—? My goodness! Just the few days we've had him, when he got loose before, he did take Sam's hat and put it in the bird bath in the yard."

Surrounded by dogs—four poodles—and with several cats watching aloofly from the porch, Feinman found both rings at the bottom of the bird bath. Billy regarded them from a tree nearby. "Billy's a good boy!" he said, preening himself.

"Well, I can't tell you how good you've been. So clever of you to see—and I'm so relieved I needn't suspect those nice people. Really, the vacuum man was quite handsome," said Mrs. Brightman, "and if I needed one— Well, I do thank you so much!"

Driving down the curving hill streets, Feinman reflected amusedly that at least, today, the great ecology rally was over. The young people had departed, leaving quite a mess up there in Griffith Park, and they could stop running the extra cars. He looked forward to telling the boys about Mrs. Brightman, but he wasn't really laughing *at* her. A very nice woman, really. Scatterbrained, thought Feinman tenderly.

■ ■ ■

Maddox had just finished talking to the *Herald*, and promised to send them a print today, when O'Neill rang him. Rodriguez, Rowan and Dabney were there; Feinman still out somewhere.

"Yes, Johnny?"

118

"You've got a homicide. By what I got, a real one—murder-one. And you won't believe who."

"Who?"

"The great screen lover you averted your eyes from as a pre-puberty lad. Carlos Moreno. His valet or cook or whatever just found him. Weltering in blood in bed."

"You don't say. What's the address?"

"You've got no romance, agrah. The idol of millions, aged and forgotten—actually I saw one of his old pictures on TV the other night, about 1935 it must have been. The media will be out on this one."

"The address," said Maddox.

It was Venus Drive up Laurel Canyon. They all went out on it and called up a mobile lab from downtown.

seven

"Hell and damnation!" Maddox swore as they came to the head of the stairs. Feinman was just coming up. "I must be getting senile. First I'm sidetracked by Janowsky, and then Mayo, and we haven't gone looking for Dorrie's bank, which was the first thing on the agenda for today. Damn it, it would be D'Arcy's day off, everything coming at once."

"We've got something new?" said Feinman.

"Not you. Listen, if George isn't busy, you both go looking for that bank. Not that you've got much time." Maddox looked at his watch; he was feeling a little harried.

"Sure thing," said Feinman easily. Maddox had kept them all up to date on that; things came up, and often they had to double in brass, switching jobs. "They close at three but the help doesn't go home, you know. I don't suppose she'd have picked one very far away, not having a car."

"So good luck." The rest of them went on downstairs and had to wait for a little handful of citizens just coming in. "My God," said Maddox, "not something else, I hope."

They didn't wait to find out. Rowan and Dabney got

120

into Rowan's car, Rodriguez into the Maserati. "Moreno," he said, lighting a cigarette as Maddox switched on the engine. "My God, he must have been in his seventies, Ivor; I can remember seeing some of his pictures as a kid, and they weren't new then."

Maddox grunted. "I'd forgotten the name. Latin lover?"

"I seem to remember he did some Westerns too. One of the rehashes of *Murietta*."

Venus Drive, when they got there, wound for a short way up into the hills off Laurel Canyon Boulevard. The house was a relic; probably built in the thirties, a Moorish castle in miniature. There were two squad cars at the curb, a uniformed man waiting beside one. "Quite a place," he said, gesturing, as they came up.

"Quite," said Rodriguez, staring at the turrets and fancy wrought-iron fencing.

"His houseman, I guess you'd call him, found him. Doesn't sleep in, just came in late and there he was. Stabbed, sometime last night, I'd guess. It's upstairs to your right. Lab truck on the way?"

"It is." They went in, past a tiled square entry hall, to tall ceilings and dim light. A cavern of a room opened to the left, another to the right; at the rear of the hall stairs wound up. They climbed. "Did you call Bergner?" Maddox asked Rodriguez.

"While you were calling S.I.D."

Two more uniformed men were in the upstairs hall outside the door to a front bedroom. "This is Francisco Ramirez, sir. He found the body."

Ramirez looked skittish and frightened. He was a youngish man. He said warily, "I don' know nothing about." He had the broad high cheekbones, the flat-planed forehead, showing Indian mixed with the Spanish. "You don' mind," he said nervously, "I call his friend. Mr. Gilday. I don' know what to do. I call Mr. Gilday. He say to call police, and he come. He is Mr. Moreno's friend."

"I see," said Maddox. They went into the bedroom. "That'll be helpful, a civilian cluttering up the scene."

"¡Porvida!" said Rodriguez involuntarily.

It wasn't a very pretty corpse. The master bedroom, like what they had glimpsed of the rest of the house, had once been furnished very expensively, but that had been some time back, and everything was shabby and old. The Oriental carpet was faded, the big fourposter bed's draperies of heavy beige silk were dirty and a little frayed in places, the velvet upholstery on chaise longue and two chairs worn. The drapes at the one wide window overlooking the street matched the bed curtains and were pulled all the way back; the window was open, and it faced west. Today had been overcast and now the sky was darkening to the north, but here the merciless thin light fell on the bed and its horrid occupant.

He had once been a handsome big man, and the ghost of his youth showed, much blurred. The straight nose and high forehead, once firm mouth. But he had taken on weight and the jawline was jowled and sagging, there were heavy lines of dissipation criss-crossing the ruined face, and as he'd fallen against the pillows the very expensive wig had slipped a little to one side, a wig of curly black hair touched with gray at the temples. The little hairline mustache was probably dyed. He was an obscenity there on the bed, for he was stark naked, the gross big paunch fallen to one side, his fat thighs white and flabby, his torso flat-chested and hairless. There was dried blood all over his upper body and the sheets. The bed had been turned down, and both pillows were generously bloodstained, as if he'd wallowed around a good deal before he died.

"That's an inviting sight," said Dr. Bergner behind Maddox. "An awful warning. Man who lets himself get into that condition, pshah! Who was he?"

"Yes, you're going on a diet tomorrow," said Maddox. "The old movie star, Carlos Moreno."

"Oh, was he? Remember him. Frightening, what years can do to a man." The doctor went to lean over the bed. Downstairs, they heard the lab men coming in.

"Just once over lightly. We'll have S.I.D. here in a minute," said Maddox.

"Well, he was stabbed to death, you can see that. Stabbed a good many times, and he probably struggled. At a very rough guess, call it fourteen to sixteen hours."

"Late last night anyway. César, see if you can get that Ramirez to open up some."

Rodriguez went back to the hall. Ramirez was watching the patrolmen out of the corner of his eye. Rodriguez was genial in Spanish. It might be easier to speak in his own tongue? He understood. There were questions to be asked.

"I am a citizen," said Ramirez, looking a little relieved. "Mr. Moreno says I should become a citizen."

"How long had you worked for him?"

"Ten–eleven years. He is on holiday in Acapulco, his other servant leaves him and he employs me there. I suit him. He brings me back here. It is an easy job. He doesn't give the parties. He is out much. It's to take care of his clothes, send for cleaning, press his shirts—" Ramirez shrugged. "Answer the telephone, like that. This was a fine house, once. He doesn't care to keep it nice now. Once in a while, cleaning women in."

"Perhaps he has lost money?" said Rodriguez.

"Oh, no! Much, much money he has. He made a great deal of money as an actor, long ago. But since he don't give parties, he don't mind about the house. He goes to other people's parties, all dressed up grand."

"Well, what are the arrangements here? How was it you only found him now? Don't you come to get his breakfast?"

Ramirez shook his head. "He don't like to be bothered in the morning. Take his time to get up. I come about noon, get his lunch. But I asked him, Is it all right I am late today? I must go to meet a bus. My sister has arrived to visit friends. He said all right."

"That was last night?"

"Yes, at dinner."

"You don't live in? Sleep in the house?"

Ramirez said, "In the garden." He pointed, and Rodriguez followed him down the hall to the back of the house. The hill behind had been terraced, and on a level site about fifty feet down from the house was a small pink stucco guesthouse.

"Oh. And what time did you leave here?"

"When I have washed the dishes from dinner. Mr. Moreno was alone, yes. Then, he was alone."

"Then? You think he expected someone to come later? What time was that?"

Ramirez shrugged again. "Nine o'clock. I—I think I do not say any evil of the dead. From others perhaps you hear." He turned away abruptly.

Downstairs a new arrival was arguing with the patrolman. Maddox came out of the bedroom and said, "Leave the lab boys in peace. They're giving it the treatment. What've you got?" Rodriguez told him. "And who's this?"

A man was climbing the stairs heavily. "Sir," called the patrolman, "he said you expected him."

"Do we?" asked Maddox.

The civilian reached the top step and panted. He was well into his sixties and too fat; he had a mop of white hair and a pink face. "You'll be the police," he said. "I don't want to interfere, just the opposite. Poor old boy! Poor silly old bastard, what a way to die. I'm August Gilday." Maddox and Rodriguez both knew the name: a director, sometimes a producer, once very well known. "I was about the only one of the old crowd who kept up with him. Not socially, so to speak. Kept track of him. Last few years, he was the hanger-on—nobody with money lacks the friends, in quotes. The races, the horse shows, the gilded doings, all that bit. Can we sit down somewhere? I just thought I might help you. Tell you about him. When that idiot Ramirez phoned me, I thought I'd better come." He looked past them. "He's—in there?"

"We won't disturb the lab boys," said Maddox. "You might be helpful."

"There's a den somewhere here." They found it; the door was open, and it looked mustily unused, the furniture dusty, so probably they wouldn't be disturbing any lab evidence. "We'd like to hear about any relatives, for one thing," said Maddox.

"Nope. Nary a one I know of. He never married, and in case you're curious," said Gilday, "his real name was Klaus Vollmer. Funny"—he looked around the room—"he used to be proud of this place. Don't know why he ever built it—barracks of a house—just for himself and a bevy of servants, back when you could get servants. He built it in the thirties, when he was in his heyday. It used to be quite a place."

"He still had money?"

"A pile. Made some shrewd investments. Poor silly old fool," said Gilday, between sadness and contempt. "He might've kept on going—they can do wonders with makeup and lighting, and he was only forty or so—but it was the war. All of a sudden, Latin romances sort of passé, you know. Everybody doing the big war pics, clean-cut

American youth. Not that he minded not *working*, you get me, but it was what they call a blow to his ego. He was the hell of an egotist."

Rodriguez said, "Are you giving us hints, Mr. Gilday? Never married, did he?"

"That could be an interesting point," said Maddox.

"Nope," said Gilday. "You asking me if he was a fag? A gay boy? Nope. Just the opposite."

"Oh?"

"If you'll believe me, he still had himself convinced he was God's gift to women. Him and his wig and corset and dapper mustache. But I guess just lately"—Gilday wagged his head—"the last few years, he'd been half realizing, you know, that the females who encouraged him— or something more—were solely interested in his money. Poor lonely old idiot."

"Oh," said Maddox. "You mean he was still on the make? At his age?"

"Seventy-three," said Gilday. "I don't know whether it was for real or just for looks. You'd have to ask the girls that. I guess it was keeping up his masculine pride— you know, the still-as-good-as-I-ever-was kind of thing."

Ramirez came in. "Mr. Gilday. I am glad you are here. I think"—and his tone was guarded—"I must tell you a thing private."

"Don't be silly, man. These are the police. They've got to hear anything important. What d'you want to say?"

Ramirez looked at the police nervously. "Perhaps they think it was me, and it was not. I am not a thief. But Mr. Moreno's rings, sir, they are gone. He never takes off but to wash his hands."

"That so?" said Gilday. "Robbery, eh?" He looked at Maddox.

"Well," said Maddox. "So, while the lab boys are at it, César, suppose you take Mr. Ramirez on a little tour and see if anything else is missing. And get a description of—"

"The rings. Come on, Mr. Ramirez, let's start up here. Does he keep much cash around?"

Maddox went back to the master bedroom. Dabney came out to him and said, "They're picking up all sorts of stuff in there. No weapon yet, a good many latents. The doctor's gone, said he'd see him at the morgue."

Maddox looked at his watch. Damnation, this would come along just now. He wondered how George and Feinman were doing on that bank. Well, sidetracked or not, sometime today he'd have to talk to Lewis Nagao's uncle. It should, he thought, be an interesting experiment.

■ ■ ■

Feinman had looked into the smaller detective office across the hall, up from the sandwich machine, and found Ellis contemplating a long yellow sheet. "I've never seen so damn many A.P.B.s out all at once, from all over," said Ellis plaintively. "And we just got another word from N.C.I.C. Those escaped cons, they still think they're heading west. Last positive ident was in Nevada."

"Well, sufficient is the evil," said Feinman. "Like to help me out on a little job? It's these wild geese of Ivor's. That's a funny one, George, you look at it close. And yet nothing to say really definitely. Well, we haven't seen her bank record yet."

"Oh," said Ellis. "I've just heard the highlights on that one." Feinman told him a little more as they went down to the lobby.

Here they found O'Neill beleaguered by three civilians, all arguing at him at once.

"Look, it was checked out, and he was just confused. That concussion—" O'Neill was looking annoyed.

"Well, Ricky remembers better now. That man tried to kill him." A fat dark woman, shrill.

"I do remember plain, and it's so. That guy oughta be arrested." A husky young man, aggrieved.

"And I'd like to know what police are for if you can't report crimes." An older young man, enough like the other to be marked as a brother.

"Look!" O'Neill raised his voice and beckoned Ellis and Feinman. "Hell, this is nothing, it's wild—it was all gone over yesterday. D'Arcy was on it—but you've got to get these nuts off my neck. I'm sitting on the switchboard."

"What's it all about?" asked Feinman.

"Oh, hell!" said O'Neill as the board lit up. He plugged in, answered, and put a call through to Lieutenant Eden's office. "For God's sake, do we have to hash this all over? I'd better call Loth in. He can give you the gist. It's only an hour to change of shift."

"You let me handle this," said Ellis, also looking annoyed; one of the many petty nuisances of police work is that things often happen all at once. "You haven't got much time to look at banks. Now, let's sort this out, Johnny."

■ ■ ■

Feinman went on his way alone and in the car got out a map of Hollywood and studied it. The nearest main drag to the apartment on Lexington was Santa Monica or, going the other way, Western. Dorrie Mayo, lacking a car, would have taken a bus along Santa Monica Boulevard to get to her job in Beverly Hills. So he tried Santa Monica first. There were three banks in the first block west from Western, and he methodically took them in order. By the time he came to the second one, it was closed, but he rapped patiently on the door, until an angry-looking guard pulled the curtain aside, and held up his badge to be let in. As he'd reminded Maddox, all the staff would be there until six o'clock or so. He didn't find an account for her there either, so he went on to the third bank at the corner.

It was a Pacific Security bank, and he had to rap quite a while before one of the girl tellers pulled the curtain back. She stared uncomprehendingly at the badge, went away, and presently a man came and looked and unlocked the door at once.

"And what does the law want?"

"The chief teller," said Feinman.

The chief teller, who was female and adored Jack Webb and *Adam-12* and in fact had a Thing about the L.A.P.D., was very helpful. With no trouble she produced Dorrie Mayo's account for him. It was, as she pointed out, a very simple account. She found back records, and the microfilms of checks, and Feinman got interested in details.

The first thing he wanted to know was the state of the account as of a week ago yesterday. It was a checking account, she didn't have a savings account, and there was $293.64 in it. The latest check she had written, not yet returned to her, was the check for the rent; it was dated February 27.

The back records were monotonous but enlightening in a way. But they offered no leads, no suggestions at all. She had been paid every two weeks, a check for $255. She always deposited most of it, taking sums in cash varying between twenty-five and fifty dollars. In the off week she had cashed a counter check for thirty or forty. She didn't write very many checks at all. He came across rent checks, in the last six months three checks to a Dr. Brubaker (that would be the baby doctor), checks to a shoe store, a drugstore, a market.

But the point was, of course, that she hadn't cleaned out her account. Wherever she was going, for whatever reason, she'd need money to live on; and by these records, she didn't habitually carry much cash.

129

It was something else to make it look funny, thought Feinman.

"I'm sorry," said the chief teller with real regret, "but we close at five thirty, sir." He looked up. It was getting on to that time, the staff streaming out. He thanked her for the cooperation and went out too. It was nearly dark, and while he'd been poring over records it had begun to rain; it was coming down solid now, pounding on the pavements. He turned up his coat collar and made a dash up the block to the lot where he'd left his car.

■ ■ ■

Ben Loth, exasperated, explained the thing to Ellis, who said, "My God, people."

"You know concussion does funny things—and it was all checked out yesterday. Detective D'Arcy—"

But they had to go over it again, slow and easy, for the confused citizenry. Ellis, on the insistence of the Caprios, drove them out to the Wechslers' place. Anybody could see what kind of place it was, and anybody could tell the kind the Wechslers were: ordinary elderly couple, salt of the earth. He apologized to Wechsler, who was a fattish old fellow with glasses sliding down his nose and benevolent faded blue eyes, and Mrs. Wechsler, who was vague and forgiving.

"My Ricky isn't no idiot, forget what happened just a day or two ago," Mrs. Caprio began belligerently. Ellis tried to calm her down.

Wechsler looked a little bewildered. "But we told the policemen yesterday how it was. I don't understand how you think I'd do such a crazy thing—we both saw the boy fall down hard."

"Yes, yes," said his wife. "It's all right, the detective said the doctor explained it, when he hit his head maybe

130

he doesn't remember so good what happened just before. This happened once to my nephew Jackie. He was in a car hit a tree."

Their gentle looks defeated the Caprios, who turned a little sullen. "Tell *me* I don't remember!" muttered Ricky.

"Now look," said Loth patiently. "We went through it when I picked you up on Saturday, Caprio. I checked it then. You know you told me you'd got a little confused. You must have fallen down like Mr. and Mrs. Wechsler said. The doctor told you—"

"Why would I do such a thing?" Wechsler appealed to them. "I'd only hired the boy, come work for me, keep the store clean, help stock shelves! Would I want to do him any harm?"

"Of course not," said Ellis. "It's ridiculous."

Wechsler smiled at Ricky. "I hope you don't let this stop you, come work here."

Ricky backed off. "No, I guess I won't—I mean, I don't want the job."

"Oh, hell," said his brother. "Come on, Mama, we aren't getting anywhere."

What a damned waste of time, thought Ellis; Loth should have gone off duty an hour ago.

"Some people," said Wechsler sadly, "take funny notions."

"Well, let's hope they won't bother you again, Mr. Wechsler."

When he and Loth came out to the street, it had started to rain.

■ ■ ■

Maddox, Rowan, Rodriguez and Dabney got back to Wilcox Street at five o'clock. They'd get a lab report on what S.I.D. had picked up at the Moreno house sometime.

131

They had compiled a list of what was definitely missing from the house, and it added up to quite a little loot. Moreno had kept quantities of cash around, by what Ramirez said, and Gilday confirmed that. Neither of them could estimate what might have been there, casually in his top bureau drawer; it might have been several thousand dollars. There'd been a complete set of sterling flatware, a dozen sterling serving pieces, dishes; Moreno's jewelry, which was considerable—an 18k wristwatch, a dozen rings, diamond-set and otherwise, gold cuff links, four sets of studs set with black star sapphires, onyx, jade and rubies; a set of expensive matched luggage, naturally initialed; a 14k pocket watch, engraved; and miscellaneous items such as a portable color TV, a console TV, a portable transistor radio, a tape recorder.

No weapon had been found, though the lab men had been crawling around all the bushes back and front before it began to rain.

"Damnation," said Maddox, looking at his watch. By four o'clock the press had had the rumor on the grapevine and were up there in force. That elderly silly old Lothario, he thought, newsworthy because he'd once been the screen idol. Unbidden, the wistful line slid into his mind: *Time's wingéd chariot hurrying near....*

Rodriguez went to get the list added to the pawnbrokers' hot list and relayed to Central Robbery–Homicide. Ellis came in and began to tell him all about that Caprio business; D'Arcy had covered it yesterday. Maddox listened to him absently, wondering if Feinman had located the bank.

"It would be D'Arcy's day off," he said. "Probably sitting somewhere over a drink discussing F stops and lens openings with his lady love." Ellis laughed. Maddox heard Feinman's footsteps on the stairs, but Feinman didn't come in right away.

■ ■ ■

Feinman looked into the little office, at Sue's bent dark head and Daisy's blond one. "Say, you know it's raining cats and dogs."

"We can hear it," said Daisy.

"Everybody just got back," said Sue.

"From the new homicide? Hell, it's after five thirty. I hope that genius of a husband of yours doesn't get side-tracked again. He said—"

"Off what?"

"Well, as he said, the brightest idea he's had all year."

As she listened to Feinman, Sue began to look alarmed. Her normally mild and amiable spouse had a tendency now and then to jump precipitately into a fight; of course he was a Celt.

■ ■ ■

D'Arcy, as a matter of fact, was not sitting over a drink with his lady love at all, and he was rapidly coming to the conclusion that she was not his lady love.

They had gone to a photographic exhibition at the County Museum, and in the first place Sheila Fitzpatrick was wearing pants, a shocking-pink pantsuit. D'Arcy was a reasonable man, and when a girl was out hiking or riding a horse he could see that pants were practical; but when it came to visiting a museum or going out to a restaurant or whatever, in town, he was convinced that nine out of ten men felt the way he did: it didn't look feminine. Proper. Or attractive. Granted, Sheila Fitzpatrick had a nice figure, but most females were too plump in just the places pants revealed.

"Darling Drogo, you are archaic," she told him, her mop of topaz hair falling over one eye.

"And you can stop calling me—"

It was, of course, no place to propose to a girl, though

the exhibition hadn't attracted any crowds; the hall was, in fact, quite bare of people. He thought she might be interested in some of the current cases—sometimes she was —and started to tell her about Dorrie and Monica; that was rather bugging him, as it was Maddox.

"Oh, for heaven's sake," said Sheila. "It's your day off. Such dreary little people—who cares where she's got to?"

D'Arcy stared at a very good black-and-white study of a child with a kitten. "There's Monica," he said absently. "The little girl. I mean, you wonder—"

"Probably a brat. Doting mother. Light, please, dear."

"And I don't like the way you throw *dears* around, not meaning anything." He struck a match.

"Oh, Drogo, you are a stuffy bore sometimes," said Sheila amusedly.

"Well, thanks for letting me know!" My God, he thought, what had got into him—actually fancying himself in love with her, asking her to marry him? My God, suppose she'd said yes? A damned rattlebrained adolescent, even if she was a good pro photographer. He must have been out of his mind. "Come on," he said grimly, "you're going home. You can go look for somebody else to boss around who doesn't bore you so damned much."

He never said another word to her until he stopped in front of the old house where she lived with her father. "It's raining," she pointed out a little sulkily.

"I see it is," said D'Arcy. "Good-by. You can give your father my sympathy."

"Oh, you're just *impossible!*" said Sheila, and got out and slammed the door and ran for the house.

My God, what an escape, thought D'Arcy. He might have got stuck with that bossy scatterbrain for life. He drove home through the rain to the old house above Silver Lake, where he'd stayed of inertia after his parents were gone, and as he shut the garage he felt suddenly relieved.

Safer to emulate Rodriguez and play it canny, not to commit yourself. He built a fire in the fireplace and made himself a large drink. He thought there was a T-bone still in the freezer; he'd go get it out presently.

He wondered what had gone down today—and if they had anything new on Dorrie and Monica. Something unnatural about a girl who wasn't concerned for a baby, possibly in danger. Possibly? Danger of what? Nothing they had turned up said that at all. . . .

■ ■ ■

Maddox looked in at a quarter of six and said, "I'm sorry, love, I'll be late. I've got an errand to run." Daisy had already left; Sue had been about to leave.

"Yes, and I know what. Joe was telling me something about it. Now, Ivor, you're not getting *into* anything? From what Joe said—and do I know you, the underdog shows up and the next thing you're wading in with both fists. Funny, you don't look like that kind at all, but— listen, you know how touchy Internal Affairs is."

Maddox laughed. "Don't fuss, woman. I'm just going to supervise the fun, all unofficial." He tossed a little pile of papers on the desk. "You can oblige me by looking through these. I'd like a female opinion."

"What are they?"

"Dorrie's recent letters to the in-laws."

"Oh. I will." Sue was interested.

"And be careful driving, visibility's nil."

"Yes, yes," said Sue. "You just be careful about what you're getting into."

The rain was certainly coming down hard. She set the windshield wipers up, feeling the brake gingerly, but it was only eight blocks to Gregory Avenue. She slid the Chrysler into Mrs. Patterson's garage and locked the door; she always carried an umbrella in the back seat. She hurried up the block to the Clinton house and up the drive.

No hurry about dinner; time to put a package of frozen au gratin potatoes in the oven. Hamburgers when Ivor got home; she could start warming some peas or asparagus presently. Sue changed into a cotton duster, rather enjoying the drumming of the rain on the roof, changed her shoes, sat down on the couch and lit a cigarette and dialed her mother's number.

"Aunt Evelyn get in all right?"

"About one o'clock, ahead of the rain. Well, we need it, but it came up in a hurry, didn't it? And why aren't you busy getting dinner at this hour?"

"Your favorite son-in-law," said Sue, "is going to be late."

■ ■ ■

Maddox drove, in the dark and pouring rain, neon lights on now flickering and iridescent on the wet streets, down Western Avenue. It was the worst time of day to go anywhere, rain or no: traffic pouring homeward, surface streets and freeways, and a lot of drivers hungry and impatient and anxious to get home. He was hungry himself, and he'd be glad to get home, to his darling Sue and dinner, after this day.

But there was the desperate and faithful Mr. Janowsky, who knew that, in spite of everything, America was not supposed to be the being afraid.

The address was quite a way down Western, past Olympic, and he probably wouldn't be home by six thirty after all. This late, he'd be damned lucky to find the place open. Lew Nagao hadn't said anything about hours. Maddox swore, catching a light. Have to look up Lew Nagao's number, if it was closed, get the home number; explaining over the phone was one thing, face to face another.

When he found the address, of course it was on the

other side of the street, and he did some more cussing, with difficulty got into the left-hand lane, found a *No left turn between 4–7* P.M. sign facing him, and was swept helplessly down to Fourteenth before he could make a left. He went around the block, got back on Western headed north, and—something to be said for this homeward-heading hour —found a parking place on the street right outside his destination.

It was the corner unit of this block of stores and offices, and there were signs plastered all over the windows and side of the building, both the double doors. Signs in living color, a pair of fiercely snarling tigers and clouds of battle. POWER! said the signs. PROTECT AND DEVELOP YOURSELF! EXPERTS! CHAMPIONS TO GUIDE YOU! TIGER JACK NAGAO, INTERNATIONAL CHAMPION! LEARN FROM THE BEST! JUDO— JUJITSU—KARATE.

He put his hand on the door, expecting it to be locked; it was nearly six thirty now, what with the traffic. It opened, and he went in. The tiny front office was partitioned off from whatever was in the back, with a contrived room divider covered with vinyl wallpaper. The wallpaper bore a cheerful frieze of fierce American eagles.

There were two men in the place, one at a small desk. The sitting one was a serious-looking Oriental in immaculate sports clothes, gray jacket, blue shirt. He was medium-sized, but his shoulders bulged some.

The standing one was out of an old movie, circa 1940. He stood about three inches over Maddox and four times as broad. He was nakedly bald. He had a fearsomely sinister Oriental countenance, yellow and frowning. He looked like a first cousin to Genghis Khan, in a business suit.

They both looked up at Maddox. "Forgot to lock the door," observed Ghenghis Khan in flat American. "Sorry, we're closed." Maddox produced his badge. "Oh, the law. What can we do for you, sir?"

"I—mmh—got talking to Lew Nagao the other day," said Maddox. "He was telling me about his uncle."

Genghis Khan scowled. "That kid. Grossing a grand a month at that gardening service, and can I get him to make any investments? Blows it as it comes in. So?"

"He said something—I gather you're Tiger Jack?— about your being in the Air Force."

" 'S right. Nisei command one, World War Two. I'm a major, Air Force Reserve, now. Why's the L.A.P.D. interested?"

"Well, I just thought you might like," said Maddox, "to hear about Mr. Janowsky."

The slant eyes turned suspicious. "That badge for real? You selling something?"

"A kind of faith maybe," said Maddox gently, "that America means what it says. You interested?"

"Shoot," said Genghis Khan, intrigued.

eight

It stopped raining in the middle of the night, but Tuesday morning was still gray and overcast. Sue had spent the evening poring over those letters, but when Maddox asked her for conclusions she said, "Wait until I can tell everybody. The more heads the better—and there are a couple of suggestive things, at least."

"Suggestive as to where she went and why?"

"Well, no," said Sue.

In the morning she had to ask him how many eggs twice before he answered her, and he forgot his coffee until it was lukewarm. "Are you still half asleep?" asked Sue.

"No, I'm trying to think of something, damn it. It's right on the tip of my mind, but I can't— Damn it. It was something to do with the Narco office downtown." Five minutes later he kissed her hastily and was gone. Sue stacked the dishes, put on makeup, gathered up Dorrie Mayo's letters and left ten minutes later.

Just as Maddox stepped into the station, he exclaimed loudly, "Carlisle! The Wilshire beat. He said—"

"Morning. Something just bite you?" said Sergeant Buck genially. It was Johnny O'Neill's day off. Maddox lifted a hasty hand at him and ran up the stairs. Rodriguez and D'Arcy were already in.

"—and I tell you, César, the more I thought about it, the more I realized what a damn narrow escape I had. Actually proposing to that scatterbrained adolescent. My God, you don't know how good it feels to be off the hook! I tell you—"

Rodriguez looked at Maddox, resigned and amused. "I told you it wouldn't last. Now you know what's going to happen next."

Maddox gave them a preoccupied grin. "Wait for it," he said. "It may be days before he falls in love again."

"Nevermore!" said D'Arcy. "Right now I feel like that old song—I've got no use for women."

Feinman came in. "You called it," he said to Rodriguez. "They started calling in yesterday afternoon. Another batch of phony checks over the weekend. I don't know that it's any use, but if we showed the new marks these photostats we might get some better descriptions this time."

"You ought to know better," said Rodriguez. "There've been stories in most of the local papers. Don't people read any more? Damn this cute bunch of amateurs."

"So far it adds to just under a thousand, this weekend's batch of bouncy checks."

"I'll go show 'em the photostats," said D'Arcy. "I don't mind what jobs I get today. I tell you, I feel ten years younger. When I think that I might have got stuck with—"

"Hold everything," said Maddox. "I've got a phone call to make, and then my wife's got some deductions to pass on about Dorrie's letters." He picked up the phone and told Sergeant Buck to get him the Wilshire precinct house. When the desk sergeant answered, he said, "You had a sergeant there name of Carlisle. Still there?"

"He just came in. Who wants him?"

"Maddox, Wilcox Street."

"Just a minute."

In thirty seconds a voice said, "Sergeant Carlisle. Do I know a Maddox?"

"Sergeant, Wilcox Street. We ran into each other downtown, on some Narco thing, just before Christmas. You were grousing about a murder-two you couldn't make stick. It was a gang of punks pulling the protection racket on storekeepers."

"Oh. That. Damn you for reminding me of it. There's too much of it going on. Another case of Satan finding work for idle hands."

"Mmh. You mentioned some of the punks, and it occurred to me just now that one of them was a Buck. Buck who?"

"It was Buck De Lacy's gang. About as worthless and brutal a bunch as they come. What's your interest?"

"They might be operating on our beat."

"That's very possible," said Carlisle. "Punks are all too mobile these affluent days. A lot of 'em with cars, or access to same. You want to hear the tale to check on the M.O.— not that there is much M.O."

"Too much of it, sure. And the courts—"

"Well, let's not damn all judges," said Carlisle soberly. "We've got some good ones, just as annoyed and frustrated as we are at having to let the punks loose. But you can't, by how the law reads, hold anybody without bail on a misdemeanor, after all. Everybody's got rights, even the punks who couldn't care less about anybody else's. So, Buck De Lacy's gang. There are eight, nine, ten—the number varies—a loose gang of mindless young savages. Ask anybody who's run up against 'em. A run-of-the-mill gang, and try to count the number of 'em in any metropolis. Buck's turned nineteen. Some of 'em are still juveniles. You know the pattern. There's a kind of inner nucleus of ringleaders, Buck and Joe Caravelle and a young Frankenstein they call King Kong—he's black, the other two white. Yeah, they were at that racket over here, getting protection money from a couple of dozen merchants. You know the lyrics—pay up or we break your windows, bash in your merchandise, put you in the hospital maybe. A couple of them held out and the punks broke in overnight and really did a job on those stores. Prove it was them? What a laugh. So the merchants were paying out, quiet as mice, except one who ran to us, Walter Meeker, had a pharmacy out on Robertson Boulevard. He was willing to identify the ringleaders who'd talked to him and swear a complaint on them. I told him they'd be out on bail in no time, and even if they were bound over and stood trial, what the hell would they get? But he was mad. I didn't blame him. They were back on the street in twenty-four hours, and they ganged up on him at closing time that night. No other place around was open till nine, so there weren't any witnesses. I don't say they meant to kill him—a gang of louts like that never means much, do what comes naturally—but they did. Most of them are big strong kids, and they get a kind of savage pleasure out of destruction, you know? They beat him up, and he fell into one of his glass cases, cut his throat and bled to death."

"And you hadn't any evidence it was them."

"Are you asking or telling? Of course not. We're morally sure, but the D.A. can't act on that. And they're not the only bunch of punks pulling that stuff, either on your beat or mine."

"Hardly. But I rather think this is the same bunch."

"My sympathy," said Carlisle.

"Mmh," said Maddox. "Save it until after lunch. I may have a tale to tell you. Thanks very much." He put the phone down.

"What's all that about?" asked Rodriguez. "Listen, somebody's got to question that Ramirez again. He was on the premises, technically speaking, and if he heard or saw anything—"

"Well, I'd like to hear what Sue's found in those letters," said Maddox mildly. He went across the hall and came back with her. "So, what did the female intuition come up with?"

Sue laid the pile of letters on his desk and sat down in D'Arcy's desk chair. D'Arcy perched on the desk; Rodriguez stood frowning slightly and Feinman pulled his chair closer, lighting a cigarette. "Have any of you read these?"

"No," said Maddox. "We only got them yesterday."

"Well, they're interesting," said Sue. "People's letters tell a lot about them. She sounds like a nice girl. A—a sensible girl. Apparently she wrote her mother-in-law about once a week, and these go all the way back to January. I don't know how much any of this says, but there are a few things that seemed suggestive to me."

"Such as?"

"Well"—Sue took up the top one—"she wrote about things that happened at the store, the customers, all sorts of little things. She was lonely, and I think she made the letters a sort of substitute for—somebody to talk to. People do. She mentions several customers several times, as if they came in fairly often. A Miss Wyatt. She says she's 'a real character.' A Mrs. Barnes, who was just crazy about Monica—Dorrie took the baby in to the store one Saturday afternoon when she wasn't working, for Sandra Cross to see—and there was that picture, with the note on the back. And a Mrs. Hamilton, who was a terrible gossip. Then in another letter—this one, dated February tenth—is something a little offbeat. She says this Miss Wyatt—here, I'll read it—'asked me to have tea with her, of all things, and it was time for my break so Mr. Simon let me off and we went up to the restaurant. And if you can imagine, the old lady had got it in her head I'd make a perfect companion for her to travel with! She wants to go to Europe, and her idea was for me to do all the work—tickets and luggage and taxis and so on! I had to be tactful—after all, she is a regular customer—and I said of course I couldn't leave my little girl, and she sniffed and said, "Children, can't stand 'em! Put her in boarding school!" Honestly, can you imagine anything so absurd?' "

They didn't react to that. "You don't see any lead there?" asked Rodriguez.

"Well, it was funny. Then there's this. There was a shoplifter, a very obvious one, and they had to call the store detective, but she says, 'It was funny, Mr. Simon was so polite to her, he always is, poor man, and so endlessly patient.' You don't like that either?"

"Try again."

"All right. Here's a letter dated January nineteenth, and I think it's the one she sent along with that snapshot of the baby, because she explains that this Mrs. Barnes took the snapshot. She'd remembered Dorrie saying she took the baby to the playground at Barnsdall Park on nice Sundays and turned up there. Then she says, 'She's been very kind in her own way, I suppose, but it's queer, some people think money is everything.' And then, here is really something for you. The first time she mentions it is in a letter dated February first. 'You'd never believe what happened today. When I came home I looked for mail and along with the ads I got an anonymous letter! It was in a plain envelope, not sent through the mail, and it's just a piece of tablet paper with a funny scrawl, as if a child had done it. And what do you think it says? "I think you very beetiful"!!! I *am* flattered!' "

"The mailbox!" said Maddox. "I never thought to—my God, I'm getting senile! And that damn realty company's got the key, at least I suppose so. Damnation! Well, it's been overlooked this long, we'll try to get to it sometime today. An anonymous letter. I don't know that I think that's so funny. What else?"

"Almost every time she mentions Simon, she says 'poor man' or something about his being so kind. And twice she put, I think, 'poor Mr. Simon' and then scratched out the 'poor.' "

"That's a little subtle for me," said D'Arcy.

"Well, why is he so poor? He owns that jewelry concession, doesn't he? Now, here are the last four letters she wrote—February seventh, February sixteenth, February twenty-second, and the last one, March first. And in every single one she says something about difficulties and being fed up. 'Sometimes I wonder whether life wasn't easier in the old days before we had department stores and cars and bank accounts to worry over and the awful alone feeling you can get in a big city. Oh, that's terrible grammar, and I sound sorry for myself, don't I?' And 'I really have been thinking of changing jobs. I'm a little fed up with this one lately.' And 'Life is being rather difficult these days. I won't bore you with the details, but I'm feeling rather unsettled.' And in the last letter, she wrote, 'Life is a difficult proposition at times! I've been seriously thinking about doing what you people want and coming back there. If you are sure I could find a decent local job, I'd almost commit myself right now.' What do you think of that?"

"Not much," said Maddox. "What do you read into it?"

"Look," said Sue thoughtfully, "she wasn't telling them any details. She didn't want to worry them. But I think there'd been some trouble at the store, to do with Simon. And I'll tell you who she might have written all the details to—the matron of that orphanage. Evidently it's a good one. Dorrie calls her 'Mother Goulding.' I couldn't make out who she meant until she made some reference to the home. Apparently she corresponded with her too, and she'd be closer to her, a kind of mother figure."

"You just lost me," said Rodriguez. "I think you're reaching, making that rigmarole spell out trouble anywhere. Except for that anonymous letter. I don't like that either."

"Oh, for heaven's sake!" said Sue. "Some child in the neighborhood—"

The phone went off on Maddox's desk. "Yes, Fred?"

"You got a donnybrook at Hollywood High. Two cars there. A couple of kids high on something, and at least one corpse."

"Hell!" said Maddox between his teeth.

■ ■ ■

He and D'Arcy went out on it, and it was a mess. Two senior boys were on an LSD trip, and the ambulance attendants needed some help getting them tied down for the ride in. A math teacher was dead of stab wounds in his classroom, half the girl witnesses were in hysterics, the school nurse had fainted dead away across the corpse and another man was critically wounded in the hallway outside.

They called up another ambulance and cleared away the dead and wounded. They got the names, and the names of the parents and of a dozen kids who seemed to be reliable witnesses, and went back to the office to do the notifying.

"This is going to make one sweet mess of the whole day," said Maddox. "We're going to have wailing parents all over the place, and damnation, I just remembered it's Daisy's day off. It'll all fall on Sue." He went across to break the news to her and found her just picking up the phone.

"I'm going to call that Mrs. Goulding at the orphanage in Fresno," she said absently.

"Why, for God's sake? You're about to have some work to do." He told her why. She put down the phone. "The teacher was a Robert Kingsley, married, and the one they didn't quite kill is a William Holderby, also married, and—"

"Well, for goodness' sake," said Sue, and laughed. "The little man who called us Gestapo and said we were prejudiced against Youth. I wonder how he feels now."

"And the parents—my God, what a mess! There are enough of you to deal with it. I'm cutting out."

"You coward," said Sue.

Maddox looked harried. "I've got legitimate business, and I'm the senior sergeant." He went back across the hall. "Joe, we've got a date at eleven thirty."

"I won't forget it," said Feinman. D'Arcy was on the phone, Rodriguez sorting out half the numbers to hand over to Sue. Notifying the bereaved, breaking the news to the parents—it was another of the difficult, dirty jobs cops come in for. They would do it the best they could. Ellis had just come back from showing those photostats to the recent marks; he'd got nothing. They pressed him into service, and Rowan.

Maddox phoned the realty company and got handed from voice to voice until patience prevailed and he got Miss Winkelstein. "The mailbox key!" she said blankly. "My God, I never thought about it until you said the word. No, it wasn't with the other one." Maddox suppressed a hasty word. "And look, when can we get in there? After all—"

"The rent's paid through this month," said Maddox. "How do I get into the mailbox?"

"It's not a very complicated lock. I suppose a skeleton might open it."

"Might isn't good enough," said Maddox, annoyed. He

thought for a moment, after putting down the phone. Wherever Dorrie Mayo was, there were her belongings in the apartment; David Mayo had better take them for safekeeping. Whatever he'd want to do with them. He was surprised, now he thought of it, that Mayo hadn't been in today, demanding action. He tried Mayo's hotel, the old Roosevelt; Mayo wasn't there.

The first parents arrived, the man loud and belligerent, the woman tearful. Maddox just shut his eyes at the overheard wail: "But children from good homes don't go taking dope, not *our* kind of children—it just can't be!"

He heard Sue's voice, murmuring tactfully. He felt sorry for Sue. It would go on for days, this one, on and off: getting statements down and signed, all the paperwork. He felt tired thinking about it. The kid who'd had the knife (packaged and on its way down to S.I.D. now) was turned eighteen; he'd be prosecuted as an adult if it ever got that far. Most likely, he'd be sent off for psychiatric evaluation and the treatment for addiction. Ditto for the other one.

Another set of parents arrived. Maddox opened the top drawer of his desk and looked at the contents. The only items vaguely resembling tools were a pair of pliers and a brass letter opener. He sighed and stood up. It was ten minutes past ten.

He went out and downstairs, past two women coming up slowly; one of them was crying, a handkerchief held up, and the other one had an arm around her shoulders. Either the teacher's wife or the other one, thought Maddox sadly.

He drove over to Gregory Avenue and went into the house. He rummaged and carried off with him an awl, a pair of long narrow shears and a long iron nail (where that came from he had no idea). He drove over to Lexington Avenue, parked and went into the apartment.

The mailboxes were the usual kind in these old apartments: on the wall to the right of the lobby, half a dozen rows of them. He looked at the one halfway down, its door numbered *12*. There was quite a little bunch of mail in it. Why the hell hadn't he thought of the mail before?

He tried the awl first, in the tiny lock. He pried and pushed and pulled at it, with no success whatever. He tried the nail; its end was too big to go into the lock. He opened the shears and using one blade only succeeded in inflicting a little bloody gash on his knuckles. "Damnation," he said. He took up the awl again and this time tried inserting it in the tiny crack at the top of the box. There seemed to be a little play there; he bore down with all his strength and the awl buried its top inch into the crack, which widened. He took a breath and bore down again; there was a loud crack and the front of the box fell open.

He thrust his tools into his jacket pocket and fished out the mail. It barely fit into the box: a week's accumulation, of course. He wondered why the mailman hadn't noticed. Maybe he had and just didn't care. People went off on vacation and didn't notify the post office.

It was all deplorably illegal, tampering with the mail, but he'd take shortcuts to find out about Dorrie, and in any case Mayo would back him up, the near relative. He sorted the mail rapidly. A letter with Mrs. Mayo Senior's return address. The next personal letter was addressed in a large crooked hand, no return address on the envelope, postmark L.A. He slit it open with his knife, neatly, and brought out a single sheet of stationery, plain and inexpensive. His brows rose. Just one line of crooked, shaky writing: *You'd better leave my husband alone or I'll kill you, you—* The obscenities were explicit. "Well, well," he muttered. "First person we've found who doesn't like Dorrie."

The next thing he came up with, past the junk mail, the

catalogues of giftware and sale announcements, was another plain envelope. It bore no address or name, and it hadn't been through the mail. It wasn't even sealed. He turned it over and lifted the flap, and brought out another (How many altogether? Had she mentioned others? Ask Sue) of Dorrie's anonymous letters.

This one was on a piece of ruled paper torn from a tablet, but the writing, large and unsteady, was across the lines. It said simply, "I think you the most pretty ledy in hole world."

"Now what the hell?" said Maddox to himself. Did it mean anything? Was it at all relevant, or just extraneous to whatever had happened to Dorrie?

And there was Moreno; Ramirez would have to be questioned again, but obviously Rodriguez wasn't going to get to it until they'd got the parents out of their hair sometime today. The kite flyers . . . and without any doubt the phony cops still cruising around looking for out-of-state cars. . . . Sue said she'd started the red tape at Juvenile Hall so Edna Gifford's respectable sister could eventually have the baby. Probably they'd pay for a funeral too. An A.P.B. out on Antonio DeLucci, who had most probably (not certainly) shot Gifford and Hahn. The muggers of Ilinsky—that was also anonymous. They'd had, yesterday, a sarcastic report from S.I.D. on that two-by-four; anybody should have known it wouldn't take prints, said the lab boys. There had been blood on it, matching Ilinsky's type.

And now all the paperwork to do on this messy, unnecessary little killing: damn fool kids, seduced onto the drugs, and how many of them with their lives and whole futures a permanent ruin from now on? That was one thing; but when they interfered, in consequence, with other lives and futures, something else.

He looked at his watch. It was eleven fifteen.

■ ■ ■

About eleven o'clock Sue called Daisy. "I'm sorry to ask you, but we've got this thing." She explained tersely. "I've just got rid of one set of parents, who'll shortly be annoying people at the General Hospital. César and D'Arcy are dealing with some of the other kids who'll be witnesses, but there are about a dozen more. And you know, Daisy, George Ellis is a dear but not the best person to deal with the bereaved widow. I'm just about to go and rescue him. But there's the other parents and—"

"Oh, Lord!" said Daisy. "What a morning. I've had Johnny here weeping on my shoulder the past hour."

"What's wrong?"

"He finally got his medical report, and they won't pass him for active duty. The rest of the lead has to come out first, and he's allergic to practically every anesthetic there is."

"Oh, poor Johnny! But, Daisy—"

"Yes, I see. I'll come in right away."

Sue was starving; she hadn't taken time for breakfast. She hurried down the hall to the sandwich machine, put a half dollar in the slot and pulled the lever labeled *Ham*. The machine growled, clanked and stopped. "Oh, damn!" said Sue and shook it impotently.

"Miss—"

She turned. A middle-aged couple, looking agitated and anxious: the woman had been crying; the man had his arm around her.

"Excuse me, could you tell us when the officers might be talking to us? That one—Sergeant Ellis—said they'd want to see us, but it's been a while, and my wife wants to see our boy at the hospital if they'll let us. We're Chris Hansen's parents, the—the other boy who—"

The woman sobbed once, dryly. Sue could hardly continue a fight with the sandwich machine under the eyes of

151

such witnesses. "I'm sorry," she said gently. "We've had to talk to quite a few people all at once. Suppose you come into my office and I'll get whatever we need to know from you."

"Oh, are you a—an officer?"

For my sins, thought Sue. And that coward Ivor Maddox—

■ ■ ■

"There they come," said Feinman. He was sitting beside Maddox in the Maserati. "Right on the dot. You think this is the same bunch on that murder-two over in Wilshire?"

"Ninety percent." The Maserati was parked in the red just around the corner from Melrose; Mr. Janowsky's store was on the corner across the street from them here. Up from there they had marked the independent bakery, the little watch-repair shop, the dress shop, the variety store, the tailor's.

It was a quarter to twelve, and just now two cars had stopped briefly along that block; they could see around the corner. Both were old beat-up jalopies, a Ford and a Plymouth, both sedans. They let out passengers—six, seven, eight males—and came around this corner and turned into the public parking lot there. The drivers wouldn't bother to feed nickels into the meters. Here they came back, across the street, two big hefty late-teen-age boys— and that was a wrong word, thought Maddox; they were men—eighteen, nineteen, both over six feet and built like wrestlers.

"Where are they going first?" asked Feinman. "Collect from the marks already set up?"

"I don't think so," said Maddox. "Let's see." He got out of the car and Feinman followed him. He glanced over at the parking lot and lifted a casual hand. Car doors slammed.

He and Feinman walked up the side street, up to the corner across from Janowsky's store. The gang of punks had grouped in a circle there on the sidewalk, and Maddox and Feinman could hear the coarse braying laughs and excited mutters. There were, Maddox counted, ten of them: three black, the rest white. One of the blacks was enormous, looking taller than D'Arcy and twice as heavy; then the two big white boys, and the rest smaller but none what you'd call small. They all wore dirty, sloppy clothes: jeans and stained T shirts.

At least two of the merchants along here had heard the rough roar of those motors, probably familiar. A man came to the door of the watch-repair shop and looked out, and a man with a fat spectacled face peered out the bakery door and retreated hastily.

Suddenly the whole gang pushed into the door of the hardware store and it shut behind them.

"Time it," said Maddox. He didn't look around. He and Feinman went across the street and into that store. This chilly day, the outer door had been originally shut; as they passed through, a little bell jangled, but nobody heard or paid attention.

They were bunched down there at the back of the store, making a semicircle round Mr. Janowsky in front of the counter.

"I will not pay money to bribe thieves!" said Janowsky loudly. He had been expecting them, and he held, absurdly, a baseball bat in his right hand. A wife and two children. Was it the boy's bat?

The punks were utterly contemptuous of him, one man against their wealth of brute strength. The biggest white swore at him obscenely, but not in anger, only annoyed at momentary frustration. He reached out and yanked the bat away; Janowsky held on stubbornly and was pulled forward with a jerk. The boy backhanded him viciously across the face with his left hand. The rest crowed, excited, happy at the prospect of action, blood-hungry. Three of them had weighted leather saps in their hands.

"You lousy foreigner, you pay double. You be goddamned glad to pay up when we finish with you, you stinkin' foreign bastard." Deliberately he lifted the bat and, whirling, brought it down to smash in the front of a tall glass case displaying small appliances.

"That's right, Buck, let him have it! We show him what he get!"

Maddox and Feinman stepped to the right of the door, and the door crashed back against the wall with a crack like a shot. The one with the baseball bat looked up.

Tiger Jack Nagao walked down the center aisle to the middle of the store. He was clad in dark pants and a black turtleneck sweater, and his torso bulged incredibly. Behind him marched four medium-sized impassive-faced Orientals similarly dressed. "A little difference of opinion with a customer, Mr. Janowsky?" asked Tiger Jack blandly. "I'll tell you one time to put down the bat, punk. Just one time."

They turned from their helpless quarry, from the delight in reasonless destruction, momentarily confused. "Hey, Buck, where'd all the Chinks come from?"

"You get outta here!" yelled Buck, furious at interruption, and he took two lunging strides and lifted the bat murderously. Three seconds later he was flat on his back gasping, and the bat was in two pieces ten feet away.

"If you don't want to be reasonable," said Tiger Jack, "we'd just as soon not."

Buck shook his head and crawled up to his feet. His henchmen, paralyzed temporarily, gave a howl of fury and surged forth to the fray.

The methodical Orientals, considerate of Janowsky's stock, scientifically aimed the punks toward the door, and within about ninety seconds the action had moved outside to the sidewalk. All the noise was coming from the punks, and it didn't last long. A couple of them—Buck and the big Negro—were strong as bulls and kept getting up and asking for more, and it must have been all of five minutes before all ten of them were laid out cold, in various picturesque attitudes, on the sidewalk and up against the building. By then nearly everybody on this side of the block had come out and was staring.

Tiger Jack stirred Buck with one foot and said, "This the big man? I figured." He leaned down and hauled him up to his feet. Buck opened hazed, dull eyes and got a smart slap on each cheek. "Listen, you cowardly bastard! You leave these people alone, and everybody else you've been shaking down, or you'll get some more of the same —understand? It's the only thing reaches your kind, and you can have just as damn much as you ask for, little man! You get me? Tell me yes or no!"

Buck couldn't focus on him; he nodded weakly.

"So all right! You make damn sure all your gang of cowards and bullies knows it! The first move you make wrong, buddy, you get double what you just got, in spades! You got that?"

Buck nodded again. Tiger Jack let go of him, and he folded at the knees and sprawled flat on his face.

A kind of collective sigh went up from the little crowd. Tiger Jack turned to Maddox. "Do I know you, pal?"

"No," said Maddox. "It was a beautiful thing, friend."

"Oh, my," said Feinman reverently. "Oh, yes."

Mr. Janowsky leaned shakily on the door of his hardware store and saw Maddox and Feinman for the first time. "Sergeant, it is you who—"

"Not at all," said Maddox. "Detective Feinman and I just stopped by to ask you a few more questions about that little matter. It seems these—mmh—blackmailers have been annoying you again. We'll take them in for it now. That baseball bat. It just might add up to a charge of assault with intent, which is a felony. For a change. But you seem to have some adequate protectors."

Tiger Jack proffered Janowsky a business card. "You have any more trouble, you let me know, see?"

Janowsky read the card somewhat dazedly and looked at Maddox. He said gravely, "Sergeant, your American ingenuity—it is impressive." And, a hand still to his head, he looked around at his fellow businessmen. "You see?" he said with a blinding smile. "You see?"

■ ■ ■

"Oh, my," said Feinman in the Maserati. "Beautiful— that's the word for it, all right."

Maddox put the key in the ignition and said ruefully, "Not the right way, Joe, I know, not the legal way. And the answer isn't the judges or the courts, or even the common law itself. It comes back to human nature. A lot of the judges who have to go by the book, if they knew about this, they'd laugh too and say, it's the only way to reach the punks. So it is. But the law—"

"Sometimes bypasses common sense," said Feinman. "I know. And we don't really want to go back to flogging and the rack. But, my God, those savage louts. It was gratifying."

"Venting your sadistic instincts, you brutal cop."

"Well, it *is* the only thing they understand. No, I know —the rights. But to the ones like that, nobody's got any rights but them. Do we get repercussions?"

"No. The louts with no respect for other people's rights are too scared and confused to read us in. I don't like operating like that, Joe, but—having been a cop awhile— I am aware of some hard-core facts that the head doctors

156

and glamour-boy criminal lawyers and some judges haven't waked up to yet."

"Such as."

"That people come all sorts," said Maddox sadly. "Human people."

"Yeah. It does say," said Feinman thoughtfully, "man He made a little lower than the angels. And some a hell of a lot lower. Like Buck and his gang."

"Extracurricular exercise," said Maddox. "With the co-operation of the Reserve Air Force." They had called up a wagon to take the remains off to the County jail; they'd have to get out a report on it, give the D.A. chapter and verse. "Let's go have lunch."

nine

About one o'clock Rodriguez finished getting statements from the batch of witnesses allotted to him and decided to go out for a belated lunch and then get back to Ramirez. The rest of them were still busy with witnesses; everybody had been too busy even to patronize the sandwich machine. D'Arcy and Rowan were still talking to people, and Ellis had gone back to the high school. As he came out to the hall, Rodriguez could hear Sue and Daisy still talking to somebody in that office.

He went down the hall for a drink of water and as he came back past the sandwich machine gave it a careless slap. To his surprise it clanked in answer and presented him with a wrapped sandwich, neatly dropped into the bottom slot. Rodriguez picked it up; it was a ham sandwich. "Well, *gracias*," he said, and started unwrapping it. Sue came out of her office and nearly collided with him as he passed.

"How on earth did you get that infernal machine to work?" she asked, eying the sandwich.

"I didn't. This is on the house. It gave it to me. I just touched it."

158

"That's *my* sandwich!" said Sue. "I put a half dollar in and it just sat there."

"Well, I bought you one. Turn about," said Rodriguez. He finished the sandwich in his car and decided it would hold him for a while. Not much had been done on Moreno at all, except for the lab examination, and something ought to be; there'd been minor headlines last night, and the press would be sniffing around.

Ramirez had been told to stay put. Rodriguez found him in the pink stucco guesthouse down the hill from the dilapidated Moorish castle. "I told you I don't know anything about it," he said when he opened the door and saw Rodriguez.

"Just a few questions. Did Mr. Moreno go out much in the evenings?"

Ramirez shrugged. "Sometimes."

"What about Sunday evening? Did he go out?"

"I don't know. Maybe. I washed the dishes from dinner and come here."

"Was he invited out somewhere?"

"I don't know."

"Where was he when you finished washing the dishes?"

"Maybe in the living room."

There was a car, a big sports Mercedes, in the garage down from the house. "You'd hear the car if he went out," said Rodriguez sharply. "Now, did he?"

"All right, he went out. Maybe nine o'clock."

"You have any idea where he was going?"

"How do I know?" Ramirez was sullen. "He doesn't tell me anything, the servant."

Rodriguez could have guessed that Moreno would be upstage, like that. "Well, do you have any ideas of your own? Come on, you'd been with him eleven years. You knew him. Probably all about him."

After a moment Ramirez said, "He wasn't a good man,

but I don't like to say bad things. He's dead. Maybe that's part his own fault, but—"

Rodriguez waited. "He'd been quite a womanizer. Come on, don't be superstitious, *amigo*. We can go back to the station and really get down to questioning you, you know."

"Ah—" Ramirez looked angry, and gestured. "All right, maybe it is better I tell. Whoever stabbed him, it's not much between, like the English says. Womanizer! That one, he thinks to pretend he's not an old fat man, the girls still like him. He brings the women home, yes, sometimes. The old fool he is, I don't believe he was any good at all, but the women—the only kind of woman he gets any more, the kind go with a man for money, see? I know a fellow works in a place down on the Strip. He says he sees Mr. Moreno there, he goes to pick up girls like that—dirty girls—places down there."

"Oh, he did?"

"Once," said Ramirez with a sly smile, "I think one of them robs him, before. I see them come back that night, and when I come in next day he's mad like anything—standing with the drawer open in the bedroom, counting money. I think it could be, that time, the woman gets him drunk—there was an empty bottle—and robbed him of money."

"Did he drink much?"

"He didn't get drunk after that when he brought a woman home," said Ramirez, and laughed. "He stayed home to drink."

Rodriguez grinned. "What about this place on the Strip?"

"It's a place with naked dancers, the Mod Palace. But he goes other places there too. I bet, you go ask, other people laughing at him there—old fat man pretending he's a young stud."

160

That Rodriguez wouldn't doubt. "Are there any recent photographs of him in the house?"

"Lots of pictures," said Ramirez. "Not new. Hundreds from the days he's in movies, young, good-looking. I don't think any new ones, like he was now."

I'll bet, thought Rodriguez. All that was pretty much in character and offered a very strong lead. The setup had been fairly crude. Now they knew Moreno had gone after the girls on the make, the murder spelled itself out. And even, possibly, the reason he'd had to be killed, at least knocked out. That other girl robbed him—so this time he'd been careful not to drink too much.

The only thing was, reflected Rodriguez, the lines weren't drawn any more, on that sort of thing. The old-fashioned red-light district was a thing of the past. On the Sunset Strip, that now-sleazy and run-down section of past glamour, there'd be quite respectable females—or at least halfway respectable—roaming around of nights together with a lot of others very available, either to selected partners for free or to anybody for the cold cash. And these days, it wasn't so easy to tell which was which.

■ ■ ■

Maddox got out to Robinson's in Beverly Hills at one thirty. Looking at the directory board for Fine Jewelry, he suddenly thought that they hadn't yet seen Simon at all: speculating about him, reading about him in Dorrie's letters, yet never laying eyes on him. Fine Jewelry was on the lower level; Maddox set out to find it.

It was a cube of four glass cases set in a square, glittering with their contents. There wasn't a customer anywhere around. Behind the cases, a man and a woman. Maddox went up to the man. "Mr. Simon?"

"Yes, sir, what can I do for you?"

Maddox brought out his badge. Simon was a tall slender man in the forties, extremely well dressed but not foppish: a precisely tailored dark suit, immaculate shirt, discreet tie with a gold tie tack set with a black star sapphire. He was dark, not bad looking: a thin aquiline face with dark eyes, a sensitive mouth. He looked at the badge, and his mouth tightened, and then he said sadly, "So she has made a formal complaint. I don't blame her, but I'm sorrier than I can say that this has happened. Did you have to come to the store?"

"I beg your pardon?" said Maddox blankly. "I'd like to ask you some questions about Mrs. Mayo, sir. She's been officially reported missing now."

Simon stared at him, lost a little color. "M-Missing?" he exclaimed. "What do you mean?"

"Nobody seems to know where she is," said Maddox. "I'd like to ask you whether she said anything to you."

"Oh, my God!" said Simon. "The little girl—Monica?"

"She's missing too." Yes, Dorrie was an adult, but Monica— "If you have any information at all, we'd like your help."

"Oh, my God, I don't understand this!" said Simon. "But I had better tell you—" He looked distracted. "If you don't mind, the restaurant shouldn't be too crowded at this hour. Just a moment." He turned to the woman, evidently a new assistant, and spoke to her briefly. "I'd like to be halfway private, if you don't mind, er—"

"Sergeant Maddox."

"Yes. We'll see if we can get a quiet table." He led the way to the elevators; in the restaurant, next to the top floor, there was a thin crowd of female shoppers, but they found a secluded table in one corner. Simon absently ordered coffee. "I don't understand," he said, "but I'm very much afraid that whatever—whatever has happened, whatever reason Mrs. Mayo had to go away, is all my fault. I've been very upset about it; she understood, she was sympathetic,

162

but it was a—a terrible thing to happen. Such a nice young woman."

"Just what did happen, sir?"

Simon made a defeated, helpless gesture. The waitress brought their coffee and he poured cream into his with a slightly shaking hand. "My wife," he said in a low tone. "She's manic depressive. She has been at Camarillo, on and off, but you know it's crowded, and the ones like her, if the family can possibly care for them at home— I have a nurse with her, a practical nurse. But it's very difficult to get a competent woman. She's a—trying patient. They stay a month or two and quit. I find a new one—I've had several like that—and find she's not experienced with mental patients, and Andrea—gets away from her."

"I see," said Maddox. "And?"

"One of her—obsessions," said Simon, "is that I am—seeing other women. Any woman I talk to—" He shrugged. "You understand, I—nobody here knows about this—Naturally I don't broadcast it. But—it was a terrible thing to happen. She got away from the nurse and came here, to the store. She—can be quite lucid, you know, and then suddenly— Naturally I try to see she hasn't any access to money, but she—she doped the nurse and stole her handbag that day. I'm being as frank as—as I have to be," he said painfully.

"And she saw you with Mrs. Mayo."

Simon gave him a bitter smile. "Mrs. Mayo's a very lovely young woman. Andrea—my wife—had come up to her at the counter before I noticed, and I'm afraid—it was very unfortunate and yet nobody's fault in a way, unless we blame the nurse—I'm afraid she saw Mrs. Mayo's name."

"Her *name?*" said Maddox.

Simon nodded. "On the sales book. Each salesperson has one, you see, for writing up sales. The name is on a label on the cover of the book. Mrs. Mayo had just written up a sale and her book was on the counter. That must have been how it happened. Because Andrea made a—well, a scene right then, shouting and accusing poor Mrs. Mayo. I got her away as quickly as I could. But later, you see, she got hold of Mrs. Mayo's address—it's listed in the phone book—and began harassing her on the phone. When she could reach the phone. I had got another nurse, but she was quite—inadequate. Andrea managed to phone Mrs. Mayo a number of times, in the evenings. I can't always be there. We've just had the annual design show, and I had to—"

"Yes," said Maddox, and brought out the threatening letter he'd found in Dorrie's mailbox. "Your wife's writing?" He held it out.

"Oh, my God," said Simon tiredly. "My God. Yes. You see, after that happened—the scene in the store—I had to explain to Mrs. Mayo. She was very nice about it, but you couldn't expect her to put up with all this. She told me about the phone calls because she felt I should know, but—"

"And you thought that was why she quit?" said Maddox interestedly. He put out his cigarette, groped for another and sat rolling it in his fingers. "That was why you were upset right away, when she didn't come in?"

Simon nodded. "I—Sergeant Maddox, I've got a business to run. It's not as if I work an eight-hour day and go home. I have all the buying to do, some of the designing. I've told you it's hard to find a nurse competent to deal with a mental patient. I should have said it's nearly impossible. And Andrea can be—quite cunning. In the last couple of weeks before Mrs. Mayo left, she—Andrea—had got away from the house several times. Once she phoned Mrs. Mayo here at the store, and—well, you see the language." He nodded at the note. Maddox put it away again. "So when

Mrs. Mayo didn't come in that morning, I was afraid she had quit. I really couldn't blame her. And I—when I first saw your badge, I thought she might have made a formal complaint. And I really couldn't blame her for that either."

Maddox lit the cigarette. Did this spell out any answers? Had she cut and run because a lunatic woman had her address and phone number? But it had looked, and he had said it before, as if somebody else had arranged the walking away. Andrea Simon? Unlikely. She wouldn't have been loose long enough or probably have the facilities.

"Has your wife ever been violent, Mr. Simon?"

"Never, except in talk. You don't think—?"

"No, I don't," said Maddox. He had been through that apartment, and there was no shred of evidence that violence had occurred there. "We've been looking through some of her recent letters," he said. "She mentioned incidents at the store. A Miss Wyatt—"

"Oh, yes. Wealthy old spinster, very fond of jewelry. A character," said Simon. He passed a hand over his face wearily.

"And a Mrs. Barnes—"

Simon nodded. "Divorcée, in the thirties. Quite a lot of money, probably a settlement. The husband was Richard Barnes, the playboy who makes headlines occasionally. She's a beautiful woman. I don't like," he added irrelevantly, "to sell beautiful jewels to ugly women. Mrs. Barnes. A very nice woman really. Money hasn't spoiled her. She was very friendly with Mrs. Mayo. I remember one Saturday afternoon she was here when Mrs. Mayo had brought little Monica in—a lovely little girl—and Mrs. Barnes was quite taken with her. She's very fond of children."

And later had remembered where Dorrie took Monica on nice Sundays and took a snapshot of her. "A Mrs. Hamilton—"

"Old harridan. Always with some tale about her neighbors. Sergeant, do you think Andrea had anything to do with Mrs. Mayo's—departure? I'd been very upset about it, it disturbed me to have such a thing happen. She's a nice girl, and I'd liked having her with me."

"I don't know," said Maddox. "Can you tell me, a week ago Sunday, was your wife—mmh—supervised all that day?"

"A week ago. I believe she was. I was out that afternoon, but—"

"The nurse you had then was competent?"

"Oh, God, that Carter woman—she'd got away from her before." He looked defeated. "I don't know, Sergeant. But you don't think Andrea could have *done* anything?"

That apartment, thought Maddox. He thought about Brian Faulkner. He thought about the anonymous letter writer. And he thought about Monica. . . . "I suppose you'd asked her not to spread this around. Yes, well, she hadn't, Mr. Simon. She hadn't even told her family about it."

"I said she's a very nice girl," said Simon simply.

■ ■ ■

When Maddox got upstairs at the station, he heard David Mayo's dull voice in Sue's office and looked in. Sue was being soothing. "Where've you been, Mr. Mayo?" asked Maddox.

He looked around. "Private detectives," he said. "I thought—but the couple of firms I saw charge such rates, and both of them said you people have more facilities. . . . Have you found out anything? I was just telling—I'm sorry, I don't know your name—"

"Mrs. Maddox," said Maddox.

"Oh, you're— Funny," said Mayo. "Both cops. I— *Where is she?* And *Monica?* God, I told Mother I'd call home tonight and I haven't got a damned thing to tell her."

"Mr. Mayo. Could you tell me, did she correspond regularly with a Mrs. Goulding? I think she'd be the next person to talk to."

"Mother Goulding!" Mayo jumped up. "My God, why didn't I think—of course, she'd know everything! She'd know if Dorrie was planning to go somewhere. She's the head matron or whatever of that place, the St. Francis home in Fresno. I guess it's a good one. Dorrie said all the kids loved her and her husband, and Dorrie wrote her everything—like her own mother. Why didn't I think to tell you before?"

"So let's ask her." Maddox hoisted one hip on Sue's desk and picked up the phone. Information in Fresno obliged him with the number and area code within two minutes. He got a female voice in another thirty seconds. "St. Francis Episcopal Home."

"Mrs. Goulding, please."

"Oh, she can't come to the phone right now, I'm sorry. May I take a message?"

"This is the Los Angeles police," said Maddox. "Will you tell her, please, it's about Mrs. Theodora Mayo, and it's important."

"*Police*—" There was a hiatus of several minutes. Maddox raised his eyebrows at Sue, who lit a cigarette and handed it to him.

"And what do the L.A. police want with me?" a pleasant, deep, forceful voice said suddenly in his ear. "I couldn't make out what it was about, just that you're police."

"Sergeant Maddox, Wilcox Street—Hollywood. It's about Theodora Mayo, Mrs. Goulding. We understand she corresponds regularly with you, and we'd like the answers to some questions, please."

"Dorrie? Is anything wrong?" The voice sharpened.

"She seems to have—walked away," said Maddox, "and nobody knows where she is. Do you?"

"The apartment on Lexington Avenue?"

"She's left it. No forwarding address. She's quit her job. Or somebody arranged both for her," said Maddox.

"*What?* Monica—"

"Also gone. When did you hear from her last?"

"A week ago yesterday, a letter. But that's impossible! Dorrie? She was thinking of going back east to her husband's people—"

Mayo suddenly reached out and wrested the phone from Maddox. "Mrs. Goulding, this is David Mayo, Dorrie's brother-in-law. We haven't any idea what's happened to either of them and we're all terribly worried. We'd—very much appreciate any help you can give us, please."

Maddox took the phone back in time to hear her exclaim, "Dear God, but it couldn't be—"

"I'd like to underline what Mr. Mayo just said," said Maddox. "If you can help us—"

"But I had better *come*," she said decisively. "And bring her letters. Now there is nothing immediate that Cleo and Sarah can't handle. John can take over morning prayers, and the choir—well, one rehearsal won't matter. If I can get Martha to come in— Yes. I'll *come*. Probably on the eight o'clock bus, but if not on the midnight one. I'll see you in the morning, Sergeant." The phone clicked in his ear.

"She'll be here tomorrow. Seems to think she can help."

"Oh, thank God!" said Mayo. "Thank God! I'd better go and call Mother right away." He ran out.

Maddox put out his cigarette. It was momentarily very quiet in the building, with only the clicking of a typewriter at a distance. "We finished the preliminary paperwork,"

168

said Sue, leaning back. "Thank heaven it's my day off tomorrow."

"What are you up to?"

"Clean the house in the morning, and somewhere with Mother and Aunt Evelyn in the afternoon. Unless it's still raining." It had started to rain again about an hour ago.

Rodriguez came past and stopped to lean on the door and bring Maddox up to date on Moreno. He looked rather wet. "I've been doing the legwork down on the Strip. They knew him, just by a description. Dirty old man making eyes at the girls. At a couple of places people said, Sure, that old guy used to come in, dressed to the nines. He'd pick up a girl, leave with her. But you know those places—a blonde they call Sally, a redhead named Jeanie or maybe Doris."

Maddox looked at him. "Are you by any chance about to suggest that we do some overtime tonight, asking if anybody remembers him picking up a girl last Sunday night?"

"Well, it's the indicated question to ask. I drew a blank on it so far."

"In the rain," said Maddox. "You know Californians, César. Like cats. Those places won't be so crowded tonight."

"True," admitted Rodriguez. "Have you got anything new on anything?"

"Take him away to tell him," said Sue. "I've still got a report to type."

They went into the detective office across the hall. Feinman was there, and D'Arcy sprawling in his desk chair. "Nice rain," said D'Arcy. "Good for the crops. I tell you, I'm feeling—what's the word?—euphoric."

"My God," said Rodriguez, "has he fallen in love with one of the high school girls?"

"You go to hell. I said, nevermore! But—"

The phone went off at Maddox's elbow and he picked it up. "Maddox, Wilcox Street."

"Taggart, Seventy-seventh. You've had an A.P.B. out for Antonio DeLucci. You still want him?"

"Have you got him?"

"Just now. He got into a fight in a bar out on Avalon, and the bartender called us. He even had identification on him in his own name—Oklahoma driver's license five years out of date."

Maddox laughed. "And I like a good detective story, but they're not very realistic, most of them. The shrewd and canny master criminals. What about a gun?"

"I thought you'd ask. A Colt thirty-two with a full load. What shall we do with it?"

"Send it down to Ballistics—S.I.D. They've got the slugs. We'll see if they match."

"You want us to send DeLucci over now?"

Maddox looked at the clock. It was ten past four. "I suppose you'd better. He'll have to be questioned sometime." He yawned. This day had been longer than usual, somehow.

"Will do."

"I think," said Maddox to Rodriguez, "I'll do my wife a little favor." He looked in on Sue and said, "I'll take you out to dinner. With a drink first. Eventually."

"Angel," said Sue. "Now I can last out another hour and a half. Just. *What* a day."

"And I am not," said Maddox, "coming back to wander through these damned vulgar topless bars asking which cheap doxy Moreno picked up on Sunday night. I don't much care. César can go looking if he wants to."

"It isn't that I want to," said Rodriguez plaintively. "I get paid to do a job. It's the next place to look. After all, the man's dead. But I did have another thought. On account of the console TV and stereo. Whichever girl it was, she had a boy friend."

"Oh. Yes," said Maddox. "I see what you mean. You know, it's a wonder it hadn't happened before, come to think of it. Him dressed to the nines and probably flashing the cash around, any enterprising female out for the fast buck would spot him as a good mark."

"But to kill him? They could have knocked him out and tied him up."

"Out for a thrill," said Maddox vaguely. "It happens all the time, these days."

He was sitting back in his chair smoking, Rodriguez had opened a paperback copy of *The Nine Wrong Answers*, and D'Arcy was just sitting there smiling, when the man from Seventy-seventh Street station fetched Antonio De-Lucci in. He said, "Maddox? I'm Slaney." He offered a hand.

Maddox took it, yawning. "Rodriguez. D'Arcy. Feinman," he added as Feinman came back. They looked at DeLucci.

He was not a prepossessing specimen. He was thin and sallow, middle-sized, and he was looking resigned. He hadn't shaved for a few days. He was wearing a cheap blue suit, a dirty white shirt with no tie.

Sue came in with a teletype in her hand. "Ellis anywhere around?"

"I haven't seen him," said Maddox. "You been in the wars, Slaney?" Slaney's left hand was bandaged in swathes of gauze and adhesive.

"Well, you might say," said Slaney. He was a sandy-haired fellow, as hefty as Ellis. "I got attacked by a sandwich machine."

"You what?" said Sue and Maddox together.

Slaney laughed. "Damndest thing ever happened to me. We just had one put in the station. Handy, everybody said.

171

But the damn thing's got a mind of its own. It's supposed to take quarters or half dollars, but if you feed it half dollars it just growls at you."

"Ours doesn't like them either," said Sue.

"Yesterday afternoon I went out there—I hadn't had a chance for lunch—to get a sandwich. I thought the thing was about to deliver, I reached into that slot, and it grabbed my hand. I couldn't get loose, it was pulling me farther in by the second, and I yelled and Jack came out and helped pull, and finally got my hand out. One finger broken and one sprained. I think," said Slaney, "these damn machines are getting ready to take over and want to get rid of us first."

"I said that machine was a mistake," said Rodriguez. "Even if it did give me one free. I don't like its expression."

Slaney laughed. "Well, there's your man. Have fun with him. It's been a long day and I think I'll go home on time for a change." He took his bandaged hand out. Sue went looking for Ellis.

"Hey," said DeLucci. "Hey. When you gonna take me to jail?"

Maddox stretched. "Not until we've asked you some questions. Did they give you your rights when they picked you up?"

"Yeah, yeah, all the bit. I never been in L.A. before, but somebody was telling me you got a real nice jail. Look, I tell you all about it, anything you wanna know, see. I guess I was wrong, but I had the idea they was holding out on me, Rex and that dame. We done some heists on the way out here, and I didn't figure they was handin' me my share. Well, I guess we was all a little drunk, that night." Yes, that had showed in the autopsy.

"Mr. DeLucci, are you sure you want to tell us all this? Will you sign a statement if we get it down for you?"

"Yeah, yeah, just get it over," said DeLucci. "I don't

mind. We'd been arguin' back 'n' forth, inna car, see—we just checked outta the motel that day. We was lookin' for another place in Hollywood—an' Rex began to get mad. He pulled over an' parked. That's when I did it. Shot them."

"But not the baby," said Maddox.

DeLucci looked at him in horror. "My God, who'd hurt a *baby?*"

"But you just left it there."

"Oh, well, I figured somebody'd find it," said DeLucci. His expression turned indignant. "I took every dime—all the loot we'd got, four real nice jobs. It was twelve grand nearly. And it ain't right!"

"What?" asked Maddox.

"Them damn crooked gambling houses down that place called Gardena! Crooked as hell they are. I lost every damn dime at draw!"

"Pity," said Rodriguez with a grin. "But most of 'em level, DeLucci. Maybe you're just not so good at draw poker."

"So now you drop on me. Listen, I ain't had a bite to eat since yesterday. I was in that bar panhandlin'. Can you get me to jail in time for dinner?"

■ ■ ■

In a rear booth at Musso and Frank's, Sue took a swallow of gimlet and sighed and leaned back. "Absolute heaven, Ivor darling."

"It was quite a day." Maddox sipped Scotch and water and waved away menus. "Presently."

"Ivor. I'm worrying about Monica. Your telling me about Simon's wife. What could have happened in that apartment? You don't suppose—"

"Look," said Maddox, "if there was one piece of evidence that indicated anybody was hurt—but there isn't.

Yes, I'm worried about Monica too. But the reservation in my mind, on that run-away-from-the-lunatic bit, is—those notes, that letter, and the phone call to Mrs. Moran. There really wasn't any need to be secretive about it. All Dorrie had to do was move and ask the phone company for an unlisted number. Why all the roundaboutness, if she really meant to go away? I haven't asked the lab about that letter," he added. "On second thought, I sent it to them to print. But what the hell could any prints tell us? We haven't got hers."

"There's just no shape to it," said Sue, troubled.

"And that's enough shop talk," said Maddox. "Look, you watch yourself with that damn sandwich machine. I don't want one of your pretty hands mashed."

It was still raining, and by the steady sound of it they were in for one of California's specials, a real storm. It might go on for days, though it had been dry up to now.

■ ■ ■

Brougham and Donaldson, on night watch, were talking desultorily at nine fifteen, with no calls in yet. "That damned cat of Maddox's gets me," said Brougham. "It looks so *happy*. I wonder what it's evidence on."

Footsteps up the stairs, heavy and plodding, and a man came in. He was elderly, big and solid and square, with a mop of curly gray hair. He looked around the office and said explosively, "Hah! They haven't got around to fixing that damn window, I see." As usual when it was raining, the air had turned warm, and the left-hand double-hung window had been slightly raised for air, propped up with a stick; the cord had been broken God knew how long ago.

"Can we help you, sir?" asked Donaldson briskly.

"No," said their visitor, "other way around. My God, it's good to see the damn place again. Couple of new desks,

174

I see—and I suppose down in Communications this new hookup to N.C.I.C." He came to offer a hand. "I'm Bill Woolsey, late Sergeant. Spent too many damn years sitting where you boys are. Retired ten years ago and moved over to Nevada—four acres and a few horses, the good life."

They shook hands. Woolsey had a hard shake, looked hale and hearty at what must be over seventy. "You come back to look us over?" asked Brougham.

"No, no. Came over to have a look at my first great-grandson," said Woolsey proudly. "The youngsters get married younger and younger, seems like. No, I wasn't going to bother anybody here, maybe take a look at the old place, but I just ran into the hell of a con game, and I figured you ought to hear about it, if you don't already know. About half an hour ago I'm on my way back to my daughter's house—I drove my own car over—and I'm on Los Feliz coming up to Vermont, when—"

"Oh, don't tell me," said Donaldson. "You got pulled over by an unmarked car. With two uniformed men in it."

"You know about it," said Woolsey. "Hell of a thing. Pay the traffic fine right off, get out of going to court! Who ever heard of that? But it's quite an idea, because a lot of tourists wouldn't know how we operate."

"We've said it," said Brougham. "I take it you didn't pay up."

"Am I crazy? By the time they'd made their spiel, I'd had time to see the uniform wasn't right. I said, The L.A.P.D. doesn't operate that way, buddy. I hauled out my old badge—always carry it on me—and by God, did that pair make tracks! I'm sorry, boys," said Woolsey, a little crestfallen, "I guess I'm not quite as quick on the up-take as I used to be. By the time I waked up and said that, and they started back for their car, I got my gun out to hold 'em for you, but too late. They gunned that old Dodge and were long gone. And what with the rain, I didn't even get a partial plate number."

"Well, we know about them," said Donaldson. "Cute con game all right. But thanks for coming in, sir." He looked at Brougham. "A Dodge."

"Olive green, four-door, seven years old," said Woolsey promptly.

"So at least," said Donaldson, "probably only these two on that job. Driving the same car."

"Damn, it's good to see the old place," said Woolsey. "No air conditioning yet? We used to cuss—"

"Central Headquarters," said Brougham gloomily. "I know. The air conditioning, the plush offices. The precinct stations, no."

"Oh, well," said Woolsey, "in any job there's something to grouse about."

He was still there, reminiscing happily, when a call came in. Missing report, said Sergeant Hopewell. A Mr. Humbard, Mike Humbard.

Bored, Brougham waited for the click on the line. "Mr. Humbard? What can we do for you?"

"I have a service station on Vermont," said Humbard precisely; he sounded like a middle-aged man. "A Shell station. We close at ten thirty on week nights. I always come in to close out the register. And my night man's missing. Gene Lasky. The register is empty, open."

Brougham snapped to attention. "Have you looked in the rest rooms?"

"Yes. He's nowhere around. I don't know how much would've been in the register, around a hundred or so, probably."

"Description?" said Brougham. In the largely dull (not always) night-watch hours, the N.C.I.C. reports got read.

"Gene? He's twenty-two, six feet, blond. But if there

was a holdup, why should—I always tell my men, don't resist, the money's only money, but a life—"

"We'll be right out on it, Mr. Humbard." Brougham put the phone down.

"Something gone down," said Woolsey. He looked a little wistful: the old fire horse.

"Something," said Brougham. "Do I remember those N.C.I.C. reports! That's the M.O. of that pair of escaped cons, Connors and Fielding. They've heisted half a dozen stations between here and Kansas. Abducted three attendants and left 'em miles away. The fourth one they shot. It just could be—"

"Well, I guess I better get on back to May's," said Woolsey. He heaved himself up. "Good luck, boys."

ten

"Be good," said Maddox at twenty to eight on Wednesday morning. "Don't pick up any strange men."

"And you wandering around the bars for a lead on Moreno."

"Not in the morning."

"Mother'll be picking me up about one, so you're to come straight there for dinner. And to meet Aunt Evelyn. . . ." Three minutes later Sue said breathlessly, "Ivor darling, you'll be late."

"I know, I know. I'm off." He ducked out into the thin rain.

The rain slowed traffic; when he got to the office Ellis, Rodriguez and Feinman were poring over the records the night watch had left them. Donaldson and Brougham had stayed with it all the way, from the first call. Brougham remembering the M.O., they'd given N.C.I.C. a hail and got more details. The two escaped cons, Connors and Fielding, had pulled a heist at a service station in Oklahoma City two weeks ago, abducted the lone attendant and let him go some fifty miles away. Four days later they'd done it again, in Clovis, New Mexico; that attendant had been left sixty miles out in the desert. The day after that they had heisted a station in Santa Fé and taken the attendant along; he got away from them forty miles outside town, where they took some shots at him but missed. The next hit was last Sunday in El Centro, and the station attendant was found shot dead ten miles up the highway. The three live ones had identified mug shots; it was definitely Connors and Fielding.

This thing bore the same earmarks; it wasn't usual for heist men to kidnap their victims. N.C.I.C. had been saying Connors and Fielding were heading west and now explained why: Connors had a girl friend in Bakersfield.

Seeing that these were big-time boys wanted for murder-one (two prison guards at Leavenworth), Donaldson and Brougham had routed out S.I.D. on overtime, and they had dusted that little building at the station, the register and door and so on. They had prints, via N.C.I.C., by 3 A.M., and it was now official; they'd picked up three of Connors's prints at the scene.

There had been a thorough hunt for blocks around, the big police helicopters out with their searchlights, for Gene Lasky; he hadn't been found.

Humbard was coming in to make a statement, but there wasn't much he could tell them, except that it must have happened after nine o'clock; he'd talked with Lasky on the phone about then.

There was no telling where they were heading, but it was a reasonable assumption that they might be going to see the girl friend. The various forces along the way toward Bakersfield had been alerted, Ventura County and Kern County, and the Highway Patrol. Of course there was no make on what car they were driving.

"And God knows what they've done with Lasky," said Ellis.

The phone rang on Maddox's desk and he turned to pick

it up. "I want Mr. D'Arcy, please," said a woman's voice.

"I'm sorry, he's not in yet," said Maddox just as D'Arcy did come in. "Can I help you?"

"Oh, I don't suppose it matters who I tell. This is Mrs. Ilinsky."

"Oh, yes, Mrs. Ilinsky. How's your husband?"

"He'll be fine, thanks. Doctor says he's lucky to be alive. He's sitting up taking notice now, and he asked me to look, and I did, and asked the hospital, but it's gone, so they must've taken it, those two who jumped him. And Walt said I should tell you. Because it isn't worth anything to sell, and so if you arrested somebody and found it, you'd know it was one of them hurt Walt."

"What is it?" asked Maddox.

"It's his good-luck piece, just a kind of curiosity. It was his father's. It's a kind of medal that everybody got in 1918, everybody in the services. It's bronze, and Walt says one and a quarter inches around, and it's got the names of all the countries in the First World War on it."

"I see. Well, thanks, we'll remember that, Mrs. Ilinsky. Glad to know your husband's all right." The muggers, of course, had probably thrown the medal away when they saw it was worthless.

"Well, Walt said I should call you."

At eight thirty on the dot O'Neill called to say, "Mrs. Goulding on the way up." He sounded dispirited. They'd all heard about his medical report now.

Maddox said, "Cheer up, Johnny—next time lucky," and stood up, beckoning Rodriguez and D'Arcy.

She came into the office quickly, a tall woman, spare figure, plainly dressed in navy blue with sensible shoes, a dowdy felt hat. She carried a battered briefcase. "Sergeant Maddox?"

He took her offered hand and asked her to sit down, introduced D'Arcy and Rodriguez. She had pepper-and-salt hair in a short cut and very kind, wise eyes. Daisy came in with David Mayo and was introduced too.

"You might have asked Mrs. Goulding to take off her coat," said Daisy, scolding. "You're wet—here, I'll hang it up for you."

Mrs. Goulding divided a smile between her and Mayo. "I'm so glad to meet you, Mr. Mayo. Dorrie's told me so much about you all. I feel I know your mother."

"I know Dorrie thinks a lot of you."

"What *is* all this nonsense about her disappearing?" She looked at Maddox rather indignantly.

Maddox began to tell her, concisely.

"But the letter to the store—you could see if it was Dorrie's writing, her signature."

"The signature was typed," said Maddox.

"Dorrie'd never do that. I don't understand this. I know she'd been feeling unsettled lately, for various reasons, but she'd have told me any plans she had. . . . I suppose you're wondering," said Mrs. Goulding suddenly, "if we—my husband and I—maintain such close relations with all our orphans after they leave. Of course not. But you could say Dorrie was one of my first babies. She came to us the first year John and I had full charge of the home. She's always been rather special to me, a very dear girl. I don't have time to write her as often as she writes me, but she understands. Now, I don't know how much you know about the various problems she'd been having—"

"The manic wife. Did she write you about that?" asked Maddox.

"Mrs. Simon." Her eyes were alert on him. "Yes, she said she wouldn't tell anyone else. She was sorry for Mr. Simon, but she was a little nervous about it. As anyone would be. About two weeks ago she said she'd just find a new apartment, but she'd been thinking about going back east to the Mayos', and it seemed silly to move twice. Then there was Brian Faulkner."

"Oh?" said Maddox. "Again?"

"He'd been phoning her, trying to get her to date him. He seemed to think a year was long enough to mourn," said Mrs. Goulding dryly. "And then there was Mrs. Barnes. Have you heard about that? I don't think Dorrie would have told anyone else."

"What about her?"

"Well, she's very wealthy, a—"

"Customer at the store, we know. Divorcée of the well-known playboy."

"And she wanted, of all things, to adopt Monica! She had the nerve to offer Dorrie fifty thousand dollars if she'd let her have Monica. I'm afraid I'm not as sweet-tempered as Dorrie—I'd have spit in her eye—but Dorrie said the poor soul really loved children. She just had the idea money could buy anything. At the last, she'd upped the offer to a hundred thousand."

"*¡Porvida!*" said Rodriguez under his breath.

"Damn gall!" said Mayo, scowling. "No wonder Dorrie didn't write that to Mother. Of all the arrogant—"

"That's new, but could it tie in?" said Maddox.

"Well, I don't know. I don't understand this at all. But," said Mrs. Goulding, "I thought you might want her finger-prints." She opened the briefcase.

Maddox sat up with a jump. "You've got her *prints?*"

"We always take the children's fingerprints. My husband's a great believer in using all the scientific aids possible. The Chief of Police says everybody ought to have their prints on file, and he sends a man out. So I brought Dorrie's. Taken when she was about fifteen."

They'd been rolled professionally, too, on two little cards. "O frabjous day!" said Maddox. "César, get these down to S.I.D. *pronto!*" He got the lab on the phone and explained. "I sent you a letter, resignation to Robinson's. Have a look for these new prints on it."

"There are *some* prints on it," said the S.I.D. man. "We looked. Unknown to us or Washington. O.K."

"We also sent you a batch of latents from an apartment, Lexington Avenue. Also have a look through them."

"Will do. By the way, those slugs your surgeon sent down. Ballistics says they match that Colt thirty-two Seventy-seventh sent us yesterday."

"Surprise, surprise," said Maddox, and put the phone down. "Sorry, Mrs. Goulding. Just expediting matters. Can you tell us anything else?"

Mrs. Goulding said, "It sounds silly, I suppose, but she'd been awfully bothered by a recurring dream. It troubled her, she said, it was so terribly real. I brought the latest letter I've had from her. I thought it might suggest something to you." She looked through the little pile of letters and chose one, not offering it to Maddox.

"When is it dated?"

"Saturday the fifth. I got it on Monday, a week ago Monday. I'd been a little surprised when I didn't get a letter this Monday or yesterday—she wrote about once a week."

Maddox looked at D'Arcy. "She wrote it Saturday, and I'll bet she had it with her when she went to the drugstore on Sunday morning, mailed it then. What about it, Mrs. Goulding?"

She had taken a pair of glasses out of her purse and put them on. "There's nothing in it really," she said slowly, "to explain— But I thought it just might tell you what she was feeling." She began to read in a clear strong voice.

"Saturday March fifth. Dear Mother G., Life can be so bothersome at times! Problems, problems! Nothing big and awful, like the accident, but niggling little things, which can be worse in a way. I'm still teetering back and forth about Connecticut. It would be such a permanent move, and I haven't *seen* much of the Mayos, after all—just corresponded. I'm sure Ken's mother is just as nice as her letters sound, but you know, once I'd done it, it would be hard to undo. But I think I'll have to decide soon.

"Just as I sat down to write this, Brian Faulkner called again. He seems nice, a gentleman and all that, but he just can't understand that *I'm not interested.* Maybe after a few more years I might be, not necessarily in him, but right now I just don't care.

"I had that dream again last night and woke up in a *state.* I don't like to feel superstitious, but it frightens me. It's all terribly real. I'm in the dark somewhere, confused and frightened, and then I hear Ken calling me. 'Dorrie, Dorrie, it's me. Come to me, Dorrie!' And I look and look in the dark, and then suddenly there's a big light and it's Ken, coming toward me just as if he's flying, and laughing and so happy. And at first I'm so glad to see him, all alive and bright and laughing, I start to cry, and then just as he puts his arms around me I remember he's dead, and pull away and run— Oh, I can't tell you what a terrible feeling of remorse I wake up with, running away from *Ken!* I know it's just a dream, but it bothers me.

"Now I'll try to be more cheerful. Monica is fine, as energetic as ever, and if you could see her with that absurd 'Kee-kee' Mrs. Mayo sent her—! I've been thinking about getting a camera. We really should have pictures of her as she's growing, and Mr. Simon says these new Kodaks are very easy to use and not expensive. Sandra has one and says she'll show me. I told you that Mrs. Barnes—oh, dear, Linda Barnes is another of the niggling little things! She's still pressuring me, as if she thought I'd *sell* Monica! It's too ridiculous to talk about, but she's been kind in her way.

184

I told you about the snapshots she took of Monica in the park; I should have copies for you next week.

"You think I should go back east, I know. To what family there is. Well, I'm thinking about it! For one thing, I have to do what's best for Monica. I'll decide soon, and I feel better now I've put all my troubles on you as usual. Good night, darling, and God bless you."

There was a little silence. Maddox said into it, "Did she mention the anonymous love letters to you?"

"Oh, that. Some child in the neighborhood, I suppose. She said one of them was signed 'Denis.'"

That was new: a very small lead to work.

"But what *can* have happened?" She looked bewildered and a little frightened. "There wasn't any reason—just an ordinary young woman living an ordinary life. There wasn't anything at the apartment to make you—"

"Think anything violent happened? No," said Maddox. "They're just—gone." His poor little wild geese, vanished into thin air.

"This Barnes woman," said Mayo abruptly.

"Yes, we want to see her. And Mr. Faulkner," said Maddox. No need to tell them about Faulkner's record. As he'd thought before, whatever had happened, it didn't bear Faulkner's mark: the too-sudden violence and no cover-up. "There's an A.P.B. out on both of them," he said, dissatisfied because he didn't think that was going to be any use. But at least, now, they had Dorrie's prints.

■ ■ ■

Mrs. Goulding understandingly took Mayo away with her. Ellis and Feinman had taken a statement from Humbard and called Daisy away to help deal with Lasky's wife, a pretty blond girl about six months pregnant.

The bars on the Strip, where—somewhere—Moreno had

probably picked up a girl, weren't open yet. The bartenders, the customers who might have noticed, wouldn't be around until this evening. Have to do some overtime at that.

"I want to see this Barnes woman. Where does she live?" She wasn't in the book; that figured, the unlisted number. He called Simon at the store and got the address: Anthony Place up in Benedict Canyon above Beverly Hills. But just as he got up, the phone rang. D'Arcy took the call and leaped up.

"Shooting going on—black-and-white there and one of our men hit."

Maddox ran after him. It was a few blocks up on Hollywood Boulevard, a tall office building on a corner. There was a bank on the ground floor, and as they came into the lobby a bank guard in uniform hurried up.

"You cops? It's the fourth floor. The doc called security when he pulled the gun."

The elevator rose in dignified style but finally decanted them on the fourth floor. There were knots of people out of other offices in the long hallway and two men in uniform up to the left, one leaning on the wall.

"What's going on?" asked Maddox.

"It's just a crease," said Ben Loth impatiently, clasping his upper shoulder. "He's in there. I don't know what it's all about—a guy with a gun."

"With all these civilians around," said the other man, "I didn't think we'd better rush him."

"Quite right." The door Loth gestured at bore a message on its frosted glass: *Dr. Clare St. John, Psychologist, Marriage Counseling*. The gun spoke again inside, and automatically Maddox and D'Arcy, guns out, took up positions on either side of the door. The second uniformed man, gun in hand, rapped loudly on it. "Police officers. Come out with your hands up!"

186

The frosted glass shattered with a crash as a bullet hit it, and a woman screamed. Maddox ducked around for a quick look inside.

There was a man with a revolver in the middle of a typical waiting room: meaningless pictures, sterile vinyl-covered chairs and couch. In a doorway at the rear a fat man in a white coat was leaning on the wall and saying in a trembling voice, "Now, Mr. Engelhard, you don't want to hurt me," and against the wall in the waiting room a woman was sprawled.

The scream had come from a statuesque brunette huddled up on the couch, a man beside her.

"Oh, hell," said the man with the gun, and dropped it on the floor. He sounded merely disgusted. Maddox and D'Arcy went in fast and laid hands on him. The uniformed man came with the cuffs.

"Oh, Harry!" sighed the brunette, and collapsed into the arms of the man beside her. "Take me home, darling, I don't want to stay here! I'm sorry, darling, it was all my fault! Let's go home, Harry!"

"Come to think," said the man named Engelhard, "I *oughta* started with you." He looked at the white-coated figure, doubtless the marriage counselor, angrily. "Damn fool idea, come to a place like this. But that's Betty, always getting damn fool ideas."

"I have to give you your rights, sir," said the uniformed man. "You have the right to remain silent—"

"Just make things worse. And another thing, damn it—"

Maddox and D'Arcy looked at the woman. She was dead, probably several slugs in her. The gun was an H. and R. nine-shot .22.

"She never fills the damn ice trays full—little niminy ice cubes melt as soon as you put 'em in a drink—and you, you goddamn idiot, talkin' about repressions. Who in hell's got repressions?"

"—and to have a lawyer present before you answer any—"

"And tomato sauce in baked beans instead o' molasses. Time after time I told her. And another thing, always fiddlin' with the TV, the color's not right, and the last service charge—"

"—If you cannot afford a lawyer and desire the presence of an attorney, the court—"

■ ■ ■

What with talking to Engelhard—not to any extent, because he was still mad and might claim duress afterward, and besides there were witnesses to the shooting—it was getting on for eleven o'clock. They'd get statements from St. John, the brunette and her husband later; all three of them were so unnerved they wouldn't make sense right now. Maddox wanted to canvas that block on Lexington, looking for Denis; he was interested in anything to do with Dorrie; but then the Connors-Fielding thing came to life again and for a while they were huddled down in Communications watching that unfold.

Connors and Fielding were having bad luck, or Nemesis was on their trail. Gene Lasky shouldn't have been found until next spring, where they'd left him, back from the road in a heavily forested area up in Angeles National Park. But a Dr. Roundtree, innocently collecting snapshots of wild life, had stumbled over him about nine thirty and called the rangers. He'd been shot in the head.

"What the hell?" said Ellis. "This storm—what was he doing roaming around in the woods?" But it seemed that what was a thin rain down here was only a few flakes of snow near Crystal Lake.

So they alerted the forces up there. No make on the car yet. They might be lost, speculated Ellis; intending to head for Bakersfield, how had they ended up in the mountains?

He tried N.C.I.C.: did Connors or Fielding know California at all? This area? The computers answered back briefly: neither of them was known to have been here before.

"They're lost," said Ellis. "God, I wish we had a make on the car."

There was a Federal warrant for them now, so a couple of FBI men showed up to take what details they'd heard from Humbard. Daisy went with one of them to break the news to Lasky's wife. She wouldn't enjoy it, but she'd do it as well as it could be done. A few years ago, sympathetic people had come to break news to Daisy, and her husband's name was on the Roll of Honor, officers killed in line of duty, at headquarters downtown.

Then nothing more showed up for a while, and Maddox went out to talk to Brian Faulkner, if he was at his job at Giese and Weekes.

He was. Jim Fogarty was coming from the rear of the big office, as Maddox came in, and gave him a suspicious glance. Maddox asked for Faulkner, and Fogarty pointed out one of the partitioned cubicles mutely.

The cubicles had no doors, and Maddox stood there for a moment watching Faulkner, who was unaware of him. A very good-looking man, Faulkner, a man who might be surprised when a girl rejected him. And other things. The way he'd reacted before—

Faulkner was typing, copying some document beside the typewriter. He was quite evidently a rapid and experienced touch typist. His fingers flew, and he never glanced at the keyboard.

"Mr. Faulkner," said Maddox. Faulkner jerked around and looked up.

"Oh," he said. "You." His mouth tightened. "Have you —found Dorrie yet?"

"Not yet. You said you'd seen her last in January."

"That's right."

"But you have been calling her, we've just heard. Trying to persuade her to go out with you."

"Well, damn it, I have. She's—it's over a year since she lost her husband, and I thought it'd be good for her. Have a good time now and then, go out to dinner. No harm. But she wouldn't."

"How many times did she turn you down?"

"I haven't kept count," said Faulkner stiffly. "Where do you think she's gone? I can't imagine why—"

"Maybe to get away from you, among other things," said Maddox.

Faulkner flushed. "Well, I don't know anything about it."

Maddox, as the experienced cop, still didn't like Faulkner too well for—whatever this was. But they really didn't know what it was, except that all this while, since he'd first talked to Sandra Cross and Teresa Fogarty, he'd had the little feeling up his spine that it *was* something. Not just a young woman dropping from sight, cutting all ties, because she was harassed by an unbalanced woman, paid unwelcome attentions by a good-looking man, bothered by a silly divorcée. Niggling things, she said. Yes.

And—was he reading it right?—it was on Sunday that she walked away. A week ago last Sunday. She talked to Teresa on the phone that morning, and Mrs. Littleton saw her with Monica in the stroller starting for the drugstore, probably a little later. That was when she had mailed the letter to Mrs. Goulding. And nobody had seen her since.

That recurring dream. For the first time, now, he felt a small superstitious cold conviction. They weren't going to find her; she wasn't coming back.

But Monica? Monica, probably fretting for her beloved pink cat?

"Where were you a week ago Sunday?" he asked Faulkner.

"Didn't you ask me that before?" Faulkner got out a cigarette. "We were still having that heat wave. I just stayed home. The apartment. No, I didn't see anybody. Oh, the man next door—the next apartment, I mean— came to borrow ice cubes; it was about five o'clock, I think."

Which said nothing at all. Maddox turned away.

■ ■ ■

The house was the kind he had expected, modern and elegant and big, a tri-level on a hillside lot. It was beige stucco and fieldstone and redwood siding, with a carved double set of front doors, what looked like real mahogany, with ornate brass knobs. Maddox had left the Maserati one level below and climbed broad steps past lower windows (recreation room, kitchen, library?) to the shallow porch, the double doors and tall windows either side hung with heavy silk drapes, pulled. There was a bell push at one side; he shoved it and there was a peal of chimes inside.

After thirty seconds the door opened and he faced a plump youngish woman with a round pale face unmade-up and a mass of light brown hair escaping from pins. She wore a kind of uniform dress, pale blue, zipped up the front, and house slippers.

He showed her the badge, which spooked her to panic. "Oh, my goodness, *police!* Oh, my heavens, has something happened to Mrs. Barnes?"

"No, no," said Maddox soothingly. "Mrs. Barnes isn't home? I'd like to talk with her, that's all."

"Oh, no, she's not. That was why I was upset, thinking maybe an accident—but what's it *about*? Why do you want to see her?

"Just a few questions about a friend of hers. Excuse me, do you live here with her?"

"Oh, yes, I'm sorry, I shouldn't have—but you startled me so! My name's Anna Hoyt. I do everything for Mrs. Barnes, I mean we have cleaners come in, but I supervise them and do the cooking and all. I've been with her ever since she married Mr. Richard. Oh, she did try, poor lamb, but it was no use. You'll never change him. What's your name? Oh. Well, I suppose you'd better come in."

Maddox went in. Possibly a chatterbox was better than nothing. The entry hall had deep sculptured carpeting, a tiered chandelier and little walnut tables. "This must be quite a big house to take care of."

"Oh, yes, but it's so lovely and all in such refined taste, it's a pleasure. Not but what it seems a waste, I've often said to her, because she doesn't entertain much. She's a very simple sort of lady really—I mean she doesn't like a lot of parties and so on. Of course she wasn't born to money. I suppose that makes a difference, and it isn't as if she pretends any different either—chat with anybody as free and easy as you please. And what she gives to charity, especially anything to do with children!"

"She's fond of children?" said Maddox.

Anna Hoyt nodded vigorously. "Never had any of her own. Not that she's so old now, of course—thirty-four, she is, and you'd never think it to look at her. She's a pretty woman. The old man was terrible pleased when Mr. Richard married her—that was old Mr. Barnes, with all the money. My mother was his cook for years and years— he was pleased, you see, Mr. Barnes, because she'd worked for him and he liked her. He thought maybe she could straighten Mr. Richard out, but nobody could. But he left her a lot of money even after the divorce—old Mr. Barnes, I mean. And if ever a person did good with their

192

money, it's Mrs. Barnes. Oh, she buys things for herself too, but charities get a lot."

"That's very good of her," said Maddox. "Did—"

"Oh, she's a good person," said Anna earnestly. "So good to all of us, and I tell her, she ought to look over the grocery bills, I always bring them to her, but she just says she knows she can trust me, and I'm sure I hope she *can*. Some of my friends think it's funny, with all the money, she doesn't give grand parties and know all the rich people —socialites, like, you know. But she doesn't like that kind of thing. The beach she likes, only she has to be careful of the sun, she's so fair. But, my goodness, you aren't interested in all this, I shouldn't think. I do ramble on. But like I say, she's not home right now."

"When do you expect her back?" asked Maddox.

"Saturday," said Anna. "Saturday, she said she'd be home. Next Saturday. I've just got back myself. She said I should take a vacation while she did, and stay over till next Friday, but I wanted to get back to be sure the house was all clean and ready for her."

"Where is she?"

"Oh, didn't I say? I'm sorry. She's in Hawaii. On a vacation. She said to me, Anna, she said, you know the only places I've ever been is Sun Valley and Disneyland— it was so funny the way she said it, of course, the time she went to Disneyland it was helping some of those Catholic sisters look after a bunch of kids, some orphanage here, and she paid for everything—but she said, she thought she'd give herself a little vacation, and everybody says Hawaii's so beautiful—"

"When did she leave?" asked Maddox resignedly.

"Now let's see. A week ago Sunday, it was. She flew over. The plane was leaving at five o'clock. She was all packed and ready when I left, and the taxi ordered. I went to stay with my sister in San Luis Obispo. I drove my own car up."

"I see. Thanks very much," said Maddox. Another dead end. Damn it, if he could see any pattern, any possible shape to this!

A mere Missing report. Not what you could really call a case—but the time they'd spent on it—and when you thought about details, it was offbeat. Funny.

That quiet, neat apartment.

He turned and went out past the double doors, pursued by her incoherence. "Old Mr. Barnes left Mother an annuity. She lives with my sister now. But I wanted to be back in good time, see the house is all clean when Mrs. Barnes comes home."

But, thought Maddox, going down the steps toward the street, that apartment; what else did it say? Taken with the notes, the letter and—not the cat; that had been just overlooked. Had it?

Dorrie hadn't meant to go anywhere; it was a conviction backed up by details. She had gone—somewhere. And Monica?

And somebody had covered her tracks. Guessing, taking the chance that it would look natural. Somebody who didn't know that those two pictures hadn't come with the apartment, nor the vacuum cleaner. Somebody who didn't know there wasn't a resident manager. But somebody who knew about Mrs. Moran, and where Dorrie worked, and about the Mayos back east wanting her to move there.

Well, quite a few people might qualify on that score. Qualify for what? Maddox asked himself.

Just a Missing report.

■ ■ ■

He came into the office, and the stuffed pink cat smirked at him. D'Arcy was there, and Rodriguez. "We've got a make on the car," said D'Arcy.

"Don't tell me! How?"

"The Feds are out, a horde of them, and the rangers up there too. All of 'em with mug shots. We just got a flash a minute ago. Service-station attendant identified Connors as the driver of a car that got its tank filled about half an hour ago, a station in Hesperia. It's a Ford Galaxie, white over blue, a 1967 four-door."

"No plate number."

"How much do you want? It's one step on."

Maddox agreed.

"And one of the Feds," said Rodriguez, "claims we're running a con game. He put three half dollars into that machine before he got a cheese sandwich."

"And it's raining, so you're ignoring everything else we've got on hand," said Maddox.

"*Amigo*, on Moreno it's no good trying the bars on the Strip until the right bartenders come on duty."

"Oh, the D.A.'s office wants you," said D'Arcy. "I don't know about what. I told 'em you'd call back."

Sitting down at his desk, Maddox reached for the phone. "Johnny, the D.A.'s office called me—you have the extension? And don't sound so gloomy, boy, give it time."

"Time!" said O'Neill. "It isn't the time I'm worried about, it's the goddamn operation. About half a slug left in, and I'm fine, I'm O.K., I don't even limp, and these bastards say—oh, hell. . . . It was somebody named Wein. I've got the extension somewhere."

"Oh, yes, Sergeant Maddox," said a crisp voice a minute later, sounding rather cautiously amused. "It's this— um—gang pulling the protection racket that you handed us the other day. Too much of that going on, all right. But somebody seems to have given these young thugs quite a scientific going-over."

"That's right," said Maddox. "Some of the latest mark's

pals, I suppose."

"Yes. Well, what about the mark? Is he willing to testify against them?"

"Very much so," said Maddox.

"A Mr. Janowsky, by the report. Well, we'll contact him about the hearing, then. We're mulling over the charge. In my opinion there's enough for an assault-with-intent. We'll let you know."

Maddox put the phone down and it shrilled at him.

"Maddox, Wilcox Street."

"I want Mr. D'Arcy, but it doesn't matter. This is Steiner." The voice was mysteriously muffled. "I make an excuse, come to the back room. I've got that one here, the girl passes me the bad check. That Coralee Lambert. She's looking at cosmetics, my girl Lois with her. I'll try to hold her for you, if you come right away. . . . Sure, I'm sure! Mr. D'Arcy showed me her picture on the license."

A break, a really true break on their gang of kite flyers. Maddox slammed the phone down and ran, beckoning D'Arcy. "Where's this Steiner's place? You talked to him, he said. And you," he added to Rodriguez, "you damned doubting Thomas, I said there's fellow feeling among the merchants!"

"What?" said Rodriguez.

"Steiner—oh, it's out on Fairfax," said D'Arcy. "A pharmacy."

"He's got one of our passers. Come on!" said Maddox.

eleven

Without consultation they all piled into D'Arcy's Dodge. "It's not far out," said D'Arcy, gunning the engine. But there wasn't a siren, and it was a good ten minutes, while they all cussed the traffic lights, before he said, "This corner. The pharmacy." Cars were parked solid along the curb; D'Arcy double-parked and they all piled out.

As they came to the door of the pharmacy, they heard the girl, loud and furious. "You let me go! What're you trying to do, you dirty old man? Let me go!"

"No, you don't, young lady. We're waiting for the police." Steiner's voice was hard.

"Police!"

Steiner relaxed his hold on her arm, seeing them come in; she wrenched away and fled, and Maddox fielded her neatly in the doorway, remembering his injunction to Sue. "Oh!" she gasped. It was the girl, all right, bad as the photograph on the license was: a fat blonde about twenty, hair in a froth of curls on top of her head, baby face, a too-small mouth.

"You identify her positively?" he said to Steiner.

"Absolutely. I said to Mr. D'Arcy, If that one ever

197

comes in again I'll know her. But I'm bound to say I never thought it'd happen."

"Oh!" gasped the girl. "Oh, for the love of—was I in here before? Oh, my God, and I got the same wig on as in the picture. Oh, my God!"

"You're under arrest," said Maddox. And as she'd resisted they could frisk her; he took her handbag and opened it. There was the usual miscellany, and a bulging billfold; he opened that. The first I.D. he saw was a driver's license issued to Sally Hawk of an address on Edgemont. "This your real name?"

She nodded sullenly. "Of all the damn fool things to do! I had to come walking in here. My God, I could kill myself! Of all the *goddamn* fool things—"

Maddox found the other license, the phony one. There was nearly a hundred bucks in the billfold. "We'll take you in now, Miss Hawk. And you can do some thinking on the way about telling us who the other five are."

"What about my car? It's parked out there—the VW."

"You live with your family?" asked Rodriguez. And, at her reluctant nod, "I suppose somebody'll take care of the car."

They took her in, and gave her her rights, and called Daisy to sit in. "Oh, what the hell about a lawyer," she said. "You know about it now."

"But we don't," Rodriguez pointed out. "We've only got you. Now I suppose we could go ferreting around, finding out who your friends are, and eventually—"

She looked at them disgustedly. "You don't think I'm going to take the whole rap for it and let the rest of them off? The hell with it." She was still furious at herself for pulling such a silly trick; she brooded. "I'll tell you. It was Sam Garcia's idea. He's the smart boy thought about the licenses."

198

"Sam Garcia. And?"

"Oh, damn. Nina Simmons. Randy Dunphy. Howard Schwartz. Michelle Brand. We all go to L.A.C.C. part time."

"That we had figured. Where'd you get the student union cards?"

She shrugged. "Nina works in the registrar's office. She waited till nobody was there and took them."

"And where will we find the other boys and girls right now?" asked Maddox.

"Suppose you do a little work yourself," she said, glaring at him.

They left her with Daisy, and Rodriguez said, "You know, this is going to occupy the rest of the day. I vote we go and have lunch before we follow up on it."

They went up to the Grotto on Santa Monica for a quick lunch. The waitress there who liked the cops coming in regarded them with a motherly eye and was pleased when Mr. D'Arcy ordered a steak; he needed building up, in her opinion. And there was something about Sergeant Maddox: you couldn't exactly say he was handsome, but there was something about him.

They were halfway through lunch when Ellis and Feinman came in. "We've been following the chase on short-wave," said Ellis. "They've got helicopters out and road blocks up, but no smell yet. But now we know the general area, it shouldn't be long.

"There's a lot of open country up that way, George," said Maddox. "You missed the excitement. We've got one of our passers, and we're just about to collect the rest."

"Well, that's a step in the right direction," said Ellis. "I'll have the steak sandwich, please."

"Yes, Sergeant. Medium."

"Oh, you can bring me the same."

"Yes, Mr. Feinman. Well done."

"Thanks for all the enthusiastic praise," said D'Arcy as he got up.

"Well, we were bound to get them sooner or later," said Ellis.

As Rodriguez had prophesied, the check passers took up the rest of the day and would take up more in days to come. First they had to find them. Three of them—Simmons, Dunphy, and Schwartz—were in class at L.A.C.C.; Garcia they found at a part-time job at a market on Vermont, after getting his address at the college and calling his home. The Brand girl was at home, and her mother insisted on coming in with her, the first of the bunch of parents to arrive.

It was quite a mess. None of them were minors, but young enough that they were all living at home, and the parents were upset. At least, as Daisy pointed out later, all the parents were upright citizens who were surprised and grieved and angry about it. But they complicated matters, coming in, asking questions.

They heard about the casual inception of the bouncy checks from Sam Garcia, who was a very bright boy indeed, darkly handsome and not even vaguely repentant. "It's a drag, the job after class to earn a little bread," he said. "What's the lousy job pay, two twenty an hour? We were all at Randy's one night. His old man's been needling him about a trade, got him working in his place afternoons, learn printing. A printing business he's got, see? So Randy knows how to set the stuff up, and I had the idea, we could print anything we wanted. That goddamned idiot Sally has to break it up, damn it. It's been working smooth as cream, all the bread so easy...."

The only one of the six who seemed to realize in a hazy way that she'd done something wrong was the Brand girl. She just sat and wept and hiccuped. "I didn't w-want to—

I was scared—but I w-wanted that f-fifty-dollar dress at Robinson's and S-Sally said it was easy—"

They had to get statements from them all, and there were still statements to get on the Engelhard thing that morning. Ellis and Feinman reluctantly came up from Communications and lent a hand. They said Connors and Fielding hadn't showed yet.

Randy Dunphy's father came in when his wife reached him on the phone. Maddox was the one who talked to him; not that there was much to say. He said heavily to Maddox, "I worked my tail off, Sergeant, saved my money, to build up my own business, have something to leave my boy. It's a good job. I thought I was doing him a favor, teach him the trade. And then, *this*. His mother—What gets me, he doesn't seem to understand it was wrong. We tried to raise him right—honest. What—what do you think he'll get?"

Maddox shrugged. "Not much, Mr. Dunphy. It's not a felony charge, and it's a first count for all of them. But—"

"Yeah, but," said Dunphy. "But is right. When he can go off the rails like this once— Well, maybe I can talk to him, make him see."

Maddox wouldn't take any bets.

He was having a breather, Rodriguez and D'Arcy taking the last couple of statements, at five thirty, when O'Neill put through a call to him.

"I've just finished this latest cadaver of yours," said Dr. Bergner. "This Moreno. My God, Maddox, but it's frightening. Time. Those pictures of him in the *Herald* the other night—glamour-boy screen idol. When I had a look at that corpse, I'm surprised he lived long enough to get murdered. The state his liver was in, and an enlarged heart—and he was full of bennies when he died."

"The pepper-uppers," said Maddox, and laughed. "Is that so?"

"Man should have been dead five years ago," said Bergner, "the condition he was in. It was a wide-bladed knife, by the way. You haven't come across it?"

"Not yet. The way it reads, he picked up a trollop who probably fetched a boy friend in to help rob him."

"He was still going after females?" Bergner was scandalized. "All I can say is, he must have had a powerful imagination. I'll send the report up."

Maddox was still laughing when Rodriguez came up to ask what the joke was.

■ ■ ■

He got to Janiel Terrace at six twenty, and Sue and Gor met him at the door. "And how's my favorite mother-in-law?" he asked, kissing Sue first.

"Aunt Evelyn's dying to meet you."

Evelyn Rice looked quite a bit like her sister. Maddox smiled at her. "So you're the paragon," she said.

"It's hopeless," Sue told her. "I knew it before we were married. Every time we have an argument, Mother jumps in on his side. Do you want a drink before dinner, Ivor?"

"I think I deserve one. We've picked up the kite flyers."

"No! How?"

He told them about that, and the furious hunt, with hundreds of men out, up around Hesperia, over the drink and part of dinner. "And did you warn your aunt about our con men?"

"I did."

"At least they missed a mark last night. Ken left us a note. Made the mistake of approaching an ex-L.A.P.D. sergeant now living in Nevada."

The women had finished the dishes while Maddox and Gor watched *Adam-12*, and Sue was just saying, "I've got to be up early, if it is your day off," when the phone rang. Mrs. Carstairs came back from the hall and said it was the office.

"Maddox. What's up?"

"I just thought you'd like to know," said Brougham, "that it's all over. They got them."

"Good. Where?"

"Out on the desert the other side of Victorville, on a back road. They'd evidently spotted all the activity and were trying to slide out of the area by a back door. Helicopter spotted the car. There was a little gunfight—one highway patrolman in critical condition."

"Neither of them?"

"Connors has a broken arm. They're stashed in the Barstow jail till the Feds execute their warrant."

Maddox went back to the living room and passed that on. "Well, at least they're out of circulation," said Sue.

"Which must be a satisfaction," said Maddox, "to Gene Lasky's wife."

■ ■ ■

Rodriguez had dinner at the Grotto and then drove up to the Sunset Strip and left the car in a public lot. He had wandered in and out of some places down here yesterday afternoon; at night it wasn't quite so bad, he thought. The dim lights, the flashing neon outside, obscured some of the dirt and shabbiness, the age of run-down old buildings. Irrelevant to the bars and restaurants and discotheques and tawdry dress shops and movie houses, across the street here and on up in the next block were tall new modern office buildings. But the old places on the Strip had forgotten their days of glamour.

He looked sadly around the fifth place he had tried tonight, looked as best as he could in the gloom. At two of the others, the bartenders had known Moreno, cynically shrugging at the dirty old man ogling the girls, but they hadn't known who he was. Nobody acknowledged having seen him last Sunday night; the customers had stared blankly at questions.

The customers. "*¡Dios!*" he said to himself, looking around. Every generation deplores its youth, but some of today's young people were indeed hard to excuse.

They sat around like zombies here, impassively listening to the over-loud rock blaring from a stereo down from the bar. Hard to tell the sexes apart, in their mostly mud-colored pants and tunics and love beads and head bands. The prevalent drink was Dago red, but none of them looked happy enough to be drunk.

It was getting on for ten o'clock, and Rodriguez was feeling frustrated. He didn't really care much who had stabbed Moreno, but it was his job to find out; anybody who had killed once might kill again. He also felt that he needed a bath, after this little excursion, but he went over to the bartender and raised his voice over the rock music.

The bartender was young and surprisingly had short-cropped hair and no sideburns, beard or mustache. He gestured at Rodriguez and led him behind the bar to a door. On the other side it was quiet. They could faintly hear the beat, but that was all.

"I think I'll have to quit this job," said the bartender. "The money's all right, but it's playing hell with my concentration. Besides, I been reading that you can get deaf from listening to that stuff they call music. I'm only here at night—I run a bulldozer, days." He looked at the badge, interested. "You're a cop? Say, is this about that old movie star got murdered?" Suddenly he was excited. "It said in the paper he might have been down here."

"That's right," said Rodriguez. "We're hoping somebody saw him pick up a girl."

"That guy? I'll be damned. My name's Gustafson, by the way."

"Rodriguez."

"He looked about a hundred. You wouldn't hardly think —yeah, I'd seen him around, a few times. This was what night?"

"Sunday."

"Yeah, well," said Gustafson thoughtfully, "I did see him in here. On Sunday night. I didn't see him go out with anybody, or hook up with any girl, but I can tell you who he was talking to awhile." He pointed at the door. "In there, first table left of the front door, a couple of girls. They're regulars, but all I know 'em by is Junie and Claire. Junie's the one in red pants and vest. I saw that guy sitting at their table."

"What time?" asked Rodriguez.

"Oh, middle of the evening—nine, nine thirty."

"Thanks very much," said Rodriguez.

"How you going to talk to them?" asked Gustafson.

"That's a question." In the end, after gesturing at the pair and pointing to the door, he produced his badge and got them out to the sidewalk by frowns and will power. At least it had stopped raining, but it hadn't turned cold yet so probably more was on the way.

"What's the fuzz want? We aren't doin' anything." They were mad. They didn't like cops anyway.

"Just some questions," said Rodriguez. One of them was dirty blond and one brunette; they both looked a little scruffy. He asked about Moreno and they denied knowing him. "Come on, he was sitting talking to you in there last Sunday night. An old man, with—"

"Oh, that guy," said Junie. "So what about him?"

"Did he proposition you?" asked Rodriguez bluntly.

"Him? He was about a thousand years old, and besides we aren't that kind of girls," said Claire.

"I can take you in to the station, you know," said Rodriguez mildly.

"Oh, what the hell?" said Junie. "Not that I want to help

out the fuzz, but he glommed onto a girl at the next table. She left with him. He was flashin' a roll, all right, but I'm a little bit choosier than that."

"Who? Know her name?"

Junie shrugged. "You see her around. They call her Dusty."

"Yeah," said Claire, "I've seen her with that guy carries the prayer wheel. You know. Tibet and all."

"Know his name?" asked Rodriguez wearily.

They shrugged at each other. "I heard somebody call him Moose," said Claire.

That was all he could get out of them, except vague descriptions: Dusty blond and tall, Moose big and fat. He called it a day and went home to his apartment and had a bath.

■ ■ ■

Maddox was supposed to be off on Thursdays; sometimes he was. But there was a little pressure of paperwork on them right now. There'd be the statements to get on the Engelhard thing, reports to type, and they weren't finished with the kite flyers by any means; they'd be bringing all the victims in, those who'd cashed the bouncy checks, for identification parades, get as much evidence as possible. Maddox would go into the office.

Sue left at a quarter of eight, and he had another cup of coffee and then—he knew she didn't like dishes standing around—washed the breakfast dishes. He finally got around to shaving, put on a clean shirt and tie and checked his pockets. It was a quarter to nine and drizzling very slightly. He went out to the car and started for the office.

There he found Mayo and Mrs. Goulding just ahead of him. "Oh, Sergeant Maddox—if you don't mind, we'd like to look at Dorrie's apartment."

He had forgotten that he'd better see that Mayo or

somebody removed her belongings. "I'll take you over," he said, but Mayo had rented a car. On the way Maddox explained about the pictures, the vacuum cleaner.

"I don't know what to do about it," said Mayo. "When she comes back—oh, God, *if* she comes back—but you said the rent's only paid through this month."

"Well, you could put them in storage," said Maddox.

In the apartment, they just stood and looked. "The lab men have been in here—you can see the powder—but we haven't disturbed anything."

"Where was the cat?" asked Mrs. Goulding suddenly. He told her. "But Dorrie's a very neat housekeeper," she said.

They looked in all the rooms. Maddox gave them time. There wasn't anything to see, but they looked. "Did she keep an address book?" he asked.

"Why, I suppose so," said Mrs. Goulding. "Everybody does. Wasn't there one?"

The refrigerator should be cleaned out, he thought; its contents all spoiled by now. And Mrs. Goulding told him what he knew: "Dorrie'd never have moved without cleaning out that refrigerator!"

When there wasn't any more to see, they took the pictures down, got the vacuum cleaner and put them in the trunk of Mayo's rented car. Mrs. Goulding said, "She saved from her housekeeping money to buy that Wood print and have it framed. She loved it. The print was fifteen dollars and it cost nearly forty to have it framed. They'd bought some new furniture, appliances, for the house, and they were just getting by, but Dorrie's a good manager."

"But *where—why—how?*" said Mayo suddenly, pounding the steering wheel. "And Monica. She's only fifteen months old!"

Mrs. Goulding was going back to Fresno. "But, please,

207

Sergeant, please keep in touch. You know how concerned I am."

When he got back to the office, Rodriguez told him about the lead he'd turned up on Moreno. "And what a thing to follow up—but we'll have to. Dusty, my God."

"If he'd acted his age," said Maddox, "we wouldn't have all the legwork to do. But then if human nature wasn't so unpredictable, César, we'd all be out of jobs."

Sue and Daisy were taking a statement from the statuesque brunette, on Engelhard. Feinman was typing a report. "Burglary went down first thing," said D'Arcy, "before you joined us. Couple spent the night at their daughter's place after watching the late movie, came home and found the house ransacked. They're mad. Why don't we *do* something about this rise in crime?"

"Why indeed?" said Maddox. He told O'Neill to get him S.I.D. downtown. "Have you had a chance to look at those prints yet?"

"Just before you called," said the lab man. "The letter to Robinson's had three prints on it, still unknown. The set you sent us don't show anywhere on that. There were quite a lot of those among the bunch from the apartment. Also what are probably a child's prints, and just one that matches one on the letter."

"Do tell," said Maddox. "Where was that print from?" As trained men, D'Arcy, Rowan and Dabney would have labeled them all.

"Let's see—oh, yes. It's a pretty clear print, and it was on the knob of the door to the closet."

Maddox thought about that. "Does it look male or female?"

"I wouldn't have a guess. Sometimes it's obvious, but you never know. Hands and fingers come all sizes. It's a fairly large print, and it looks to me as if the finger could be splayed a little, from manual work of some sort."

"Mmh. What about the typing on the letter?"

"We had it over to Questioned Documents. It's pro work all right, an experienced touch typist. The machine is fairly new. It's a Hermes three thousand, the special pica type, and Documents pointed out one rather interesting thing. It's a model made for the European market."

"Oh?"

"Yep. It'll have, they say, Spanish punctuation on it, a pound sterling mark, and a German umlaut. The reason they know is that the typist made just one mistake and erased it with that erasing tape. They spotted it by infra-red, of course. He, she or it hit the upside-down exclamation instead of a hyphen. On that model, the upside-down exclamation is right where a pro typist expects to find the hyphen. So the typist was not too familiar with the typewriter."

"Do you boys have to make things more complicated?" said Maddox bitterly.

He thought about it as he went out with D'Arcy to get a list of the burglar's loot, get a statement from the victims. But the new rigmarole of the typist and the unfamiliar typewriter didn't ring any bells in his head at all. It was just confusing.

Dabney and Rowan came out to print the burglarized house, and the victims objected vociferously to being asked for their fingerprints.

"Do you think we broke into our own house?" exclaimed Mrs. Brophy. "I always knew cops are dumb, but that's too much!"

"No, ma'am," said Dabney patiently, "but you and your husband will have left a lot of prints around, and we have to know which are yours. In case the burglar left any, then we'll know which." He rolled the prints rapidly and offered Kleenex to wipe off the ink.

Maddox, D'Arcy and Rodriguez went out to lunch together at the Grotto. "You can have the rest of the day off," said Rodriguez. "Some of us had better do some leg-work tonight, looking for Dusty and Moose."

But absently, from force of habit, Maddox trailed back to Wilcox Street with them, half his mind still on that letter. On those prints. On that typewriter. He sat down at his desk and stared at the stuffed pink cat, and the cat smiled back at him.

The phone went off. "Yes, Johnny?"

"You must have had a premonition," said O'Neill, "coming in today. You've got a new homicide."

■ ■ ■

Patrolman Ben Loth had got used to this beat in central Hollywood now, but occasionally he still felt a little home-sick for a two-man car. Riding with a partner, you had somebody to talk to, eat with.

Today his shoulder was just a little stiff where the slug had creased it yesterday. It had barely bled at all, but it had singed his uniform, which was a nuisance. Ought to have known better, he thought afterward. Shots reported. He'd been a damn fool, just open that door to look in; a wonder he hadn't got himself killed. He did know better, but this usually quiet beat around here, maybe he'd got soft.

It was nearly one o'clock and he was getting hungry. He was cruising down Cahuenga Boulevard, coming up to Fountain, and suddenly he thought about those fat sand-wiches in old Mr. Wechsler's deli case, pastrami and cheese. He unhooked the mike and announced his car number. "Request Seven at Cahuenga and Fountain."

After a moment the impersonal female voice said, "Car X-four-four-seven, shows Seven at Cahuenga and Fountain."

Loth turned right on Fountain. There was a space by

210

the curb a couple of car lengths up from the little store. The small market and delicatessen was in a block of small stores, a couple of them empty and for lease now. There used to be a lot more walk-by trade here than there was now, since the new lead-in to the freeway had gone through and more apartments been built nearby.

He went in. There wasn't anybody in the front of the store, behind the counter. He walked over to the deli case; the sandwiches were there. "Mr. Wechsler?" he said. They were probably in the back room, maybe having a bite of lunch. With the familiarity of the cop on the beat, Loth walked behind the counter and into the rear room of the store.

"Mr. Wechs—" He stopped, aghast.

■ ■ ■

"But," said D'Arcy, "this is where there was all the fuss the other day—that kid with concussion claiming the old storekeeper had biffed him. I told you about it."

"So you did." There was a squad car up the street and an ambulance just turning the corner. Maddox slid the Maserati into the curb, and they got out and walked back.

It was Patrolman Ben Loth who came to meet them, and he looked utterly shocked and incredulous. "I still don't believe it," he said. "I couldn't. My God, old Rudi Wechsler, they've had this store so long it's a landmark—the kids stop by for snacks after school, the neighborhood people. I couldn't take it in, but—"

"What is it?" asked Maddox.

Loth just gestured, numbly. They went in.

The front of the store was empty. A typical little place, the neighborhood store. Shelves of cans and packages; a small refrigerator with the dairy goods. At the left side, another modest refrigerator case with the delicatessen goods, cold meats, cheese, sandwiches, potato salad. Maddox stepped behind the counter where a door led to a rear room.

It wasn't a big room, about nine by twelve. There was a back door, open, and beyond it they could see a bare shabby back yard and, at the rear of the lot, a little old frame house much in need of paint.

But the tableau in here was more interesting.

On the floor sprawled the body of a big gray-haired man. He was shabbily dressed in pants too short for him and a dirty work shirt. He was lying face down and there was a little mess of blood, still wet, at one side of the back of his head.

Sitting in an old straight chair by the back door was a fattish elderly man, his face in his hands and his shoulders bowed. There was a woman standing beside him, an elderly thin woman in a faded cotton dress.

Maddox squatted over the man on the floor. He was dead, only just dead: still warm and flaccid.

"Mr. Wechsler?" said D'Arcy in naked astonishment. "You mean—?"

The old man looked up slowly. "So," said the woman in a stolid voice, resigned, "it's come to nothing and you've killed a man, Papa. You see where it leads you. Now we both go to jail and you don't have to worry about money to live."

Maddox was going through the dead man's pockets. They were empty; he had nothing at all on him.

"Mr. Wechsler?" He stood up and went over to the old man. His voice was sharp, to penetrate Wechsler's dull abstraction. "Mr. Wechsler, who is this man?"

Wechsler said simply, "I don't know, sir. You see, it had to be a man nobody would miss. I made a mistake with that other young fellow. I put the ad in the paper. I

212

thought, If anybody comes, ask questions, find out if anyone will miss him. We don't need help. The business is
dead. Dead. After all the years, we work so hard, build it
up, save, have money for our old age—we never had any
family. But it's gone. We don't hardly make the rent any
more. And I worry about Selma—my wife. I'm ten years
older. It's only natural I go first and leave her with nothing
—nothing to show for all the years. But I made a mistake,
that young fellow. He came, he said he's just out of the
Army, never had a job here before, and I think it means
he's all alone, nobody here knows him. But I didn't—I
didn't hit him hard enough."

"I told him, give it up," said the woman. "When those
people came, I was afraid."

"But I had the plan all ready," said Wechsler painfully.
"It was wrong, but I thought, Somebody with nobody to
care about him, a—a bum, nobody misses him. It was for
Selma, that she shouldn't have to ask the charity, the pen-
sion. After all the work so we can have a good old age.
You've got to understand."

"Yes, Mr. Wechsler?" said Maddox quietly.

"The car, it's worth nothing—an old Ford. I'd put the
man in it, down some side street, pour gasoline on, set it
afire. It would all burn, and everybody think it was me
there—an accident. And the insurance would get paid. It's
ten thousand dollars. I stopped smoking my pipe to keep
paying the premiums on it, when things started getting
tight. It was the only way I saw. I could go off somewhere
quiet, like maybe up to Hemet—it's pretty up there—and
after the insurance got paid Selma could come. I know it
was wrong, but a man has to look after his own. Take care
of his wife, like it says in the marriage service. For better
or worse."

"And where did you meet this man?" asked Maddox.

The corpse was quite obviously a derelict: unshaven, dirty.

"After—after that young fellow, all the trouble, I thought I'd better be more sure," muttered Wechsler, "that it was a man nobody would care about. I—I went down this morning, to Main Street, downtown. I talked to men there."

Skid Row, where the derelicts drifted. "Yes?" said Maddox.

"This man, he said he wanted work. That he wasn't a drunk or a beggar, he wanted a job. I told him I had a job for him. I didn't believe him," said Wechsler. "He looked like a bum. But I told him—and I brought him here. In the Ford. I told Selma to give him lunch. And then—"

"And then you hit him. With what?"

Mutely Wechsler pointed. A hammer lay there on the floor, bloodstained.

"I had it all planned. And then, just then, Mr. Loth has to come."

"I said it was all wrong—foolish, Papa. We don't like to ask charity, but this was wrong."

The ambulance attendants were waiting. "Mr. Wechsler," said Maddox, "you'll have to come with us now. And we have to tell you about your rights. Are you all right, sir? You understand what I'm telling you?"

"I understand you," said Wechsler submissively. "But *you* got to understand. It was wrong, I knew it, but it was for Selma. Not fair, all the years we work, and at the end nothing—nothing! The neighborhood changes, people don't shop close to home, and it's not right we should ask charity paid for by good people can't hardly pay their taxes."

"Get the corpse's prints," said D'Arcy, sounding shaken. "Washington may know him."

"Yes. Come on, sir." Maddox urged him up gently. "You'll have to come too, Mrs. Wechsler."

"I know," she said mournfully. "I lied for him, before —because he is my husband, after all. But it was foolish."

In spades, thought Maddox, taking Wechsler out to the squad car. The lab examination, the autopsy, would have exposed the truth right off.

twelve

They'd just got the Wechslers into the station when the old woman went to pieces and Daisy and Sue took over.

"I'll leave the paperwork to the rest of you," said Maddox. "It's my day off, after all."

Rodriguez came over to ask what they'd got. "And we really ought to do some legwork tonight, if we're going to chase down that pair."

Maddox lit a cigarette. "I'll volunteer. But let's do it the easy way, César, minus the badges."

Rodriguez laughed and agreed. "Meet you here at eight, O.K.?"

Maddox had a little idea he wanted to look into, and now was as good a time as any. One of those anonymous letters, Mrs. Goulding had said, had been signed "Denis." He drove out to Lexington Avenue and parked and began ringing doorbells.

It was an old neighborhood, zoned for multiples as well as single houses, and there were old apartment buildings, one or two new ones and a scattering of old California bungalows. On the principle that homeowners were apt to be less transient and might know more about the neighborhood, he started out with the single houses, but an hour's effort turned up nothing: most of the houses were rented and nobody knew a Denis in the neighborhood.

It had started raining again. Maddox went home and settled down somnolently with *The Jungle Book*, and went to sleep on the couch.

He woke up with a start; the phone was ringing and it was pitch dark. He switched on a lamp hastily and went to pick up the phone. It was six twenty and Sue was at the other end, sounding exasperated.

"I'm stuck, darling. The car won't start. It's absolutely dead."

"I'll be over," said Maddox.

By the time he got there, she'd got Slade from the precinct garage, and he had the hood up. It had stopped raining. "You need a new set of spark plugs," said Slade. "These have had it. But so far as I can see that's the only thing wrong. Don't let some fast talker sell you anything else, Mrs. Maddox. You'll have to have her towed in."

"Damn!" said Sue crossly. "Of all the annoying things— and I'm starving to death."

"So am I," said Maddox. "Take you out to dinner again."

"Well, we'd better see about the car first."

Maddox went across to the office and called the Gulf station where they both usually stopped. The service manager was apologetic. "We'll come tow it in, sir, but I can't promise just when I'll get to it. Try to have it for you by Saturday, but I won't say definitely."

When Maddox broke that news, Sue said "Damn" again. "I'll have to borrow Mother's. It's a good thing Aunt Evelyn's here. She can take her to market and so on." They went to Musso and Frank's again, and Maddox said thoughtfully, over a drink, "At times it's useful to have the kind of beard that needs shaving twice a day."

"Yes, you look rather ruffianly," agreed Sue. "Why?"

"We're hitting the Strip tonight, hunting that pair on Moreno."

"Oh," said Sue. "Well, you be careful, is all I can say. Hopheads and nuts in those places. We'd better eat and run."

"I am not in such a rush to mingle with *hoi polloi*." But they got home at seven thirty and Maddox went to look in the closet, stripping off his jacket. Sue got on the phone.

"So I'll have to borrow yours, if that's all right. Just for a day or so. They said Saturday, but I'll take no bets I get it back till Monday."

"What a nuisance," said her mother. "But you'd better take Evelyn's, Sue. You know she doesn't like to drive here, so it'll work out better all around."

"Well, that's all right, so long as I've got transportation," said Sue. "Ivor'll drop me off in a few minutes, he's getting his costume on."

"What on earth?"

"Amateur theatricals. I do wonder what César looks like. He's as fastidious as a cat."

But when she surveyed Maddox five minutes later she merely shut her eyes and said, "Very convincing. You look like a third-rate villain out of a B movie."

He had on an ancient T shirt and shabby slacks, with a disreputable tan trench coat over them and the oldest shoes he owned. "You needn't insult my raincoat. I've had it for years and it's still perfectly good. The only effect I aimed at was not looking like a cop."

"You don't," said Sue with conviction.

He dropped her off at Janiel Terrace and went on to the station, where he found D'Arcy and Rodriguez waiting for him. Rodriguez, by just leaving off a tie, putting on old clothes and running fingers through his hair, had achieved a raffish air, like a professional gambler down on his luck;

D'Arcy in old clothes looked much the same, but he never had had COP written all over him, like George Ellis or even Feinman.

They took D'Arcy's car and left it in a public lot. "Split up?" said Rodriguez. They'd be wandering around about a four-block area.

"Skip the regular bars, concentrate on the discotheques and rock spots," said Maddox.

"And hope we don't run into any undercover Narco boys," said D'Arcy. If they did, they'd be sheriff's men; this side of the Strip was county territory.

"Meet back here in an hour and a half," said Maddox. "See if we've turned anything. It shouldn't take much time to check out these places." Minus the badges, the casual inquiry should turn up what there was. Even if Dusty and Moose were running scared after a homicide.

Like Rodriguez, Maddox felt sad: aimless, unoriented young people, sitting around with glazed eyes, hypnotized by the rock or something worse. He was in and out of ten places in the next hour, and in every one he spotted a few of the customers obviously under the influence. Never the liquor; pot or pills or the hard stuff. And as he'd expected, at several places he got the casual recognition.

"Yeah, I know Dusty, saw her at the Green Burro, last night or maybe the night before—"

"Moose, yeah, sure, he was askin' around for Benny last time I seen him. Man, he had some bread. Musta had a lucky hit—"

It went like that. They accepted him as the casual drifter, not one of them but not anything alarming or unusual either, but he didn't get anywhere.

"I don't pay no attention to where people got pads—or if they got. I never been to Moose's, wouldn't know where—"

"Dusty useta have a place with a couple other swingers

over Jamboree's disco," said one girl vaguely. He checked that out, but the hollow-eyed girl who opened the door told him Dusty'd moved out a while back.

"I dunno where she went. People come 'n' go," she said indifferently.

Toward the end of the hour and a half he was in a place called The Little Grass Shack, trying to talk to a serious bearded youth with horn-rimmed glasses who said he was writing a master's thesis on Habit Formation Patterns of Twentieth-Century Youth. It sounded about as sensible research as went into many other master's theses, but all Maddox was interested in was that the researcher claimed a wide acquaintance with the street people around here. Yes, he knew Dusty and supplied her last name: Hagan. He knew Moose; his name was Sellers and he came from Moosejaw.

For the last five minutes a slack-faced kid about eighteen, who was silly-giggling high probably on pot, had been annoying them, trying to get them to listen to jokes he couldn't remember, pulling at the researcher's arm, insistent on invitation to join an unspecified party. "Go away, Jerry, we can't bother with you now," said the researcher kindly. "It's very curious how conformist the youthful mind can be. The popular music, for instance, merely by means of publicity—"

"I'm just interested in locating them," said Maddox. "Do you know where either of them lives?"

"Come on, letsh all shing!" said Jerry. He wasn't high on liquor, but the effect was much the same.

"No idea, sorry. But it's quite fascinating how, for instance, these strange street names get attached. Moose, as I told you, is—"

"You talkin' about Moose? Good ol' Moose!" said Jerry, falling against Maddox. "Gi' me a fix f'r nothin' jus' yesserday. Letsh all go shee Moose."

Maddox grabbed his shoulder to keep him from falling down. "You know where his pad is, pal?"

"Sure, sure I know. Right up Sweetzer. Holly—Holly somethin'. Good ol' Moose gi' me a fix—"

"Say," said the researcher with sudden curiosity, "why are you so interested in finding Moose?"

"He owes me five bucks," said Maddox, and escaped outside with relief. He walked back to the lot and was leaning on D'Arcy's Dodge smoking a cigarette when the other two came up.

"Better check it out," said Rodriguez. "The way these people move around—" They moved the car up to Sweetzer. The city is a strange place when it comes to areas and authorities; there on the Strip they had been in the county, but the other side of Sunset was again the city of Los Angeles, their own territory.

About a block up was an ugly, twelve-unit, square modern apartment with HOLLY DAY APARTMENTS in script over its front door. They went in to a dim lobby and looked at the mailboxes. Only one had a name in its slot, and it wasn't Hagan or Sellers. In the end they started checking all the apartments, and at the fourth door they knocked on, they were confronted by a tall willowy blonde who was just not quite falling-down drunk. Her hair was over her eyes and she had on a pink bra and a pink bikini and that was all, and she had a glass tumbler in one hand.

"*¡Vaya por Dios!*" said Rodriguez appreciatively.

"Who're you? Well, nev' mind, come in 'n' join the party," she invited generously. "Y'know somethin'? Firsh time I ever was drunky—'n' itsh nishe! Tried the grash, 'n' the speed, but y'know what they shay ab-about th' al-co-hol"—she enunciated it carefully—"Moose said, try somethin' different—the champagne—an' itsh *nishe!* Have shome champagne, friendsh, we got gallonsh an' gallonsh!"

She waved one arm toward the champagne, which was

sitting on the floor against the wall, some five dozen bottles of it, some empty and some full. A big fat young man clad simply in swimming trunks was lying flat on his back, snoring, next to what looked like the console TV out of Carlos Moreno's Moorish castle. There was also the expensive stereo—they'd identify it by the serial number—and on inspection Maddox discovered that the sleeper was wearing three of Moreno's rings.

"Well, happy day," said Rodriguez. "Is there a phone? I'll go call a wagon. We won't be able to talk to them until tomorrow."

Maddox straightened up. But it was all so stupid, he thought tiredly. Not really much trouble to find out which girl Moreno had picked up, not really much trouble to find her. And the boy friend. Who had killed him? They'd probably sort that out without much trouble too. Most of the people cops spent their lives dealing with were stupid; the cunning master criminals were few and far between, and come to think, most of them were technically on the other side of the line, as politicians or financiers or something. But this particular effort had been so very damned stupid that Maddox wondered if a majority of the human race wasn't slipping backward these days.

The wagon came, and the uniformed men loaded them in—by that time the blonde had passed out too—and Maddox, Rodriguez and D'Arcy drove back to Wilcox Street.

On the way D'Arcy said, "Dabney picked up some pretty good latents on that burglary—probably the burglar's. They were on the plate of the lock that was pried open. Funny how people don't know about locks. With no deadbolt on it, they might as well not have a lock. Anyway, we sent the prints downtown. Maybe he's in our files."

Maddox got home at ten to eleven and found Sue sitting up in bed with a book. "Do any good?" she asked.

"These stupid damned little people," said Maddox. "I get tired. Just look around a little, and there they are. I want a shower." He looked at her there, trim and dark and pretty, his darling Sue, in a new nightgown, and he added, "But I must say you cheer me up. You look very fetching. And it's stopped raining for good."

"I noticed," said Sue. "I put on the electric blanket."

"Pending my arrival home?" said Maddox.

■ ■ ■

It had stopped raining for good, this time. The residents of Southern California, knowledgeable of their climate, realized that as they huddled under electric blankets. The biting icy cold slid down from the mountains all that night, and Friday morning was bright and chilly. Sue got up in time to make pancakes for breakfast.

And when Maddox came into the office, the pink cat smirked at him and he was annoyed. There was nowhere else to go on Dorrie; just keep the A.P.B. out and fingers crossed. That Denis: any use to look some more? What possible link could the anonymous letters have with Dorrie's disappearing act? And Monica's.

It was Dabney's day off. D'Arcy said, "We had a report from S.I.D. They don't know those prints. They've sent 'em to the Feds."

Not much had gone down overnight but a hit-run out on Santa Monica, with nothing to follow up on. The victim, an elderly woman, was D.O.A.

Maddox called the county jail and asked when they could talk to Dusty and Moose. They had now been identified, by drivers' licenses and, surprisingly in Dusty's case, a Social Security card, as Ina May Brown and John Hugh Sellers, respectively twenty-one and twenty-three.

The matron he talked to said dryly, "Sergeant, have a heart. When those two come to they're going to have king-size hangovers and you wouldn't get much sense out of them anyway. It must have been quite a party."

"Champagne all the way," said Maddox. "When?"

"Leave 'em in peace this morning. After lunch, maybe. I've got a recipe for a pick-me-up."

Maddox laughed; they left it at that. As he put down the phone, a heavy-shouldered man in a tan jumpsuit came in. "The sergeant downstairs said to come up," he said querulously.

"Yes, sir. What can we do for you?" Rodriguez and D'Arcy still had paperwork on Engelhard, on Wechsler; Maddox got him settled in the chair beside his desk.

"What you can do, damn it, is find the bastards that walked off with my heavy construction equipment! My name's Nichols, Weston T. Nichols, and I own the Nichols Construction Company. And of course the damn rain stopped work at this new apartment site, up on Vista, and so this morning I go take a look at the job, see if the rain's washed out the excavation any, and the damn equipment is gone. A bulldozer and a fork lift. They'd be worth five Gs apiece even secondhand."

Maddox stared at him. Now here, he thought, was a thief who Thought Big. "Were they locked?" he asked.

"Of course they were locked! Like a car. But like a car, you can hot-wire them if you know how. I suppose that was how they did it. And of course they got commercial plates on. I can give you the numbers."

But where, Maddox wondered, could you possibly fence a bulldozer? Well, the thief must have had a market in mind. He began to take down the particulars.

Half an hour after Nichols had gone away, reiterating that he expected action on this and they'd better do something, a call came in from downtown: the highway patrolman shot by Connors had just died, after hanging on this long. They hadn't known him, but he had been a cop, and whatever else cops may be deficient in, fellow feeling is not one. There'd probably be a collection started for his widow; he'd only been thirty-six.

The stupid little pros—and amateurs—thought Maddox, made a lot more trouble for the world than was really necessary.

■ ■ ■

When Maddox and Rodriguez saw Dusty and Moose it was in one of the bare interrogation rooms at the county jail, with a rather good-looking police matron sitting beside Dusty. Neither of them looked anywhere near so happy as they had last night. Dusty was pale and wan, her long blond hair combed back into an unbecoming flat pony tail; the plain tan jail uniform seemed to bother her. Moose was slack-jawed and glassy-eyed, his fat shoulders humped. Awake, he had shallow gray eyes and a soft mouth.

"So," said Maddox to start the ball rolling, "was that the first time you'd gone with Moreno, Miss Brown, or had you marked him for a sucker before?"

She looked at them mournfully. "Gee, I nearly forgot that's who I am—Miss Brown. Sounds funny. Listen, are you nuts? I wouldn't—"

"Let's not go the long way around," said Rodriguez. "We've got all the loot you took there that you hadn't got rid of yet. We know you were with him. Last Sunday night."

"Did I say I wasn't? I've got some sense. You damn fuzz seen all that stuff now—sure you know it. But I'd never gone with him before. I'd heard people talk, other girls. Dirty old man picking up girls—what's it to me? I'm not that kind." She was a little indignant about it. "Now listen, I'm not tellin' you no lies, fuzz. You got us, but I want you to see straight how it was. God, I've still got a head." They waited while the matron got her some aspirin. She sat slumped on the straight chair, looking sorry for herself.

"All right, let's hear it," said Maddox. They'd given them their rights before anybody said a word; neither of them had reacted, only nodded.

"Well, so if I got to tell you, just get it straight. I'm not tellin' you I haven't slept around some, but I never did it for money—I'm not that kind of girl. I dunno why I took up with lover boy here, unless I was sorry for him, but there it was—and we were really strapped for some bread, see."

"Either of you with a habit to support?" asked Rodriguez.

"Gee, no! The grass once in a while, that's all. Not regular. But we were real broke. I had a job dancing in one o' those topless places, but I got fired. Just before I quit. The combo all had six hands apiece."

"So?" said Maddox.

"So"—she let out a sigh—"I owed twenty-five on my room and the landlady kicked me out. Moose still had a pad, room with some other guys, and he took my stuff to keep for me. All right, I'm *getting* there. Sunday night I was in the disco and saw that guy. I remembered what the other girls said, he's got a roll, and I was kind of desperate, see. I never meant to let him put a hand on me—*that* old guy, about a hundred, and who knows what kooky ideas he's got—but I go get Moose and I said, Maybe we can roll him."

"What about it, Mr. Sellers?" asked Rodriguez.

"Yeah," said Moose with an effort. "Yeah, that's what she said. She'd pick him up and I was supposed to follow 'em."

"You have a car?" asked Maddox.

"Sure I got a car. Who hasn't got a car? Kind of beat up but runs. 'N' I did. Follow 'em."

"Only not fast enough," said Dusty with a shiver. "The guy had a Merc, real sharp, and before I *knew* it we were up on that road in the hills and he was pattin' my knee and sayin' we'd have a real good time, and I thought, Where the hell's Moose? There wasn't a car behind us. I thought, Oh, my God, he's lost us, and I begin to get scared. I wasn't about to go to bed with this creep if he paid me five Gs—or five million, see?"

"Go on," said Rodriguez. The matron was looking amused. Moose just sat.

"Well, we got to that place—my God, like a castle or something—and just as I got out of the car, thinking maybe I better run, only I had on high heels and that road was awful steep, I hear Moose's car coming up. The guy left the Merc in a garage there, didn't shut the door, so I knew Moose'd see it and know where I was. And we went up about a thousand steps into this place. He didn't turn on many lights but I can see it's a place there's money, all right. And then all of a sudden we're in this big bedroom, and he's pawing at me and I'm scared again. I couldn't hear Moose anywhere. He said he'd get in a window—"

"Damn place on a hill," said Moose thickly. "I couldn't get *near* a window. Front door was locked. I fin'ly got in a kind of glass door to one side—it wasn't locked." Later on, S.I.D. would identify his prints from that, out of the bunch they'd picked up there, but his hadn't been on file anywhere, or hers either.

"Now I'm telling you," she said earnestly, "I been around—I worked around and all—and a long time ago I learned, a girl alone, she better carry something for the wolves. See? I used to carry a can of pepper, but you better believe me, mister, these days that isn't enough. So I got a switchblade. It's in my bag."

"Not any more," said Rodriguez. They'd asked for a search warrant for that apartment last night; it hadn't come through yet, but they'd found the knife in her bag, there in plain sight on the couch. It was now down at the lab.

"Well, anyways! I kept stalling him and listening and looking for Moose, and my God, first thing I know the old guy's stark naked and pullin' at me—he tore my dress half off, he got me onto the bed, and I'm not *about* to get myself raped—dirty old guy old enough to be my grandfather. I still had hold of my bag, and I got the switchblade out an' just—just sort of beat him off, like. I didn't mean to *kill* him! I just wasn't about to let him—" Suddenly she sniffed, even sorrier for herself. "I—we never knew he was dead, or that he used to be that old movie star, until I saw the headline a couple days later."

"So Moose finally got there?" said Maddox.

"Yeah. And we went all through the drawers and found a lot of loot—about seven Cs in cash, and jewelry—and then when we got downstairs Moose says, Get the TV and all. We had to make two trips, get the stereo too."

"You've been living high on the cash, but why didn't you fence the rest?" asked Rodriguez curiously.

She looked at them, a little offended. "We aren't pros," she said. "We got that nice new pad, and sure, we had a ball on the cash. But I only been in L.A. about four months. I don't know the place good. Neither does Moose. How'd we know a fence? I figured, when the cash ran out, hock the jewelry—"

"So we'd have caught up to you then," said Maddox. "It's on the hot list sent to all pawnbrokers."

She looked annoyed. "You damn fuzz got it figured six ways from Sunday! Well, anyways, that's how it happened. I didn't mean to kill the guy, just take his roll."

"Mr. Sellers? You back all that up?"

"Oh, yeah," said Moose. "Yeah. Nobody ever meant to hurt the guy. We just wanted the bread, man."

■ ■ ■

There'd be the report to write on it, and probably some discussion at the D.A.'s office what to call it. That wasn't their business. Conceivably Dusty and Moose might get by with murder-two—no premeditation. Mr. Wechsler, reflected Maddox, wouldn't be so lucky; they'd call that murder-one.

He left Rodriguez to write the report and went out again, feeling the eyes of the pink cat on him. Damn it, if he checked out every useless little lead, every scrap of vague evidence, on Dorrie, maybe sometime the thing would take on some shape.

He'd worked up one side of the block and down the other, yesterday. Today, for no reason, he began with a side street, St. Andrews Place. There weren't any apartments in this little backwater, only old single houses and a couple of duplexes.

And at the first house he tried, a nice-looking old lady said, "Anybody named Denis? Why, of course there's Denis Kohler, poor boy. Two doors down. But he's harmless. Why are you asking? Is anything wrong?"

Maddox thanked her and went two houses down. The woman who answered the door was fat and middle-aged, with a frilly apron round her middle. "Denis?" she said, and her expression sharpened. "Oh, he hasn't done anything wrong, has he, sir? He never does anything. I'd keep a sharper eye on him, but he never does any harm. He's, you know, retarded—he's twenty-five but the doctor says the mind of a six-year-old—but he's a good boy. I raised him to be nice and polite. I let him go as he pleases. Most people in the neighborhood know him and don't mind, and—but you're not from around here, are you? Why're you asking?"

Maddox didn't frighten her with the badge. "Nothing wrong," he said. "We think he wrote some notes to a young woman over on Lexington. Nothing bad. He just admired her."

"Oh, he shouldn't do that. He can write, yes, sir—like a six-year-old, you know." She went away and brought Denis back with her. He was a nice-looking young man, tall and gawky, with a weak girlish face; he smiled shyly at Maddox. "Denis, did you write some letters to a lady around here?"

He blushed slowly and looked at the floor. "She's—a beautiful lady. Prettiest I ever saw. I—I—I just wanted— just tell her—"

"Dear, you mustn't," she said. "I'm sorry, sir, I'll keep an eye on him and see it doesn't happen again."

"It doesn't matter," said Maddox. "She's—gone now."

And that was another dead end, and really the last one, wasn't it?

■ ■ ■

About four o'clock Patrolman Carmichael brought in a high school girl named Pansy O'Brien. He said she'd nearly given him a heart attack, jumping out of the car ahead of him down on Highland. "Might have killed yourself," he said severely, looking at her. "That car was doing about twenty. I took her to First Aid first—she's just got a couple of cuts."

She smiled shakily at him. "I was just *so glad* to see a police car, I didn't think. Thank you very much, Mr. Carmichael."

"Well, you're all right," said Carmichael, "but don't you get in a car with strangers again." He went out.

230

"What happened, Pansy?" asked Daisy. "You'd better tell us about it. I'm Mrs. Hoffman and this is Mrs. Maddox."

"Are you both policewomen? It must be a *very* interesting job," said Pansy. She was about sixteen and a pretty girl, brown-haired and brown-eyed, with a rose-leaf complexion and a nice slim figure. "Well, it wasn't—that was it—as if they were exactly strangers. They're senior boys, Steve Williams and Jack Stover. We didn't *know* them, but we knew who they *were*. Senior boys at school. Hollywood High. I'm a sophomore."

"Yes," said Sue encouragingly. There would be paperwork still going on, down in the D.A.'s office, on that messy homicide. She wondered irrelevantly how Mr. Holderby was doing.

"Well, I was with Marge—she's not my best friend but pretty good—when they came up to us and asked us to go for malts. And—well, seniors—Marge was thrilled but I felt sort of funny about it, only I thought it wasn't like going alone with one of them. But once we got in Steve's car and away from school, *goodness*," said Pansy, and blushed furiously. "Jack got terribly—what Mother calls fresh, if you know what I mean—I mean, he got his arm around me and he was—*well*, I was just scared to death, and Mother always says to *bite* if you have to, so I did, and he yelled, and then I looked out and saw the police car in the next lane behind, so I just—and Steve gunned the car so Mr. Carmichael couldn't—"

"He was too busy picking you up," said Sue. "You did just right, Pansy."

"Well, I know you can't *arrest* them for it. But thank goodness Mr. Carmichael was there," said Pansy.

She lived down on McCadden Place. "I'll take you home," said Sue.

"That's awfully nice of you, Mrs. Maddox. Do you mind if I ask you something? Does your husband mind your being a policewoman?"

"Well, I don't think so," said Sue, laughing. "You see, he's a sergeant of detectives here."

"Ooh!" said Pansy, impressed.

At the end of the afternoon Sue had just changed out of uniform. Picking up her coat, she took Pansy downstairs.

Sue's Chrysler, presently sitting at the station awaiting new spark plugs, had automatic transmission. She'd learned to drive on a stick shift, but it had been years since she'd driven one, and Aunt Evelyn's eight-year-old Chevy had a clutch. She had to remember consciously to use it; and still a couple of times, just the short while she'd been driving it, she'd killed the engine.

She remembered the clutch and drove Pansy home to McCadden Place. "Thank you *very* much," said Pansy.

"And you just remember," said Sue, "to bite when you have to."

Pansy gave her a joyous smile and skipped up the walk. Sue went around the block and headed north on McCadden for Melrose. She caught the light there and waited, remembering the clutch: forward and to the right for second, all the way back for high. The light changed, she stepped on the accelerator and shifted into second, making a right onto Melrose.

A car came up close beside her as she glanced at the rearview mirror to see if it was safe to change lanes. It was really very close, and Sue shied the Chevy away instinctively.

"I beg your pardon, miss," called a deferential voice, "but I'll have to ask you to pull over. Police officers, miss. Please pull into the curb."

She took them in with one swift comprehensive glance:

olive-green Dodge, unmarked, four-door 1967 model; two men in the front seat, navy-blue uniforms.

"Oh, dear," she said. She pulled the Chevy into the next available curbside space; it was just outside a small independent drugstore on the corner. The Dodge double-parked ahead, and both uniformed men got out and came back to her. "Did I do something wrong?" she asked anxiously.

"I'm afraid so, miss. You signaled too soon for that turn. I guess you visitors don't know all our traffic rules. I'm sorry, we'll have to give you a ticket. May I see your license, please?"

"Oh, dear, how annoying!" said Sue. What she was thinking of was the probable unavailability of the out-of-state tourists as witnesses, once it got to court. Luckily nothing on a driver's license specified jobs, but of course it was a California license. She opened her purse. "Will I have to go to court?"

"Well, a moving-violation offense, yes, I'm afraid so." They were both nice-looking, young, open-faced, polite: one sandy, one dark. "But you can get out of it, miss, if you'd like to pay the fine now—ten dollars. We'll give you a receipt for it, and that'll take care of it."

Sue batted her eyelashes at them. "Oh. I've only got two weeks here—" And what a piece of luck, the Chrysler going dead so she was driving the Chevy with Arizona plates, and them picking her at random. "Ten dollars?"

"Yes, miss. Then you won't have to go to court."

"Oh, dear," said Sue, "such a muddle my purse gets into." She got out of the car, set her working-size handbag down on the fender, produced her license and a ten-dollar bill. "You'll give me a receipt?"

"Oh, yes, miss." The dark one brought out a tablet and scribbled on it, gave it to her. "Here you are. That takes care of it O.K."

"Indeed it does," said Sue crisply, bringing out the Colt .32 from her bag. "Feet apart, up against the car!"

"What the hell?"

"You made a little mistake," said Sue, "in stopping a real L.A.P.D. officer. We've been hoping to drop on you for some time. Did you hear me? Up against the car!" She poked the gun at them. They moved reluctantly.

"But, for God's sake, an out-of-state car—"

"My God, Joe, of all the lousy luck! It was going like magic! It was a hell of a good idea."

"So it was," said Sue. She patted them down; neither was armed. "March—up to the drugstore!" They marched. There weren't any customers inside, fortunately. She said to the open-mouthed clerk, "Call the police—six-five-five oh-two-four-one—and tell them to send a car up here fast."

"But, they're policemen!"

"Not by any chance," said Sue. "I'm the cop—as you can see by the badge if you'll look."

■ ■ ■

D'Arcy was feeling morose. Sometimes, all the stupidity and violence and irrational wrongdoing made him feel pessimistic about people. That Moreno business—he'd just finished writing up the report—was pretty stupid. All of them had been stupid: Moreno and Dusty and Moose.

Reluctantly he grinned, thinking about Sue Maddox and her triumphant capture. She and Carmichael had marched them in here like gladiators, and she and Daisy were still talking to them across the hall. Well, it was just as well to have the phony cops off the street; they ruined the image, you could say. But she'd be boring Ivor with it—or maybe not; he was in love with her, thought D'Arcy.

Him thinking he'd been in love with that scatterbrained Sheila. Well, a narrow escape, that was all. Better take a long careful look at any female after this.

It was a quarter to five. An hour and a quarter more on duty. He got up and wandered out to the hall. He was hungry, and there wasn't anything pressing to do right now. He fished change out of his pocket and went up to the sandwich machine, put two quarters in the slot and pulled the lever labeled *Beef*.

The machine clanked obligingly. He waited, and when he figured the thing was about to deliver the wrapped sandwich, he reached for it with his left hand, into the long tube.

The machine grabbed his fingers and started pulling. A set of rollers, it felt like, pulling hard.

"Hey!" said D'Arcy, and pulled his hand back, or tried to. The rollers held on, and slowly the tips of his fingers were pulled in farther.

"Hey, help!" roared D'Arcy, and heard Rodriguez running, but he'd be too late. D'Arcy jerked out his gun and began firing at the sandwich machine blindly. It gave a loud clank and stopped.

With Rodriguez's help, D'Arcy pulled his hand out. The fingers were bleeding and cut.

"You'd better go down to First Aid," said Rodriguez. "I said that machine was a mistake. Maybe Slaney's right— they're all set to take over."

thirteen

Maddox got back to the office to find D'Arcy still shaken, just up from First Aid with his hand bandaged. Rodriguez and Ellis were inspecting the sandwich machine. "Well, I don't suppose he did it any good," said Maddox, surveying the bullet holes.

"If you ask me," said Rodriguez, "I think Slaney's right; these machines are figuring on getting rid of us. But you missed the rest of the excitement, and your wife's the heroine of the day."

"What? What's happened?" He went in search of Sue, who was telling it all over for Feinman's benefit.

"And talk about nerve. When we questioned them and had a look at their I.D., we found they'd been using their own names on those receipts—Robert Dillon and Norman Grenfell. They came apart right away—you know con men. They've both got pedigrees with us. But of all the luck, just because I was driving Aunt Evelyn's car." Sue was pleased with herself, as well she might be.

"Congratulations," said Maddox, also pleased with her. "I'm glad to know those birds are out of our hair, anyway.

We might have gone hunting for a year and never dropped on them."

Sue cocked her head at him; she had, after all, been married to him for a while and knew this and that about him. "You could sound happier about it."

Maddox lit a cigarette and stood looking at it. "I just found Denis," he said. "The anonymous letter writer. And that really was the last dead end. There's nowhere else to go." He told them about Denis.

"Just a big blank," said Sue. "You'd think something would have showed by now. And the baby. Oh, she must have gone of her own volition, Ivor. Somewhere. In a hurry, but—for a reason."

"I'm rather siding with our cynical César," said Daisy. "She won't thank you if you do find her."

Maddox just shook his head. "I'd still like to hear her cuss me out for finding her shacked up with the jaded millionaire."

Some benefit accrued to him from that afternoon's work, however. Sue went home early and produced the special beef Stroganoff.

■ ■ ■

"Did you hear about D'Arcy and the sandwich machine?" asked Donaldson as Brougham came in. "O'Neill got such a kick out of it he left us a note."

"Hopewell was telling me. What's it look like?" Curious, they went down the hall to inspect it. The bullet holes had somewhat altered its expression. "It looks as if D'Arcy killed it dead." Experimentally Brougham pulled a lever.

The sandwich machine uttered a subdued clink and instantly delivered four wrapped sandwiches into the slot. "My God," said Donaldson, "the slugs primed it to give 'em away." There was one sandwich of each kind. They took them back to their desks appreciatively. "Oh, and those phony cops. Of all the luck going for us, they pulled Sue Maddox over and—" The phone rang.

"Yum?" said Brougham through cheese sandwich.

"You've got shots fired and a probable assault, a bar down on Western," said Sergeant Hopewell, adding the address.

"O.K., we're on it."

The ambulance was there by the time they found the address, in Donaldson's car. But the wounded man was sitting at a table by the door laughing intermittently and clutching one arm. "D-damndest thing I ever saw!" he said. "Funniest damn thing I ever saw." He was a young man in a white jumpsuit with *Al's Electronics* on the back.

There was another young man sitting beside him, looking pale. "Jeez, Eddy, I didn't mean to hurt you! You aren't hurt bad, are you? Look, you better let the ambulance guys look at you—you're bleeding. I never meant to hurt you."

Gomez had called in the report; he was looking disgusted. "These damn practical jokers," he said.

Donaldson bent over the laughing man. "If you're hurt, you'd better—let me see your arm, sir."

"You more cops?" said the friend. "Look, I shot him, but I never meant to! It just startled me so."

"What?" asked Donaldson.

"Oh, brother!" said the bleeding one. "Never saw anything so damn funny. S-see?" He held out a box at Donaldson and opened it and a big snake jumped out, and Donaldson leaped backward like a ballet dancer and fell over a table. The wounded one collapsed in mirth again and Gomez came to help Donaldson up.

"It's a wonder you didn't get yourself killed," he said to the practical joker. "Of all the damn fool things to do."

"It's just p-p-plastic," said the joker. "Pete only creased me with the gun, but it was so damn funny—"

The ambulance attendants said it was nothing serious but they'd take him in for first aid. The friend attempted to go with him, and Brougham pulled him back. "Just a minute, sir. Let's see that gun. Have you got a permit to carry it?"

"Oh, yeah, yeah, it's all kosher. I'm a trucker, cross-country, and about half the time I'm hauling explosives or something, and what with all these damn kids blowing up things, the boss said I'd better be armed." He had a permit, and the gun was a new Police Positive .38. They got his name, and the name of the man with the snake, and went back to the office.

"It just strikes me, Dick," said Donaldson, "that we've been getting the offbeat little things this last week. The funny things."

"Yeah," said Brougham thoughtfully. "And that pink cat is the funniest. If it stays there much longer I'm going to have to hang around until the day watch comes on and ask Maddox why in hell he's got it there."

They tossed for who would write the report, and Donaldson lost.

■ ■ ■

On Saturday morning the report about the man with the snake was on Maddox's desk. It had been a quiet night after that, with nothing turning up for the detectives and just the usual run of D. and D.s and accidents for the patrolmen on tour.

Maddox was sitting looking at the cat when Dabney came in just head of Rodriguez and D'Arcy. "And I do not believe it," he said, "but fingerprints don't lie. Central didn't have this burglar's, so they sent them to the Feds. They know him. Report just came in."

"Who is he?" asked D'Arcy, flexing his bandaged hand gingerly.

"You won't believe it," said Dabney. "His name is Peter Swenson and he escaped from the Illinois pen twenty-seven years ago. He was in for life for murdering his wife."

"*¡Caray!*" said Rodriguez. "Twenty-seven years! He's going to be damn mad at himself for not wearing gloves, isn't he?"

Dabney looked at the teletype again. "I will say he should be easy to spot if we ever get any lead. He's six foot seven and weighs—well, I suppose he could be fat or thin, but he'll still be six foot seven—and he's got a port-wine mark on his left cheek. He'll be about sixty-seven now."

"And anywhere in the county," said Rodriguez, "of which the population is now—"

"Don't be such a wet blanket," said D'Arcy. "I had a thought on that burglary. It's a very modest house, doesn't look as if there'd be much loot there, but there was. Brophy had a brand-new shotgun, and a lot of rolls of silver dollars, some gold coins. I know the pros don't always pick a place with loving care, but it did occur to me to wonder, Did the burglar know what was there? I don't think it'd do any harm to go and ask the Brophys if they recognize that description."

"Talk about simpleminded," said Rodriguez rudely, "that really is."

"I'll agree with you if it doesn't check out," said D'Arcy. "What the hell am I going to say to the I.A. boys, by the way?"

"To—oh!" said Maddox. Any time an L.A.P.D. man had occasion to fire his gun, whether he hit anything or not, Internal Affairs held a hearing to decide if he'd had legitimate reason.

"It's going to sound pretty stupid," said D'Arcy gloomily, "to say I was attacked by a sandwich machine."

"Well, you can show them your hand as evidence," said Maddox. "They can hardly claim you weren't attacked by something."

Ellis came in, looking annoyed, as D'Arcy went out; he had in tow a big man in a plaid wool shirt and jeans. "This is Mr. Singer—Sergeant Maddox. Mr. Singer's lost a bulldozer."

"Right off the site," said Singer. "I'm foreman on the job, new office building on Santa Monica. And the damn bulldozer, do we move it away every night? It was locked, but—"

"But they can be hot-wired like a car," said Maddox. "You've got the commercial plate number, I trust."

"I have. And how in hell would a thief ever find a fence to take a bulldozer, for God's sake?"

Ellis waited until Singer had signed a complaint and gone, to say, "Damn it, I went over to look at the other site, and there's just a hole in the ground, nothing to see, like footprints. How the hell do we work this, drive all over the county looking at plate numbers on construction equipment?"

"I think," said Maddox, "whoever's stealing it must know where he can sell it. It could be a ring. We'll ask Central to have a look in the files for the same M.O., and if they can't turn anything we'll ask N.C.I.C."

But as he started to write the report, he felt the cat's eyes on him.

■ ■ ■

About ten thirty Ben Loth brought in a young teen-age boy and said to Sue and Daisy, "You'd better follow up on this." He looked serious, and they both got up and joined him in the hall, leaving the boy in the office.

"What's the story?" asked Daisy.

Loth grimaced. "These kids!" he said. "I came across these two in an empty lot up on Fountain. That one"—he jerked his head—"was trying to bring the other one to. I got an ambulance in a hurry. I could see for pretty sure it was an O.D., and the attendants said so too. My God, they can't be over fifteen. That one's got a few needle marks on him, so I brought him in. He said the other kid's name is Dave Dankenburg. He's Tom Ferdig."

"Nice," said Sue. "Thanks so much." They went back into the office. The boy was sitting in the straight chair beside Daisy's desk. He wasn't a very big boy, thin and dark, with lank black hair falling over one eye. He was dressed in shabby corduroy pants and a blue shirt with a gabardine jacket over it, not very warm clothes for this chilly day. He looked, in fact, cold and uncomfortable. He didn't say anything when they came in, just looked up warily; he had brown eyes and lashes a girl would envy.

"Your name's Tom Ferdig?" asked Daisy briskly.

He nodded once. "How's—how's Dave?" he asked in a thin voice.

"Well, they've taken him to the hospital. In a while we'll call and find out," said Daisy. "What happened to him?"

Tom's face tightened up. "Well, I—well, I guess you heard. I guess that last stuff was—kind of strong, and—Dave got too much, is all."

"An overdose. Of what?" asked Sue.

He blinked and looked down. "Horse," he muttered. "It's just since—about last week, that Dave—he'd only got to mainlining it maybe like yesterday, but I guess—"

They didn't have to look at each other. "How old is Dave?" asked Daisy expressionlessly.

"Uh—fifteen. So'm I."

"Are you on it too?"

"I—I guess." He didn't look at them. "Some guys at school got us to try it. They give us some first, didn't ask nothing for it. And then—"

Sue could feel Daisy boiling; she was simmering a little herself. What particular corner in hell was reserved for that kind, the pushers who deliberately got the other kids hooked so they'd turn to thievery, to anything, for the loot to support the habit?

"You live around here, Tom? With your parents?"

"There's just Mom. She's divorced from my dad. We live on Harvard."

"Would your mother be home now?"

"You gonna call her?" He looked only a little scared. "No, she's at work. She works waiting on table at a place on Santa Monica."

They wanted to hear something more about the pushers, but first things first. "Will you please take everything out of your pockets and put it on my desk, Tom," said Daisy.

He didn't move for a minute, and then he said, "I haven't got any. I been—kind of worried—about that. I and Dave were going to see the guy sold him what he'd just got yesterday—because I guess I'll be needing some pretty soon."

"Come on," said Daisy kindly. He stood up slowly and began to take things out of his pockets. There was a wad of bills, a key on a chain, a handkerchief, some loose change, a candy bar.

"Where's the hypo?" asked Daisy. "You said you were mainlining?"

"Just the last couple days. I—I got one from the guy at school. It's home hid under the mattress on my bed."

Sue was automatically counting the money; they'd have to make out a receipt. The bills added to two hundred and eight dollars. "Where'd you get all this, Tom?"

He sat down again, looking as if he wanted to cry. "I

stole some ladies' purses—one at a time, I mean—in a department store. The Broadway. Yesterday and today. I almost got caught once, but it was crowded." He looked at her, and now he was really scared. "I—I—we didn't know how it'd be—after the first couple times, like—like you *got to have it*—just, it don't seem no time since the first, and I—I never did anything bad like that before."

Maybe there was hope for Tom, with some conscience still in him, and he hadn't been hooked long. "So now you'll tell us who the boys were," began Daisy.

He looked confused. "We aren't s'posed to tell. Rat on anybody to the cops. You don't do like that."

"Look, Tom," said Daisy patiently. "You don't like having to use this stuff, do you? Having to steal to buy it?" He shook his head, thinking about it. "You know it makes people kill and steal and—do all sorts of wrong things because they have to have it. Once they get hooked. You understand that?" He nodded. "Well, do you think you owe any loyalty to those boys who got you into this?"

"You aren't s'posed to fink on anybody. Everybody says." He was more confused.

Sue began to count the change and stopped. After a moment she got up, exchanging a glance with Daisy, and went out to the main office.

Her spouse was absent, but Rodriguez was there, looking over a report. "César," said Sue, "Ivor said something about that Walter Ilinsky having his good-luck piece stolen when he got mugged. He told me about it. What does this look like to you?"

Rodriguez took the thing and looked it over. It was an old medal, bronze, a little over an inch in diameter, with a big ring fastened to the top and a much-faded ribbon of red, white and blue attached to that. On the face of it was a winged figure in robes, holding a sword and shield, with a rayed aura. On the opposite side was a U.S. shield with superimposed on it a kind of stylized Roman fasces, the X-tied bundle of sticks symbolizing unity. Around the top ran the legend *The Great War for Civilization,* and on either side of the central symbol ran the names in bas-relief —*France, Italy, Serbia, Japan, Montenegro, Russia, Greece, Great Britain, Belgium, Portgual, Rumania, China.* "I'll be damned," said Rodriguez. "Where'd you get it?" She told him. "One thing, there can't be many of these hanging around after all this time." He laughed. "The great war for civilization. I'd better talk to this kid."

In the other office, Daisy was still reasoning with the boy. "Getting hooked on heroin can not only spoil your whole life but maybe kill you, Tom. Do you think those boys really deserve—"

"Hi, Tom," said Rodriguez. "Like to tell me where you got this?" He held out the medal on his palm.

"Who're you?" asked Tom in a thin voice.

"Detective Rodriguez. Where'd you get it?"

"It isn't worth anything," said Tom warily. "It's just ole junk."

"No, it isn't worth anything," Rodriguez agreed. "Less than nothing. But I'd like to know where you got it."

Tom was silent and then he said, "It—it was in that man's pocket, I guess."

"What man?"

"Well, that—that guy we knocked down one night. A while ago. Last week, I guess. Because we—I and Dave— we needed some bread. For the stuff. It was just after we started, after those fellows—"

"And you knocked a man down and robbed him. Remember where?"

"I guess it was a street up—there was a parkin' lot and it was dark," said Tom miserably. "And he only had six dollars on him."

"Did you know you nearly killed him?" asked Rodriguez. "Which of you picked up that two-by-four?"

"Dave, I guess. Well, the guy was a lot bigger than us. He knocked me down once."

"Now look, Tom," said Daisy firmly, and the phone rang. She picked it up. "Sergeant Hoffman, Wilcox Street."

"We were asked to inform you," said an impersonal female voice. "The boy the patrolman sent in about forty-five minutes ago. We couldn't bring him around. It was a massive overdose."

"He's dead," said Daisy. "I see. Thank you." She put the phone down.

"*D-Dave?*" said Tom incredulously. "*Dave's dead?*"

Daisy nodded. "Do you think you'd better tell us now?" He burst into tears.

■ ■ ■

So when Maddox came back from Communications, with exactly nothing from N.C.I.C., there was that waiting: the names of three senior boys at Hollywood High. "And what do you bet," he said to Rodriguez, "they tie into our little homicide there the other day? If they can supply the H, they can probably supply the acid. At least we've got the Ilinsky thing cleared up. Of all the damned queer things." He looked at the medal curiously.

"They ought," said Rodriguez, "to have buried one of those in that time capsule. For our descendants to marvel at. The great war for civilization."

"Indeed," said Maddox. "There seems to be less of it around every time I look. Well, things to do about this. And I suppose Mr. Ilinsky would like his medal back."

But before they started the paperwork on it, D'Arcy came in and said complacently, "You should be so simpleminded. The Feds tell us who to look for, so here he is."

"My God!" said Rodriguez. He and Maddox both stared at the man D'Arcy had with him. He was a thin old man who topped D'Arcy by several inches, and he had a small port-wine mark on one cheek. He was looking ready to cry.

"I never did think about the FBI," he said in a cracked tenor. "About fingerprints. It's been so long."

"The Brophys knew him," said D'Arcy. "He rents a room from the widow next door. They'd got chatty over the back fence."

"Rabbits out of hats," said Maddox.

"Been calling himself Andrew Green," said D'Arcy. "You can sit down, Mr. Swenson."

He sat down and looked at them piteously. "Maybe it's for the best," he said. "I've never done anything wrong at all since I got out of the pen. Worked regular, honest jobs. But just lately, I knew I was goin' to get fired. I been working as a painter, but my eyes are givin' out on me, and the doctor says he can't give me any stronger glasses. The only reason I ever did such a thing, rob the Brophys, I wanted to get my car paid off. So I'd at least have that when I got fired."

"Well, you needn't worry about that now," said D'Arcy.

"I guess not. I guess I'll go back to the pen," said Swenson. "It'll seem funny, after all these years."

■ ■ ■

They got the paperwork started on that, and Sue and Daisy took Tom Ferdig up to the receiving hospital for examination. They had a quick lunch at the Grotto, and Sue went to locate Mrs. Ferdig at the restaurant on Santa Monica.

Mrs. Marion Ferdig was already defeated by life, expecting the worse to happen. "I never suspected a thing," she said, sniffing. "Tom's always been a good boy. But it's hard, raising a boy without a husband. Only John'd be a bad influence, I guess—he drinks some."

"Well, you do understand that you'll have to go to the hospital, give your consent to any treatment? He hasn't been on the stuff very long and there's every hope he can be cured," said Sue.

"I certainly hope so. Don't know what we're coming to, a boy fifteen taking dope. Well, I'll ask the boss if I can get off, but I don't know."

Sue hoped somebody could straighten Tom out, but it didn't look as if his mother had the energy to try.

Rodriguez went out to locate the Dankenburgs and tell them their boy was dead. It wasn't a job he looked forward to, and for once he found it an even worse job than usual.

He found the Dankenburgs in a shabby apartment on Harold Way. Whether the male Dankenburg was on unemployment funds or welfare wasn't apparent, but he was there, not at work. He didn't like cops—with reason; they found out later he had a number of D. and D. counts with them—and he didn't like cops with Mexican names worth a damn, as he told Rodriguez loudly. Mr. Dankenburg was large, belligerent and half drunk. His wife was thin and plain and had a well-developed black eye. When Rodriguez finally got his message across she began to cry hysterically, and Dankenburg rounded on her with a bellow.

"*Now* y' see what he's gone 'n' done, for all the beltin' I give him—talkin' back to me, give me his lip. He oughta know what he gets by now! So he's dead, huh? Dope? Way he was shapin' to turn out, it's damn good riddance! Shut up!" he added to his wife.

"Oh—oh—oh, poor Davy! Oh, poor Davy—"

"An' you said your piece. You can get out," said Dankenburg to Rodriguez.

"You'll have to identify the body," said Rodriguez coldly, "at the morgue, before you can claim it. This address, if you don't—"

"An' I s'pose you expect me t' pay for a fancy funeral," shouted Dankenburg, slamming the door in Rodriguez's face.

Rodriguez came out and took a long breath of cold, clear air. "Civilization," he said to himself. *"Tiene su pizca de gracia."*

■ ■ ■

At two thirty O'Neill rang Maddox, who was typing a belated report on the missing bulldozer. "You've got a four fifteen or an assault or something at this address on Vermont. And I think Gonzales is drunk on duty—he couldn't talk straight."

Maddox collected Feinman, the only one in, and they headed for Vermont in the Maserati. When they got there, they saw that it was a Turkish-bath-and-massage salon. "Oh, oh," said Feinman. The L.A.P.D.'s vice bureau was having quite a time with these places; it made a dandy front for the high-priced prostitutes.

The black-and-white was parked in front. The massage salon was housed in a new smart building of green stucco and redwood siding, which wasn't the usual case with the fronts. There were three women in white uniforms standing on the front steps, and Patrolman Gonzales had a man in cuffs up against the car.

Maddox and Feinman walked over to him. "So what's the story?" asked Maddox. Gonzales didn't look drunk.

Before he could say anything, the man suddenly roared, "I want my money back! I been gypped! I want my money back!" He was a big red-faced man about forty, and he'd had a few drinks but he wasn't tight by a long way.

Gonzales said, "His name's Blish, Ronald Blish. He's a car salesman. He"—his shoulders were shaking—"he came into this place about forty minutes ago, Mrs. Burson said—

that's Mrs. Burson there." The tall solid-looking female with a knot of gray hair and a sour expression.

"Well?" said Maddox. "And?"

"He th-thought," said Gonzales, "it was a front. You know. And he gave the receptionist a twenty, and—" Gonzales collapsed into helpless mirth—"they gave him a Turkish bath and a massage."

Maddox and Feinman began to laugh.

"A clip joint, that's what it is. I want my money back! Like to pound me to death on that table, and both of 'em with faces like horses! It's a gyp."

Feinman leaned on the squad car laughing. "They g-gave him a real massage," gasped Gonzales, "and handed back his clothes, and he started breaking up the place." He dissolved into mirth.

Maddox pulled himself together and went up to Mrs. Burson. "Well!" she said, fixing him with a gimlet eye. "You *are* going to arrest him, I hope. Making such a disturbance, breaking two of the chairs in the waiting room— and such language I never heard! He's drunk."

"Not very," said Maddox with a tremor in his voice. "I'm sorry you were—mmh—subjected to any disturbance."

"For no reason. He had our best masseuse, hospital trained."

Maddox choked back mirth. "Er—Mrs. Burson, I'm sure you must be aware that some massage salons are—er— covers for prostitutes, and Mr. Blish"—the name nearly broke him up again—"evidently thought—"

"No, I was *not* aware of that!" she said, mightily offended. "We're decent women and know nothing of such matters."

"You gimme my money back!" yelled Blish.

In the end, Gonzales ferried him to jail on a D. and D. It was the easiest thing to call it.

■ ■ ■

When they got back to Wilcox Street they found snub-
nosed, freckled Mr. Flanagan standing in front of the
sandwich machine with Rodriguez. "Gee," he said, "Mr.
Rodriguez told me what happened. He didn't have to
shoot it, that other cop. I don't know if it'll work now.
I'll hafta look." He pulled it around and opened the back,
began to take out wrapped sandwiches. "Well, it don't look
as if there's any damage to the machinery. Gee, I don't
know what made it act like that, grab a guy's hand. Maybe
he pulled the lever too hard or something. Well, I'll fill it
up again anyway, and I hope it'll work O.K."

He put in a batch of fresh sandwiches and went off looking worried. "I wouldn't take any bets," said Rodriguez.
"Want to try?" He got out a handful of change, selected
two quarters and slid one into the slot. Before he could
put the other one in, the sandwich machine gave a tenor
clink and four wrapped sandwiches slithered into the long
tube.

"¡*Por Dios!*" said Rodriguez. "D'Arcy's tamed it. Its
spirit is broken, *absolutamente*." He picked up the sandwiches. "One of each. Very nice."

"I hardly think Flanagan would think so," said Feinman.

And David Mayo said, "Sergeant Maddox—"

Maddox turned. Mayo stood at the head of the stairs,
looking tired and worried. Any vestige of laughter vanished from Maddox's mind, and he said, "Yes, Mr. Mayo?"
He could see the pink cat in on his desk, past the door to
the office. "Come in and sit down."

"What are you *doing?*" asked Mayo. "Those private
detectives said you have better facilities. But what are you
doing to try to find her? There's just no sense to it—
Dorrie—but you must be doing *something?*"

A mere Missing report. To the private citizen, the one
big thing: somebody of theirs missing. To the experienced

251

cop, another report: more paperwork to file away. Nine out of ten people reported missing—as the experienced cop Maddox knew—had walked away voluntarily and weren't always pleased to be found. About once in five thousand times there was a genuine case of amnesia.

"I ought to be home," said Mayo dully. "I've got—commitments. Clients. But— And nothing to tell Mother and Helen." He looked at Maddox in a kind of numb misery. "We love Dorrie," he said. "Ken's girl. We just met her at the wedding, and then she and Mother and Helen wrote back and forth and got to know each other. But Monica—you see, Monica's the only grandchild. Helen can't have any. We've got our name in at an adoption agency, but—what are you doing to find them?" He sounded a little wild.

Maddox didn't know what to say to him. He thought about all the dead ends that couldn't, any way, tie up to Dorrie Mayo's—walking away. And for some time now, at the back of his mind, had been the worry about Monica. Monica, fifteen months old.

He tried to think what to say to Mayo. He wondered if Sue would know better what to say to him.

■ ■ ■

When the city of Los Angeles was incorporated, the canny city fathers were entirely unwilling that the fine natural harbor should bear the names of San Pedro or Wilmington or even Long Beach, the actual towns upon it; so they retained as part of the city of Los Angeles, a mile-wide strip of land down to the harbor, which is consequently known as Los Angeles Harbor. The city of Long Beach, however, third largest in the state, claimed part of it too.

And consequently, the L.A.P.D. has a Harbor division which operates largely in boats.

At five forty that Saturday afternoon, Patrolman Harvey Evans of Harbor division said to Patrolman Bob Dolan, "There's something caught on the breakwater, Bob." They were cruising in a regular patrol craft, a thirty-five-foot patrol boat with a fast engine. "Let's head round for a look."

They were in the outer bay, and Dolan swerved the cruiser around and headed for the breakwater. It was a beautiful clear March day, the air crisp and cold and the sea like glass. They moved up on the breakwater fast and Dolan cut the engine, letting her idle up closer. "It's a drowner, Harve. The tides along here, if they go in anywhere this side of Catalina Island, they usually get washed up sooner or later. Somewhere."

They looked at it sadly, distastefully. They'd have to gather it in for possible identification, autopsy and decent burial: not a nice job, but their job. Evans got a tarp out of the cabin and spread it on deck, and Dolan climbed out onto the breakwater with a rope and hauled the boat in to ground gently. He caught the other rope Evans tossed him and bent to the broken, mutilated body. "Hey," he said. "Look at this. This wasn't an accident. It was weighted down. Only reason it came up, the gases in the body. And it's in bad shape. I wouldn't guess how long—"

"For the doctors," said Evans. He helped to haul the body on board, and they covered it with the tarp. It wasn't in a very nice state. "I'll be damned," he said. "Weighted down, with that. So it wasn't an accident. The boys at Central might be interested. I guess we'd better—"

"Yeah," said Dolan. "We'd better take everything in, the rope and all. Those boys at S.I.D. like all the material evidence."

"Well, I wish the surgeons joy of this one," said Evans.

fourteen

On Sunday morning the alarm failed to go off, not because Sue hadn't set it but because the clock hadn't been wound. "We've got to get an electric one," said Sue, rushing around measuring coffee and finding clean stockings. Maddox discovered he was nearly out of shaving cream. He got away, kissing her hastily, at five past eight, and Sue left ten minutes later. She still hadn't got her car back; the station said probably tomorrow.

By the time Maddox got to the office, there were three men from Narco downtown already there. The names Tom Ferdig had given Rodriguez yesterday tied in with the boys picked up on that homicide at the high school; nobody had done any talking and the Narco men were hoping to locate the supplier. Probably part of the day they'd be borrowing the junior division.

Rodriguez and D'Arcy were both in, D'Arcy reading a report and Rodriguez on the phone. When he put it down he looked annoyed. "It used to be that the D.A. and the courts shut down on weekends. But the D.A.'s office at least is working full blast. They want us to get a statement from Ricky Caprio on Wechsler."

"We might have known they'd want one," said Maddox. "Well, I'll see if I can locate him." Rodriguez went out.

D'Arcy handed the report over. "New body. Nothing very immediate." The body had been reported at midnight by a homecoming citizen; it had been lying on the sidewalk on a quiet residential street. Brougham's report said it looked like natural causes—an elderly man. He hadn't been identified yet.

Maddox sat at his desk and thought about the various things they'd been dealing with this last week or so. They would all drag on in the courts, all of them still awaiting the first legal skirmishes; and sometime later he and Rodriguez and D'Arcy and Feinman would probably be called to testify in some court on all of them. In some, it wouldn't come to a trial, jury trial at least. And by that time they'd have other cases on hand to work, God only knew what.

Dusty and Moose would be arraigned sometime next week. That old egotist Moreno had made the headlines again, and that had probably pleased him.

They hadn't yet identified the derelict Wechsler had killed; probably they never would now. And Wechsler might be found unfit to plead. The hospital had called yesterday; Mrs. Wechsler had had a heart attack and was in critical condition.

At least the Weavers had cut the red tape and borne away Edna Gifford's baby, said Sue. For the decent raising.

They hadn't had an autopsy on the stabbed teacher yet. Those boys would end up in a drug-cure clinic, but Maddox would take no bets that it would do any good. If he was lucky, Tom Ferdig would get unhooked.

The hot-tempered Engelhard—that would be called murder-two and he might get a ten-to-fifteen. The insouciant gang of check forgers wouldn't get much of a sentence; probably three-to-five and they'd be out in a year or so. To what further mischief remained to be seen;

none of them seemed to have any clear notion of wrong-doing. The phony cops wouldn't draw much either, but just as well they were out of circulation.

Buck De Lacy and his pals were loose on bail, but it was to be hoped they'd been effectively discouraged from pulling the protection racket soon again. Maddox grinned, thinking of Tiger Jack.

The elderly lifer would get extradited back to Illinois. The man with the snake hadn't been hurt much and refused to bring a charge; his nervous friend would be charged with a misdemeanor, firing a gun in a public place, and get off with a fine. The disappointed Mr. Blish, ditto.

Sometime, he hoped, they'd get a lead to the purloiners of the bulldozers.

The collection for the dead highway patrolman's widow had topped five thousand. Most of the citizens here appreciated their good cops.

Maddox lit a cigarette and looked at the pink cat with dislike. A Missing report. And nothing but dead ends.

Ellis and Eden were off today.

There were other reports on his desk and he started to look through them, came to one from downtown and stared at it. "By God!" he said, and D'Arcy jumped.

"What hit you?"

"I hope I'm imagining things," said Maddox, "but take a look at this." It was a routine report circulated from headquarters to all precincts, and it would have gone to N.C.I.C. too. In case anybody had any ideas about identity, a corresponding Missing report.

The Harbor boys had pulled in a body yesterday, washed up on the breakwater. It was described: "Female Caucasian app. 22–26, dark hair, 5 feet, app. 90–100 lbs. Wedding ring, plain gold. One shoe still on body, tentative label Leeds', size 4½. Dental chart in preparation." No autopsy yet, no cause of death.

"The size," said D'Arcy, "is all I see."

"All I saw too," said Maddox grimly, and got on the phone. He got a lab man at S.I.D. and asked him about the body.

"Well, there hasn't been an autopsy yet, but the surgeon thought she'd been in the water at least a week, possibly longer. It's not in very good shape. I don't know what they'll get from an autopsy."

"What about prints?" asked Maddox.

"I'm not sure we can get any. We'll try. In the water that long, the fingers are shriveled, but we'll try this latest gimmick—we've got them in a solution of glycerine, to plump them up. See what they look like later today or tomorrow."

"Yes," said Maddox. "Well, if and when you do get any prints, will you check them with that set I sent you, please? Theodora Mayo."

"You think it's her?"

"I haven't the slightest idea," said Maddox. "The size fits, that's all."

"Well, see what we can do."

"But how would she have got in the ocean?" asked D'Arcy. "That'd make even less sense than it's made all along. And if it is—"

"Yes," said Maddox. If it was, how about Monica?

Rodriguez came back with Ricky Caprio and started to take down a statement. Caprio, maddeningly, kept saying, "I told you so."

Maddox sent a description of last night's corpse down to Missing Persons at Central. Sue and Daisy were out somewhere with the Narco men. It was a quiet Sunday.

At a quarter of eleven there was an attempted heist at a pharmacy on Vine. The heisters were two young Negroes, and they'd come in and threatened the owner with a large knife, demanding the contents of the register. He came in with Gonzales to make the charge; his name was Paisley, and he was a solid-looking man with horn-rimmed glasses. "Hoodlums," he said. "Shiftless young hoods." He kept a revolver under the counter, and had pulled it out and held them for the squad car.

One of the hoods said sullenly, "We dint know he had a gun. We wouldn'ta tried it if we knew he had a gun."

"That," said Paisley dryly, "is why I keep the gun."

"They oughta outlaw 'em all over," said the other hood righteously.

Maddox and Gonzales shepherded them downstairs to the wagon, heading for jail. Temporarily. Gonzales went back on tour. Maddox strolled up to the desk, where O'Neill sat.

"Say, have you found that girl yet?" O'Neill asked. "Aunt Daisy was telling me about it. It sounds offbeat."

"Sometimes we get them. I hope I haven't found her," said Maddox absently. O'Neill looked at him curiously.

It stopped being a quiet Sunday at three fifteen, when they got a jumper on an overpass on the Hollywood freeway. They all went out on that, though there wasn't much they could do. The man was outside the chain-link fence, on the ledge, and Silver Lake Boulevard was a couple of hundred feet down, with light traffic. The Fire Department was out, trying to get a ladder up, but every time they started to move it the jumper yelled again, threatening to jump; there were several patrolmen trying to talk him in, and a minister passing by had stopped and was trying too.

Maddox and Rodriguez joined the patrolmen, but they couldn't get too close. "You come in reaching distance and I'll do it!" he kept saying. "I will! I'll jump!" He was a man in the forties, well enough dressed, nearly bald, and he looked thin and unwell. They couldn't get his name out of him.

258

"Isn't there someone you'd like to see?" One of the patrolmen, coaxing. "Your wife?"

"She left me. She left me," said the jumper, and sobbed.

"Is that why you say you'll jump? Come on, sir, you can reach my hand, I'll help you back."

"Go away! I don't want to be helped! Tell those men down there to go away!"

By the time he'd been there an hour, the TV cameras turned out. The cops and firemen tried to keep the cameras at a distance.

At four thirty an old Ford rattled up and was stopped at the roadblock. The woman driving it climbed out and glared at the TV reporters and marched through them. She ignored the patrolmen who tried to stop her, and when she got to Maddox and Rodriguez she looked them up and down. "All this fuss," she said. "All you grown men just standing around. And what it's costing in tax money, with all that expensive equipment down there—Well, *men!*"

"Excuse me," said Maddox, "but just who are you and why—"

"I knew that flibbertigibbet they got to spell me on Sundays was not responsible," she said. She was a large efficient-looking woman in nurse's uniform, starched white. "She didn't even find out he was gone until she saw it on TV and called me. Went to pieces, of course. These young scatterbrains don't get the training we got in my day."

"You know who he is?"

"Of course I do. He's my patient—chronic colon, gastric ulcer, and plenty of money. He's feeling sorry for himself because his wife went on a visit to her mother for a few days, and I can tell you she needed a rest, worn out as she was with attending to him." She marched past Maddox and looked at the jumper. "Harmon Ellington," she said, loud and severe, "you climb back over that fence and stop making a fool of yourself! You hear me?"

"Yes, Mrs. Neal," said the jumper and meekly climbed back to safety. She took him by one arm.

"Might have caught pneumonia out in this wind without a coat! You come home and stop acting like a baby!" She led him away. The Fire Department packed up all its equipment and went off, the patrolmen got back on tour, and the detectives went back to the office.

"Never underestimate the power of a woman," said Rodriguez.

Maddox called S.I.D. again, and after getting passed around finally talked to the man he'd got that morning, Fernald. "We haven't tried to get any prints yet, Sergeant. The fingers have been in glycerine about ten hours now, but we'd like to give it a little more time. Is there anything else to make you think it's this woman, or just the size?"

"Well, the wedding ring."

"A lot of those around," said Fernald. And it was doubtful that Mayo could identify it; he'd only seen it once, at the wedding. "There's nothing distinctive about it: plain gold band with a fourteen-karat mark inside. It's size four and a half, if that says anything." It didn't.

"Well, at least," said Sue as she started to leave at ten of six, "the Narco men bought us lunch this time. Not that we were with them all day. I had to see Mrs. Ferdig again. She's like a piece of limp spaghetti—and a lot of use she's going to be to the boy. I heard about your jumper. Daisy got a kick out of it."

"These bossy females," said Maddox. "It was quite a performance. Keep your fingers crossed that we haven't found Dorrie."

"Where?" And when he told her, she wrinkled her nose at him and said, "But how could it be? How could she have been drowned?"

He shrugged. "I don't know. I hope it isn't, because of—"

260

"Monica. *Ivor*," said Sue, "you don't suppose anybody could be so wicked—?" She looked horrified.

"We wait and see. I'll be home in ten minutes." It was still all up in the air, as it had been since they'd first heard her name.

As he came downstairs, O'Neill gave him a crooked charming smile. "Good news, avick," he said. "I can just hear all the boys on Traffic detail. It's great to know our younger generation is so concerned with the mounting problems of the twentieth century."

"Now what?" said Maddox resignedly.

"Why, the rumor's out—pretty solid—there's going to be another great ecology rally next weekend, up in Wattles Garden Park this time. Ecology, it's the in thing, you know."

Maddox uttered a rude word. "My God, just about as the P. and R. men finished cleaning up the mess the first bunch left."

"Oh, you mustn't expect logic out of the idealists," said O'Neill. Maddox uttered another rude word and went out.

■ ■ ■

That night the service station called; the Chrysler had its new spark plugs and was all ready to go. On Monday morning Maddox followed Sue over to Janiel Terrace, where she left Aunt Evelyn's car, and took her to pick up the Chrysler. "And I'll be reaching for a clutch for the next two days," said Sue.

The first thing he did when he got to the office was to call S.I.D. "Well, we're just about to try for some prints," said Fernald. "It looks as if the glycerine's done the job, smoothed them out enough—but even if we get some good enough to check, it'll take a while. I'll call you, Sergeant."

"As soon as you know either way," said Maddox.

Rodriguez was out on something. D'Arcy was on the

phone to the D.A.'s office, something about Wechsler. When he put the phone down, he looked at Maddox. "Mrs. Wechsler died last night."

"That's messy," said Maddox. "Another stupid thing. The only reason he made the plan."

Ellis was out presumably hunting for strayed bulldozers; he was still asking N.C.I.C. if they couldn't find a similar M.O. somewhere. Feinman was with him.

Fernald called back at ten o'clock. "Well, you called it, Sergeant. We got some good prints, and it's your girl, Theodora Mayo."

"My God," said Maddox quietly. He thought about Dorrie, all they knew about her now: a nice girl, a responsible bright girl, a good mother. And what about Monica? Where was fifteen-month-old Monica Mayo? "I want everything you've got on it," he said.

"There's not much to go on," said Fernald, "but this much I can give you. The Harbor boys spotted it right off —one reason we went to a little trouble to get her identified. It wasn't an accident. She was weighed down. There was an old anchor tied to her legs with a rope. They brought everything in for analysis, of the knots and so on. We haven't got to that yet."

"Cause of death?"

"There hasn't been an autopsy. I don't know if the surgeon can come up with that. As I said, the body's not in very good shape. There'd been fish, and there wasn't much hair left."

"Yes," said Maddox. He felt cold. And he thought, That dream, the recurring dream she'd had; it had come true. He hoped she'd already found her Ken, but he thought she'd have been worried about Monica.

He was worried about Monica. He was damned worried. D'Arcy had come over and was listening. "That's all?" said Maddox. "No leads at all? Nothing else?"

262

"That's it. Oh, the anchor—it's got something stenciled on it in marine paint. I suppose the name of a boat. *Athena.*"

"That's damned anonymous," said Maddox. "Who were the Harbor boys?"

"Harvey Evans and Bob Dolan. They're probably out in a boat on patrol now," said Fernald.

"Well, they've got a phone in it, I suppose. I'll be talking with you again," said Maddox, and broke the connection.

"It's her?" said D'Arcy. "That makes it still as shapeless as hell. How and why? And where's the baby?"

"Johnny, get me Harbor. I don't know!" said Maddox savagely. The thing made no sense at all. Dorrie, out there in the cold Pacific all this time? He spoke to a desk sergeant at Harbor; after some delay, the call was relayed through to the patrol boat Evans and Dolan were on. Maddox introduced himself, explained. "Can you tell me any more at all? You'd be more experienced than I am with bodies in the water."

"We find 'em," said Evans sadly. "What can I tell you, Sergeant? She came up when the gases formed in the body. Even weighed down, they will come up. She was caught on the breakwater, about fifteen feet inside the line dividing L.A. from Long Beach. Only reason she belongs to us. I deduce the body came up as the tide started in, or she'd have floated out the opposite way. We saw she was weighed down, so we figured, Not an accident. A homicide of some kind. Suicides don't weigh themselves down."

"No," said Maddox. He felt helpless. "What about tides, currents? Would you have a guess where she might have gone in?"

"Anywhere in the outer harbor, Sergeant. There's a pretty strong current between the mainland and the off-shore islands. Likely if she'd gone in out beyond Catalina, she'd never have turned up. But anywhere this side, north or south, she might have turned up just where she did."

After a moment Maddox said, "The anchor. S.I.D. says it's got a name on it, probably a ship's name. *Athena*."

"Probably the boat the dinghy belongs to."

"What dinghy? What do you mean?"

"Well, it's not a regular big anchor, Sergeant, it's a kedge anchor that'd be attached to a dinghy, a little row-boat. Usually a big motor cruiser or a yacht will have a dinghy on board, for—well, when the big boat's anchored offshore or—"

"And how the hell do I track down a cruiser or a yacht by its name?" asked Maddox. "There must be thousands of privately owned boats."

"Well, they'll all be registered somewhere," said Evans. "If the boat the dinghy belongs to is based in some port along here, the Harbormaster's office might know."

"Hell!" said Maddox. It looked to him, right then, as if Dorrie Mayo's story was going to stay a mystery, the book never closed on it. And Monica.

"Of course," said Evans, "there's no guarantee the anchor hadn't got moved around. The original boat it belonged to could be anywhere."

"You're a big help," said Maddox, and put the phone down. Almost immediately it rang.

"I've got something else for you," said Fernald. "We've just taken a close look at this anchor, and under infra-red something else showed up. There was something else painted on it, under the *Athena*, worn off by water action, but infra-red showed it up. I suppose they repaint these things every so often."

"What is it?"

"*Alamitos Yacht Club*," said Fernald. "It might be a lead."

"Thanks," said Maddox. He reached for the Long Beach phone book, hunted the number. Three minutes later he was talking to an employee of the Alamitos Yacht Club. "I don't know how you operate. Do you have a pier of your own, for members' boats?"

"We're just across from the Long Beach Marina, sir," a rather puzzled voice told him. "We're in the inner harbor. Yes, our members have regular assigned places where the boats are tied up. But what the police—"

"And is one of the boats named *Athena?*"

"Why, yes, sir. It's a motor cruiser, thirty-eight feet, but it hasn't been out of its berth for some time."

"Why not?" asked Maddox.

The man told him why, and Maddox looked at the telephone for thirty seconds and then said very gently, "So now we know. Now we know. Thanks so much." He put the phone down.

"What do we know?" asked D'Arcy.

Maddox got up. "Come on," he said. And then he turned back and picked up the big stuffed pink cat. He went across the hall and said to Sue and Daisy, "I think you'd both better come. We'll take D'Arcy's car."

"And what's hit you?" asked Daisy, eying him.

"We know about Dorrie," said Maddox. "What we don't know we can guess. But I think we may hear all about it. It's been a funny one all the way, hasn't it? You know, we've seen all the other people we ran across as attached to Dorrie some way. Brian Faulkner, and Mr. Simon, and even Denis. But we haven't laid eyes on this one. A name, just a name. Ships that pass in the night— and how appropriate that line is."

Sue shook him by the arm. "Talk sense, darling! What do we know about Dorrie?"

"Come on," said Maddox.

■ ■ ■

It was indeed the first time they'd seen her, and she was an attractive woman. Maddox knew how old she was; she didn't look it. She was a tall, athletic-looking woman, slim and graceful. Her frosted brown hair was exquisitely done in a smart smooth coif, and she was smartly dressed in beige sheath and black pumps, one bright pin on one shoulder, little gold earrings. Her makeup was discreet, and she had friendly blue eyes. When she opened her own door to them, after they'd climbed all the steps, she looked at the badges in Maddox's and D'Arcy's hands and stood very still.

"Sergeant Maddox. Detective D'Arcy. Policewomen Hoffman and Maddox," said Maddox. "May we come in, Mrs. Barnes?"

She said, "What—about?"

"You know what about," said Maddox. "Theodora Mayo. She's been found. And the anchor was still attached to the body. The anchor that belongs on your former husband's cruiser."

Linda Barnes stepped back into the elegant entry hall, and they went in. There was a long silence, while she seemed to be looking into space, her eyes wide and fixed, and then she turned and went slowly into a room to the right. It was a big living room with a raised hearth of field-stone, deep pile carpet, heavy drapes, expensive furniture. She sat down in one of the chairs and opened a box on the table beside it, took out a cigarette and lit it with the table lighter.

"I knew—it couldn't last," she said. "Because it wasn't right. It was all wrong. But I'm sorry. I'm very, very sorry. I don't think I've ever done anything else wrong in my life."

"Would you like to tell us about it?" asked Daisy. She and Sue sat down; the men stayed on their feet.

266

"I didn't mean to hurt her, you know. I never meant that. I don't know if you know, but I've always—wanted a child so much. I'd been—"

"We know about your trying to buy Monica," said Sue.

"Buy—but I could give a child so much, so much that she couldn't! Everything—the good schools, all the advantages, pretty clothes, and—and so much—love," she said painfully. "She's such a darling little girl."

"You had," said Maddox, "a plane ticket to Honolulu, that Sunday."

She nodded. "It was that day. Anna—my maid—had already left on her vacation. And I thought if I talked to Mrs. Mayo just once more—offered her more money. . . . I went there. She'd just come back from somewhere. Monica was still in her stroller. It was about one o'clock. I realize now, she'd been very patient with me—just as you said, offering to buy her child, I can see now how ridiculous it was—but that time she was angry. She was angry when she saw it was me at the door. She told me to go away. She wouldn't listen to me any more. I'd been arguing with her again. I hadn't been there five minutes. And I never meant to hurt her—I never meant to hurt anyone in my life—but she couldn't understand how I felt. I—I was angry too, and I just—I just pushed her a little, and she tripped on the scatter rug—silly things, I never liked them —and fell against the corner of the coffee table. And—she didn't get up. I tried to help her up."

Struck on the temple, thought Maddox, where the bone was thin. She might have died instantly. Poor Dorrie, just a silly little accident. "There wasn't—but a little blood," said Linda Barnes. "I couldn't believe it. I couldn't believe she was—dead. It just—happened. And Monica there in her stroller chattering away to herself, and everything just the same. Except—"

"And then?" said Maddox after a long silence.

"Yes. I began to be frightened. It was an accident, but I— And then all of a sudden I thought, But I could take Monica now. It was a long while before I began really thinking and planning. Everything seemed to stop, and then a long while later I was thinking what I could do. I used to be very good at plans. I was old Mr. Barnes's secretary, you know, and he didn't suffer fools gladly. You had to be good to satisfy him. And I saw—if I could make it seem that she'd gone away on her own—people she knew might think it was a little queer but they'd never suspect—"

"But you didn't know quite enough, did you?" said Maddox. "What you did know, you used, as efficiently as you could."

She nodded. "I should be frightened now," she said. "My hand should be shaking, but look, it isn't. I—she was dead—I couldn't bring her back. I thought, Why shouldn't I? And I planned it all there, the rest of the afternoon. I called the airline and said I'd have to change my ticket to Tuesday. Because I didn't know—quite how much time I'd need. I had things to do, to keep busy while I was planning. I fed Monica and put her down for her nap. And I—"

"When did you think about Richard Barnes's cruiser?"

"Right away," she said. "It was another plaything Dick had because it was a thing *to* have, the *Athena*. He never cared for it much but I loved it. I used to take her out alone, lots of times. It's so clean on the sea. She's a lovely boat to handle. I knew Dick was in Europe, and I still had an ignition key to her. I thought that'd be easiest. And it was very easy. I waited till midnight and just ran my car up the drive under the apartment windows and came in and tipped her out to the drive. She was a little thing—she didn't weigh much."

"What about Monica?" asked Sue.

"Why, I took her with me, of course. She was sound asleep, the darling, and she's only a baby. I put Mrs. Mayo in the trunk and drove straight down to Long Beach. I knew there wouldn't be a soul there at that hour—at the yacht club's marina, I mean. I got Monica settled on one of the bunks, and just pulled her—the body—up onto the deck. You can drive nearly to the pier, and the *Athena* was moored in one of the first berths. The tide was going out. I didn't start the engine until we'd drifted out to the outer harbor."

"Suppose the tank had been empty?" asked D'Arcy curiously.

"Oh, it was," she said listlessly. "But there's a siphon in with the other tack. I put some gas in from my car. I'm—handy at jobs like that. And then I thought I'd better—so it wouldn't float—and I took the dinghy anchor."

"Yes, that's what led us to you," said Maddox. "You made some efficient plans. Not quite efficient enough. I suppose her handbag—with any address book—went in with her?" The sea had taken it all, clothes, everything but the wedding ring and one shoe.

She gave a violent start. "The anchor?" she said. "The anchor? That's funny. Yes, I was thinking—of how it had to look. I knew about her husband's people wanting her to go back there. It was almost the last thing she said, that she'd decided to do that. She was going back east. So I thought, Make it look as if she'd gone. Suddenly. So I—"

"The typewriter," said Maddox. "You must have seen she didn't have one, probably didn't type. Why did you use one?"

"What else could I do?" she asked him simply. "I suppose there were people who'd know her handwriting. I took the chance. The typewriter—that's funny too. It was the last one Mr. Barnes bought for me. I hadn't had it long before he had the stroke, and I hadn't used it at all since. I wrote a note to the apartment manager—"

"There isn't one," said Maddox softly.

"—and I even remembered that she'd said a Mrs. Littleton was the only tenant there she knew. So I wrote a note to her and found the name on the door—"

"And you didn't know she worked, but of course you taped it to the door, not to be seen."

"And I wrote a letter to Robinson's saying she was quitting her job. A big place like that, they wouldn't think twice— And I remembered her mentioning Mrs. Moran, once, in the park."

"But you didn't know any of her other friends," said Maddox. "to try to fob them off with that story. Teresa Fogarty or Sandra Cross."

"No. But people do—just move on and not bother to tell people. I had to take the chance." She stubbed out her cigarette, and now her hand was shaking slightly.

"And did you think how her in-laws might act? That they'd believe she'd just moved on and forget all about her —and Monica?" asked Daisy.

"I—took the chance. How could they—ever know? And it was a good plan, about Monica. You know they don't charge for babies on planes. I had it all done by Tuesday. I dusted every place in the apartment I remembered touching—"

"I think you missed a few," said Maddox. That, they'd find out.

"And the place she hit herself on the coffee table, I washed that. I packed all her clothes, and Monica's bed, and the stroller, everything she owned there, and I brought it all here. This is a big place, and Anna doesn't go into the garage. I put it all there, in the third slot, covered up with tarpaulins. I thought I could get rid of it later, give it to the salvage people, and then nobody could ever know."

"But you didn't know she owned those two pictures and the vacuum cleaner," said Maddox.

"And Monica and I flew to Hawaii that Tuesday. And when I came back—last Saturday—I was going to tell everybody—I'd told Anna—I'd adopted her over there. She was an orphan, and I'd—"

"And isn't she the lucky little girl, getting adopted by such a lovely mama?" Anna Hoyt was at the door, fond and sentimental.

And there was Monica, rosy from her nap, dark curls and rosebud mouth and bright eyes; oblivious to everything else in the room, she uttered a joyous shriek and tottered on her fat legs toward Sue.

"Kee-kee!" she crowed. "Kee-kee!" And she embraced the fat pink cat in rapturous arms.

■ ■ ■

David Mayo said, "Well, there's nothing to say about it. I can't help it. In spite of everything I'm sorry for that woman. Even Mrs. Goulding said the same thing. But—Monica's all right. Monica's just fine. Helen's flying out tonight. We'll take her back with us tomorrow. What do you think will happen to Mrs. Barnes?"

Maddox shrugged. "Depends what the D.A.'s office will call it, murder-two or manslaughter. She won't get life, anything like that."

Mayo nodded. "I'm glad," he said.

And Rodriguez said, "Well, I'm sorry I missed it. And I'll beg her pardon—poor girl, just trying to do her best, and a senseless accident just because a silly woman got a bee in her bonnet."

"Females," said D'Arcy darkly. "Dangerous, all of 'em."

Maddox looked at Rodriguez. "Take a bet he'll go falling in love again within a month?"

Rodriguez grinned. "*Muy posible*. I won't risk a dime on it."

"You can both go to hell," said D'Arcy.

Sue and Daisy had brought Monica back with them, that day, and fussed over her before reluctantly taking her down to Juvenile Hall, pending the arrival of Mayo's wife. "She is a darling," said Sue.

And at three o'clock on Wednesday afternoon, with another two lots of heavy construction equipment stolen from building sites and irate foremen asking what the cops were doing about it, Maddox and Rodriguez came back to the office from questioning a couple of suspects on the market heist that had gone down last night to find a gloomy-faced Flanagan unloading the sandwich machine.

"We got to move them all out," he said. "We just found out they're defective—reason the other company went bankrupt, see. They don't work right at all."

"We could have told you that," said Rodriguez. "Not that D'Arcy didn't improve its performance."

"Fred says we shop around and find some that're O.K. If we do, I'll be back," said Flanagan.

They were fairly busy that day, and Maddox looked into the junior division's office at five thirty and said he'd take Sue out to dinner.

It was still cold and crisply chill out, and when she came out of the station she looked pert and smart in a bright red suit and white blouse, his darling Sue.

They went over to Musso and Frank's again, the closest place.

"Ivor," she said, taking a swallow of her gimlet, "I know we *said*—"

"The T-bone for both of us," said Maddox to the waiter, "well done and medium. Blue cheese dressing, and coffee with the steaks, please. What did we say?"

"That I'd go on working for a year and then start a

family. Two, maybe. But I've been thinking. I'm not getting any younger, and maybe—"

Maddox laughed. "Maybe," he said. "Your mother'd be
very pleased. Let's go home—after we've had a leisurely
dinner—and talk about it, love."

R